Our
Burden's
Light

Our Burden's Light

Patrick Thomas Casey

THOMAS DUNNE BOOKS
ST. MARTIN'S PRESS
NEW YORK

This is a work of fiction. All of the characters, organizations, and events portrayed in this novel are either products of the author's imagination or are used fictitiously.

THOMAS DUNNE BOOKS.
An imprint of St. Martin's Press.

www.stmartins.com
www.thomasdunnebooks.com

Book design by Claire Vaccaro

Library of Congress Cataloging-in-Publication Data

Casey, Patrick Thomas.
Our burden's light / Patrick Thomas Casey.—1st ed.
p. cm.
ISBN 978-0-312-53390-8 (alk. paper)
1. Shenandoah River Valley (Va. and W. Va.)—Fiction.   I. Title.
PS3603.A8637O87 2010
813'.6—dc22

2009040297

First Edition: April 2010

1 3 5 7 9 10 8 6 4 2

FOR MY FATHER

Acknowledgments

I would like to thank Tom and Norrine Mack, without whose unusual generosity this book could not have been. Also, my editor, Katie Gilligan, a dream.

Barefooted through the snow where birds recite:

Come unto us, our burden's light—

—ROBERT LOWELL, "THANKSGIVING'S OVER"

Our
Burden's
Light

Eden

I. If childhood is time's mercy, then perhaps it, too, must be repaid. But the blind tumble forward is not the whole debt alone, we must know it, too; must stand eventually eyes and mouth open beneath the sudden awareness of what rolls over us. Memory is a compromise with time, nostalgia a collusion with the past; they are only cracked shields beneath which we crouch, staring at our first selves. And there is always this moment we return to, a chorus through the generations, this moment before the world became. Only seconds, really, that are held close, clung to, and us with them, stilled, frozen, almost delivered from dreams, already borne into them. For we are singers. So, we come to sing.

The birds, they lit from the trees behind and his open eye closed, shuddering. When it opened again, the rabbit was gone and all that was left of it was the low, trembling bushes and the nearly invisible sound of loose, scattering earth beyond them. The birds screamed and then stopped and fell quiet again as they lay themselves with heavy wingbeats onto new branches. Hayden could feel the weight of the shotgun returning. He let his finger fall off the trigger and straightened his spine until the stock slid down from his shoulder.

The tension, the concentration that had sharpened every leaf, every shadow, as he raised the gun, began to slip away. He laid the barrel against the crook of his arm and turned back toward the path he had followed out. Where it opened in the brush, Hayden stopped, listening for what had upset the birds.

The wind whistled against the trees, and several warblers made their throaty calls from the creek nearby and were answered somewhere in the distance. Above, long, whispering branches shuffled against one another. Already, into the tallest of them had come the first patches of color, the slow, burning reds and oranges, the soft, dreaming splashes of yellow; but beneath them, autumn was nothing more than a coolness. Grainy shade hovered above the wet ferns and twisted arms of fallen trees. Where the sun angled through, its light fell in long, smoking columns and left discs of gold shining on the earth and damp, early-fallen leaves. The quiet was made of birdsong and creek sounds and wind and was laid like a gauze over the air.

Crossing the path, Hayden began to walk through the woods on its other side. There was a clearing there where kids he knew sometimes threw parties and made bonfires. Nearly a quarter-mile from the closest road, nobody worried about being underage, and Hayden wondered if someone were there now. It was far less than a mile from the cabin where Hayden and his father lived, the clearing, and some nights, with the right wind, you could hear the parties from the house, the soft laughter and inaudible conversations growing almost eerie in the distance they were carried.

The large, serrated leaves of summer-heavy ground ferns scratched against his pant legs and wet his ankles. The low plants dripped even this late in the day with the dew and mists that came in every night now and never fully burned off in the darkness. The bark still on the fallen trees was black and soft, covered in the softest places by heavy carpets of thick moss that had already begun to fray in the cold nights. Hayden thought the first frost would come soon and tried to remind himself which plants in their garden would have to come up before that.

With the barrel of the shotgun, he held the thorny tangles of nettles to the side and pulled the thinning summer tree vines open around him, their last, lacy, spade-shaped leaves hanging curtainlike from the low branches above. He could just make out the clearing ahead, though he stopped well before it. Beyond the trees the sun bleached the colors of everything into descending shades of gold and white, laying a pale dust over the greens and browns. The shade he stood in felt dense beside it. A single, warm drop of sweat tickled his ribs as he walked slowly forward before being caught in his shirt.

He had been right; there were people, but it wasn't what he expected, no group of laughing boys, no bottles and joints being passed around. A girl lay on her back in the tall grass about twenty feet into the clearing and beside her a boy was lifting himself up, his hands digging into the ground as he crawled on top of her. Hayden knew them, too, as he thought he might. Her name was Evelyn

Warren and his was Grant Shelley. They went to the same high school that he had just graduated from. Hayden looked away but didn't move. Already the beginnings of an erection pressed against his jeans.

He leaned the shotgun against the top of his thigh as he looked back into the clearing. Evelyn's face was turned away and behind her the dark mass of her hair sprawled out wildly in the grass. Hayden watched Grant begin to unfasten his pants, awkward and hurried, above her. She looked almost as if she had fallen where she lay, her legs tossed apart and bent, one arm over her face and the other lying haphazard in the grass beside her body. Her dress rose up her legs as she began to move, and Hayden could see the white flesh of her thighs and the taut, white fabric of her underwear clinging to the darkness beneath them. Her breasts swelled as she pulled in one quick, deep breath and then another. Grant kneeled above, staring down between her legs, too, and as he pushed his jeans apart, he said something, hissing almost, that Hayden couldn't hear.

It wasn't right to watch like this, and Hayden knew that if Grant saw him there would probably be a fight but still he didn't move. For one second everything seemed rooted, frozen exactly where it stood, as if the breeze had stopped blowing and they had all stopped moving with it. And then, just as suddenly, the moment collapsed and there was no more slowness, nothing left still.

Evelyn began to push herself back on her elbows, her face turning up to Grant. Her eyes were wide and panicky and even from where he was Hayden could see the quick lines they traced over the clearing. His insides cinched and he felt dizzy, as if it were all the blood his body had beating into his groin. He lifted his free arm and balanced himself against the oak beside him, the rough bark digging into his palm.

And everything was too clear now, too precise and fast, the head of each stalk of grass leaning singularly in the wind, the single shadow of their two bodies like some dense and definite thing cut out of the light; motes of dust spiraled out into the brightness and then fell back, and the sun pressing slowly, purposefully down in the west and its light crawling up the faces of the eastern trees. Hayden tried to focus on the small blue flowers stitched into Evelyn's sundress, to let his gaze become as small as one of them while the fabric pulled beneath her digging heels, collapsing in taut, shapeless folds beneath Grant's body. Somehow, he had gotten between her legs without Hayden seeing it and his body canted as she tried to close them. He held his bottom lip with his teeth as he struggled toward her and the white teeth shone in the sun and a single thread of sweat had risen along his cheek and shone also. Beneath him he held his pink erection in a loose fist and the pink-white skin of his exposed thighs was garish and bright and all together it made him look grotesque, like some fast and struggling animal.

"What are you doing?" she said. Her brow knotted together as she pushed back on his shoulders. "Grant, wait—"

"Why'd you come out here, then? What'd you come here for?"

"Don't."

"It's not like I hit you," Grant said. "This isn't like that." He turned his ribs in her legs, making an edge of his body, and pushed down farther into her. Hayden watched Evelyn's face change, a dawning response to something in Grant's expression that he couldn't see. Her eyes shot over the clearing again, searching the trees.

"You know I like you," she said, softer. "You know that, right? I do. I just—I'm just, you know—I want to be slow. That's all."

"You knew it," Grant said. His voice was hushed, sibilant.

When he said it, she tried to kick him out from on top of her, but he was already too close. She squeezed her legs against him, her thighs clamping onto his ribs just below the armpit, and each time he pushed toward her, she was pressed farther into the tall grass until it bent, arching over her face. She thrashed back and forth, her hair plaiting itself into the long, brownish strands.

"No," she had started saying. "No."

Along the edge of the clearing, tall white flowers swung their heads in the wind.

"No," she said. Just *no,* over and over, as though it were suddenly the only word that she could find and she screamed it out.

She pressed her palms against Grant's shoulders, trying to force his body down, away, and they rocked together against the cradle of her spine, and her voice grew louder until it eclipsed even the birdsong, and it stopped finally only as Grant slapped his palm down against her mouth. Her eyes grew wider and frantic and she began to writhe beneath his hand. Her voice was muted, but you could still hear it. She threw loose fists against Grant's head and he dodged them and even when they hit him it was as if they hadn't or he hadn't noticed. He was whispering, but it seemed to Hayden that it was to himself. Along his neck and shoulders and face, deep red welts rose behind her reaching fingertips.

Hayden closed his eyes. In the darkness, he could feel his body again, shivering still, shaking in fact, his groin distant now but still there, tight and throbbing, and he was ashamed that it would be like this, that his body could be so base and separate. With his eyes closed, he could suddenly hear everything. The screeching of a bird was like a blade sound in his head; and below it all were the sounds and almost screams that Evelyn was making and swallowing under Grant's hand, and then the sound, like threshing, of their bodies in against the stalks of grass, the padded earth sounds beneath even that. When he opened his eyes, he felt as though he were dreaming and waiting for some small detail to rise up and make sense of it.

Evelyn's jaw opened and closed until Grant's hand fell inside of it and when he pulled it away the crescents of her teeth were outlined in red and her lips were painted in the deep red as though they had been lipsticked with his blood.

"Scream," Grant yelled, the veins in his neck standing out as he leaned over her. "Go. Do it. Say that you didn't know." He pulled at Evelyn's dress until one of the straps fell from her shoulder, the dress slipping down over one of her breasts, which hung against her ribs.

"Please don't do this," she sobbed. "Grant. It's just me. We can stop this. Right now we can stop."

At their feet, Hayden saw a small pile of empty beer cans, the metal squeezed and bent into sharp, bright angles. He waited for Grant to stop but he didn't.

Her body shook with the force of her legs around his ribs and the white flesh of her breast shook and her thighs looked thick and pale flexed in the glare of the sun. Grant leaned his weight down on her, his palm against her throat. "Don't," he said.

Breathing in short, pointed whispers sucked between her teeth, Evelyn's eyes rolled back in their sockets until there was only the gross, flickering whites. Beneath his fingers the reddening outline of Grant's hand spread across the skin of her throat, and beneath the hand she was choking, gulping the throaty sounds. A thin bubble of saliva rose from her lips and caught the sun in a delicate rainbow. Grant ran his tongue over his open palm and reached down between their bodies.

Hayden looked away, into the shade again. His hand felt empty around the shotgun and he could feel his sweat slicking the wood stock and soaking his shirt. He was cold.

Evelyn screamed suddenly, a gargled sound loud enough to drive the birds again from their trees in small, rising clouds around the clearing. Her neck was arched and her head pushed into the earth and her hair mixed more intimately still with the grass until it seemed as if it grew from her also. Her body convulsed in huge, absent arcs as Grant pushed himself in against her and again. Her eyes closed and tears fell from their corners, glowing, and crossed over her temples before disappearing.

A shadow passed over the clearing and Hayden looked up into the sky and its brilliance was blank, vicious. The sun a glowing, hollow point in the west as though the world were not yet accustomed to its light. A line of far-off cirrus clouds grasped at the pale blue, which was otherwise totally empty.

2.

Robert Shelley leaned against his car with his eyes closed and tried to concentrate on the simple, clear feeling of vomit burning his throat. As the metallic, strangely sweet taste settled over his tongue, his empty stomach pitched again and he felt a fresh, clean burn as the bile splashed onto the gravel of the turnoff. Robert cleared his throat and spit out the last, thick strings that still hung from his lips. His eyes had filled as his body wretched and tears dropped slowly from their lashes.

Against the woods across the road, he and Dan stood as giant, misformed shadows cast by the emergency lights hung behind them. Above the trees the sky was black and flat and the stars of the clear night had been erased by the electric halo suspended over everything. Robert stood upright and he could feel himself shaking inside. He looked over at Dan and then down at the vomit splashed on his loafers.

"My shoes," he said. His voice sounded distant in his ears.

"They couldn't keep a shine even before. And now look. I'll have to throw them away."

Dan dropped the cigarette he had lit when Robert started getting sick.

"Jesus," he said. He shook his head slowly. His brows and jowls had grown heavy and tired as the night went on and now slanted down over his features, turning his face, in the strange lights, into just a series of pouches laid one on top of the other. His right hand rested on his chest beside his badge. "Robert, Jesus Christ. Tell me what I can say?" He shook his head again.

"Tell me I'll be waking up soon," Robert said.

Dan didn't respond, not even a half-smile, his face only sinking another small measure into itself. Robert didn't know what he wanted him to say, anyway.

"I know," Robert said. Inside Dan's pocket, Robert could see his other hand working something absently. "Your good luck?" he said, nodding to the shifting fabric.

Dan brought out his hand and showed Robert the worn rabbit's foot inside it. "I guess," he said. "Something like that."

Robert nodded and turned to look over the cars at their shadows. His mind was awash of the things he had just seen. His son's body lay not three hundred yards away from him in a clearing in the woods, half-naked under the cold blanket of the emergency lights. He really did feel as though he were waiting to wake up, though of course he knew that wasn't true. It was just that this all seemed so distant, so numb and unrelated to his own life. That thing out there, that crumpled, broken thing, tucked inside the rising grass, it was like an already shattered gift only half-unwrapped. Yes, he had said it was his son, said his name even, but what does saying have to do with believing?

"How?" he said, finally. He was crying. "How does a person even start with something like this? I can't make any sense of it."

Dan stepped toward him and wrapped his arms around him. Robert could feel his friend's warm, dry breath on his neck and he closed his eyes. "I'm sorry," Dan said. "I'm sorry if it wasn't right to bring you here. I just thought you'd rather do it here, and not—"

"No," Robert said. He held in his breath and nodded. "No, you were right. I'd probably rather've seen it here, I think. Not laid out, not so cold, you know."

He stepped back as Dan let his arms go loose. "I should go back," Robert said. "Deb. I guess she'll be waiting. Jesus."

"Sure," Dan said. "You'll be all right for now?"

Robert lifted his shoulders and thought he would start to cry again.

"Just take care of them tonight. All right?" Dan said. "You'll have time."

"Fuck," Robert said.

Dan stood where he was and watched Robert walk around the trunk of the car. As he started the engine, Dan pulled out another cigarette and cupped a struck match in his hand. Lit by the flame, the flesh of his face leaned in toward the cigarette. Robert looked at him one more time and wondered when they had grown old.

Outside of the lights, the night was swollen with darkness and the stars were brilliant and clear, except where a few thin wisps of cloud covered over them. The big Mercedes Robert drove coasted softly over the pavement. He had bought it as he had grown wealthy breaking down and selling off farms for the second homes that were filling the valley, but as he drove along the hills back toward home, the car, the soft leather seats and the dull purr of its insides, made him feel somehow fraudulent and embarrassed.

He tried not to think about anything, but he couldn't stop. His headlights filled the hollow troughs of the valley with brief pools of light, and around the turns in the road they lit clusters of tall, naked woods and the sharp, red eyes of cattle that turned their faces toward the oncoming sound.

The streets of town were empty, the yellow stoplights blinking in the air over each intersection. Just before his house, Robert turned off his headlights and pushed the car into neutral, sliding almost silently into the driveway. He turned off the ignition and the last small noises of the engine dropped away. Outside, the crickets' screaming was like a pillow held over the other sounds.

His hands were shaking and Robert was afraid to take them off the wheel. In the semidarkness of the lit street, he looked up at his house for what seemed a long time. It was a big house, nearly a century old, with a formal front parlor and a large wraparound porch framed in ornate wood slats and railings. The wisteria and bougainvillea vines, which laid deep curtains of shade and color over the porch chairs in the summer, had lost nearly all of their richness and begun already to recede to the thin brown skeletons of their fall and winter selves. The house leaned almost imperceptibly forward and nothing Robert could do, he was told, short of rebuilding the foundation, would stop its gradual slouch into the earth.

The front parlor was the only room lighted and the dark glass of the other windows were empty holes in the white face of the house. He stepped out of the car and closed the door, flinching at even the small sound as the lock clicked shut. The loose dust and cement on the walkway scratched against the soles of his loafers and he stepped carefully onto the soft wood of the porch steps. So quiet like this, he felt like a ghost who is present but invisible, impotent in the world, though the thought was all too pretty and he knew it.

The air had gotten cooler and Robert stood on the porch and pushed his hands deep in his pants pockets and watched his wife through the big, lit windows of the parlor. She was sitting on the couch with her feet tucked under her like a little girl. Over the quilt she had wrapped around her legs lay an open book. She stared, unblinking, out at some middle distance, her hand rested on the book, fingers spread over the white pages. She looked remarkably like a blind woman reading Braille, Robert thought.

As he walked through the entranceway and into the parlor, she smiled, her eyes tracing his body and then moving behind him.

"I wondered when y'all might get back," she said. Robert stood just inside the parlor and Deb craned her neck to look into the entranceway. Unfolding her legs slowly, she began to stand up, the quilt falling at her feet. The book, caught inside it, thudded against the floor.

"Love," he said. "How can I do this?"

"Do what?"

Robert thought he could see the fear carried through her body, cell to cell as though it were some basic, physical command, and he had never felt a greater pity or love than that moment in his entire life. "Where's Grant, Robert?" she said.

She tried to look around his shoulders again. "Robert, where's Grant?"

Tears filled his eyes and stood briefly on the edges of his lashes before falling. Deb watched the first tear fall, following it with her eyes as it slid down his cheek. Her brows pulled together and her lips began to shake. She tried suddenly to run past him, hurling her body toward the entranceway and the door, but Robert caught her in his arms.

"Baby," he said. He pushed his mouth against the side of her face, breathing in loose strands of her hair. "Deb, baby. Grant's dead." He wanted to say something more, but there was nothing more and he knew it.

Deb pushed herself out from his arms and looked at him with a fierceness that until right then might have been unimaginable in her. "No," she said. Her jaws were locked shut and her lips pulled back, baring her white teeth in an almost animal grimace. She pointed her finger into the middle of his chest. "You go back out there," she said slowly, nodding her head with each word, "Robert, and you get our son."

"I can't do that, Deb," he said. He thought again of what he had seen in the clearing; the false, blue daylight of the sulfur lights, the cleaved skull and its insides emptied like some riverside pile of fish bellies tossed into the grass, the opal and pearl colors of his son's naked legs and bottom and the scratches and welts all down the boy's face and neck. There were places the vultures had already gotten to. His son, finally, so open and exposed, so helpless, it was as though he were a child again. Robert shook his head. "He's dead," he said. "I saw him there, in the woods off 211. He was shot, love. And he's dead."

Deb slapped him fast and Robert barely registered the pain or the sound. His eyes caught only a still photograph of the empty, blackened fireplace and the chair beside it. He looked back up and Deb was holding her stinging hand against her belly, her eyes clamped shut. "No," she said again. The words came as barely articulated, tearless sobs. "No, he's not. He's not—" Her fists shook in front of her and she blindly threw them out against Robert's chest as she began to cry. "You promised," she told him. "You said it wouldn't be anything serious. When that sheriff called, you promised it. Robert, you did."

"I know," he said. "I know I did, baby. But I was wrong. I was so wrong." He stepped forward and tried to take her in his arms again, as Dan had done with him, but she turned quickly away and stood with her back to him. Her head sank against her chest and she covered her face with her cupped palms. Robert leaned against her.

"Don't, you," she whispered. "Don't you touch me now."

Piece by piece, it seemed, she lowered her body onto the ground and curled over herself until her head lay against the floor. Her back struggled with the shallow breaths she could swallow and the clear bulbs of her spine rose through the fabric of her shirt. Robert crouched beside her and lay his forehead against her back.

"How could you do this?" she said, swatting at his leg. "How could you say this?"

"I wish I wasn't."

"But you are," she said.

"I know," he said.

"Don't."

Robert nodded against her ribs. "I'll go get Rachael," he said. "I'll bring her down here."

At the foot of the stairs, he stood waiting, he didn't know what for. Rachael sat on the top step already, her head leaning against the wall. Her black hair was matted with sleep and lay swept across half her face, stark against the pale, alabaster color of her skin. Robert could only see one of her deep brown eyes, wide and almond shaped, and he watched as her swollen bottom lip slipped from between her teeth and she wiped the tears from under her eyes. They looked at each other for a long moment while she calmed the shaking of her breath and then she nodded and stood up. At twelve, her tiny breasts only managed to exaggerate her androgyny and as the white undershirt she slept in fell down over her thin, pale legs, it all made her look like some Old Testament angel, frightening and beautiful, and still willing to descend.

Robert reached out and put his hands on her shoulders as she came nearer. "Daddy," she said when she turned and saw her mother lying on the floor in the parlor. He let her go. She kneeled beside

Deb and stretched her body over her back and they began to rock like that together on the floor. It looked like a trance they shared; like some kind of ecstasy, painful, almost rapturous. They just fell into it, whatever communion this was, naturally. Watching them, he thought how close women seemed to God, how quick and intimate with the things beyond this world, as if they were given some recourse men didn't have.

Leaning back against the wall, he let his body slide down to the floor, and he wrapped his arms around his knees and hugged them against his chest, watching them, these women. He felt lost inside the blank space of his mind. He thought his father, or his grandfather, would have known something more than this nothingness, and he wondered whether this failing that rang through him now was his alone, or if it was shared. Had they all been left like this, weak and silent and neutered, the diluted grandsons, the mute shadows of actual men?

Raising her head off the floor finally, Deb swayed from side to side. A sound rose from her upturned mouth that was like nothing he had ever heard. It was not a moan, but deeper than that. It sounded as if the earth beneath them were giving way. The skin grew tight along Robert's arms and his neck.

That's it, love, he thought. Yes, that's it exactly.

The Children of God

 Paul leans against a windowsill in the small kitchen, wishes he could hear the sound of the world outside, the wind, anything other than the close, steady drone of the refrigerator. He stares at the green linoleum curling off the floor in the corners. His eyes search the rough concrete browned with ancient glue below it. He would like to draw those corners sometime, if he remembers, the curves and angles that he's never noticed, wonders if that's what waves look like. He's never seen the ocean.

He does not look at his mother as she pulls her work uniform over her shoulders. It is a dark green and black cocktail waitress uniform, tailored to be sexy. Tight around the hips, low in the front. He hates the dress. Hates his mother in it, watching her push her breasts up in the mirror and kiss at her reflection. Outside the sky is molten with dusk. Paul can feel the cold coming through the glass.

"You're working the night again?" he says. He is ten years old.

"Paul," his mother says. "You know I work nights, Fridays."
She is a waitress at the neon bar just outside of town.

"Can't you tell them you want to switch or something?"
he says.

"No. I can't just tell them I want to switch," she says. "Tonight's the best money of any shift all week."

"Oh."

His mother walks over to where he's standing, touches his
cheek. He raises his eyes for the first time since he came into the
kitchen. "I know you miss your mama when she works," she says.
"But somebody's got to pay the bills."

She turns, squats down, the back of her dress open.

"Maybe we'll all go to a movie or something tomorrow," she
says. "Zip me up, okay, honey."

Paul looks at his mother's back. It is spotted with freckles and
moles, textured with her muscles and ribs. The clasp of her bra
stretches across it, black, like a border on a map. He pulls the zipper
of her dress up slowly, watches as the shapes close in on each other.

"There," he says.

"Thanks, honey," she says. "What would I do without you?"

Paul doesn't say anything. His mother moves around their
kitchen with her purse in her hands, checking her things. "Keys," she
says. "Yep. Wallet, lipstick, glasses," she says. She is a lovely woman,
once beautiful; her straw-colored hair lies flat across her cheekbones.
Paul can see the veins in her hands as she moves them among the
things in her purse. He notices a shopping bag next to the door with
clothes in it.

"Mom," he says. "You'll be home before I'm asleep, right?"

"Um, yeah," she says. "I'm sure." She opens the refrigerator, looks in, double-checking. "I may stay and have a few drinks with the girls after work, though. So."

"Mom," he says.

"Paul." She stands up straight, tries to fix him with a look. "I need to have a little fun, too, honey."

He looks out the window at the darkening sky. Their building stands on the cusp of the valley and across it the last razor cut of red still clings to the uneven horizon, laying an almost iridescent last light into the folds of the hills. He watches as it gets smaller, the red, as the valley below disappears. Years from now, after his first gallery show, someone will write, "These paintings are a memoir of what is almost gone, what will one day be taken away from us, forever. They ask us to face what is missing, warn us not to love too much what is lost." When he reads it, he will be remembering this, not this moment, but this time, this place. This boy.

His mother takes his face in one of her hands.

"Okay?" she says.

"Okay."

She leans down and kisses him. "Good," she says. She goes back to her purse, to her search around the little kitchen. "So, listen to your sister when I'm gone, and there's tuna for you guys to eat in the cabinet, and some vegetables from the other day in the fridge," she says. "Okay?"

"Uh-huh."

Paul looks down the hallway of their apartment. Music throbs from behind the closed door of his sister's room. She is twelve years old. His mother walks down the hallway, opens her door, says something he cannot hear over the grinding sound of guitars. Then she is back again, standing in front of the mirror. She pushes her lipstick along her lips, runs the tip of her tongue over her teeth. She turns to face Paul, her arms up and out like a game show hostess.

"So," she says, frozen in that pose. "How do I look?"

"Fine."

"Fine?" she says.

"You look beautiful, Mom."

She says, "That's more like it."

She locks the door behind her.

Paul goes back to the window, watches his mother as she walks out the back door of the apartment building to her little gray car. He watches until the headlights fire the small space between her and the wall.

He opens the refrigerator, his hand never leaving the door, closes it again. Their refrigerator is old, and there is a pause before the light flickers on. Paul opens and closes it several times, waiting for the reticent light. He turns and walks down the small hallway. Past his mother's room, which is meant to be the living room; past his small bedroom, to Melissa's room.

He opens the door. Her music heaves between them. She is sitting on her bed, staring at a muted television. He steps in. She looks up from under the canopy of her heavy, dark curls.

"Hey, lover-man." She smiles.

"Hey," he says.

Sometimes, midafternoons, Paul sees his sister naked. She calls him into the bathroom when she is showering. He opens the door, steps into the steam. She talks about nothing. Their mother is at work. She pulls the shower curtain aside. She is pale as paint, almost a ghost in that fog. She watches him, smiling, as he watches her body. She gives him chance enough, each time, to take her in. Her small breasts, reaching out for the world. The tight skin that climbs across her body. The water, which drips down and pounds her flesh, accentuating the curves pushing on her frame and her little girl's ribs. She watches as his eyes fall slowly, as they hover over the wispy hair. "You shouldn't look at me like that," she says, soft. Maybe, for a second, she touches her collarbone.

She asks him for something, a towel, the hairbrush. He finds it and then gives it to her. She turns, arcs her back, lets the last of the water slide down her spine, across the new roundness below it. She says, "Thank you." He leaves. He doesn't talk about this. But, later, when he is starting as a painter, he paints nudes of her from memory. When they ask, he tells people they're of a lover.

Paul climbs up on her bed, leans his back against the wall.

"Is she gone?" Melissa says.

"Uh-huh."

"Cool."

She bends from where she is sitting and reaches under the bed, comes back with cigarettes and a lighter in her hand. She pulls one out, lights it. Paul watches the flame fall into the end of the cigarette, watches the smoke come out of her nose like steam in the cold. It reminds him of a bull.

"Liss," he says. He looks behind him. "What're you doing?"

"Smoking," she says.

They sit back on the bed and watch music videos pass across the television like a safari. She ashes too often in the Coke can pressed into the crotch of her jeans.

"It sucks mom has to work nights," Paul says.

"Why do you care?"

"I don't know."

He traces invisible shapes on the legs of his soft corduroys, notices the shade that remains behind his finger.

"Oh," she says, as if she has just remembered something. She sits up. "Come here."

Paul scoots toward her. "What?" he says.

She puts her hand out, palm up. "Give me your hand."

Paul puts his hand in hers. They are almost the same, these hands, bony and fragile, what spreads through the wings of a bird. They have their mother's hands.

"What're you doing?" He squirms a little in his corduroys.

"Shh," she says.

She pulls his hand up to her face, singles out his pointer finger with a little fist around it. Held like this, both their hands shake in the air. She folds the rest of his fingers into a fist. She brings his finger to her mouth, runs her tongue around the tip of it. Slowly, she pulls it into her mouth, presses her lips to the knuckle. Paul can feel her tongue, smooth and muscly and wet, working his finger, can feel it swirl and spread over his skin. Shivers crawl through him.

Melissa pulls his finger slowly out of her mouth, her tongue on him the whole way. Her lips give up nothing until the end, kiss his finger away. She falls back on her bed, laughing.

"I saw it on TV," she says. "How did it feel?"

"Eww," he says. Though he can still feel it along his spine, in his belly.

"It felt good," she says. Her lips, which were just on him, hot and strong, are wide, smiling.

"No."

"C'mon," she says, leaning so close he can feel her breath. "You can tell me."

"It was gross," he says. She pushes him back, laughs.

"Uh-huh," she says. Paul rolls his eyes, the lids delicate as moths at a light. He leans back, tries to focus on the television, his hands covering his lap.

They sit there together, quiet and close, for some time. Paul pulls her comforter over his legs. His body feels cold and empty as the winter-dark windows.

"You want to eat dinner soon?" he says, turning to his sister. He notices the line of her jaw into her neck, the soft hollow there, only half-hidden under her hair.

"Sure," she says. "I'm hungry."

She takes his hand as they walk to the kitchen, and he is grateful. He is glad to be led, even just to the kitchen, to be shown how, where. They are swallowed together by the dark that has grown in the apartment since sunset. Melissa hits a light at the end of the hallway, and it takes the darkness slowly, hesitant, as it flickers on.

She makes the tuna fish, squeezes the thin, gray juice into the sink. He toasts bread, pours water. They sit at the little Formica table facing each other. They don't speak. They eat quickly, almost ferocious. Paul watches the tendons of his sister's jaw, stretching taut, snapping her mouth closed. He looks at the shadows play on her neck as she moves.

When they are done, Melissa stands up. "I'm going back to my room," she says. "You want to come?"

"No," he says.

"C'mon." She turns her hip a little, tilts her jaw. Her eyes look big like this, two First Communions where eyes should be.

"I'm gonna watch TV in Mom's room."

"All right," she says.

She rinses her dishes in the sink. The sound of the water running into the metal is a small music, and he closes his eyes. He opens them again when she turns the tap off and the only sound is her feet padding down the hallway. He watches her as she goes, her shadow splayed across the floor behind her.

Paul rinses his dishes in the sink. The water runs over his hands. Even when the dishes are clean, he lets the water run. Then he shuts it off. He walks to his mother's room. The bed is big next to the small dark nightstands in the large room with clothes and bags scattered over the heavy tan carpet.

He lies down on the bed, turns on the television, and closes his eyes. He pulls one of her pillows to his body, between his legs. Her smell rises off of it, like apple juice but salty, and he pulls it into himself. He listens to the people on the television.

For a while he is lost in this noise. He will find something like this freedom in painting, in the forms and the resuscitation they are. And he will be lost in that also, perhaps hurt by it, in it, because form is a freedom and because he will believe in that, because he is a believer.

Paul walks to Melissa's room, pushes the door open against the wall of sound around her. She is lying on her bed, reading a magazine, playing with her hair. One curl runs slow through her fingers.

"Liss," he says. "I'm gonna go to bed."

"All right," she says. "Good night."

He closes her door again. In their little bathroom, Paul brushes his teeth, washes his face. His blond hair hangs over his eyes. He strips his clothes off and puts them into the hamper in his bedroom. In the dark he is a skeletal blue, bare but for the thin white cotton of his underpants. His bed is cold under its covers, and he curls up on himself until sleep comes. The darkness tight as a skin.

Paul wakes to the sound of the pins shifting heavily in the lock of the front door. He is still. The sound moves like horses through the small silence of the apartment. The door creaks open, and Paul hears his mother's voice, though he cannot hear her words. He waits for the other voice. It is rough, sibilant.

"All right, all right," the man's voice says. "We'll be quiet."

He hears his mother fumble on the entrance table, walk into a chair. She laughs a little, then shushes herself. Their footsteps drift through the hallway. Paul pulls the blanket tight around him. He looks out the window to the overcast sky, lighted from the street below.

He lies awake for an hour, their slight sounds like something crouching over him. The bed shifts, cloth ruffles, a floorboard creaks. There is his breath in his ears. It is a makeshift rhythm he counts the seconds by. A gasp, his mother's. He knows her sounds. Then a muffled grunt, something like pain. After, the silence washes the air. Paul lies in this watery quiet another half hour, listens for the footsteps. They are heavy and come down the hallway like a stone skipping. The door to the apartment closes softly.

Paul waits some time and then stands up. He walks into the hallway, without making a sound, to his mother's room. He looks in from the darkness. She is either asleep or just still, lying on her bed, her back facing the door. Her golden hair is scattered across the sheets. Paul feels his thin underwear against his skin, and the air, cold and insubstantial. His mother is half-covered by her blanket. He wants to cry but doesn't. Her naked back pushes against the dark; her spine notched, her ribs lifted against the skin.

He turns away from the door. For the first time, he feels how big the space in this little apartment is; or, how small he is. He feels them both just below his stomach. It is a feeling he will have again walking through New York City for the first time. And the first time he makes love to a woman. It is a feeling he will grow to love, but not yet. He walks down the hallway to his sister's room. The dark huddles around him. He opens the door.

"Liss," he says softly. "Are you sleeping?"

He can see her shape in the bed, outlined by a streetlight through the window. Her curls are dying sparks in its light. She is balled up, facing the wall. She raises her head to look at him. The skin around her eyes swollen with shadows.

"No," she says.

"Oh," he says. "Me, either."

"Yeah."

They look at each other in the dark.

"Can I sleep with you tonight?" he asks.

"Yeah," she says. "Come."

She lifts up her blanket for him to get under. He feels delicate and light as he walks around his sister's bed. Melissa does not turn to face him as he climbs into it. He can see that she is not wearing underwear beneath her oversized t-shirt. He watches the silver light on her skin crawl, like mercury, from her knee to her hip. He lies in bed with her.

"He left," she says.

"Yes."

He presses his body against hers. Her skin is hot. He can feel the hard round hollow of her backside through his underwear. Her body almost soft, almost water soft. She reaches behind her, takes his hand in hers. She pulls it, slow, almost shaking, up her leg to her waist, under her shirt. His hand hangs off of the precipice of her hipbone, the fingertips gently touching the soft curls below. She presses his hand onto her. She arches her back so she is open against him, and begins to rock, slowly. Years later, she wants to take him aside. She wants to talk about all of this.

But for now she says, "Is it nice for you?"

"Yes," he says. "Yes. Please."

Eden

3. Whoever thinks about how a house breathes, how it bleeds into and accepts the world outside it? But Robert stood watching the barely open door to Grant's room sway back and forth doing exactly that. Carrying up the stairwell, the voices from the television downstairs sounded hollow and distant as echoes. Flowers had started to arrive the day before and already the air in the house was overrun with their sweet, perfumed smell. Only now, only standing at this door, did he realize how grateful he had been for the small tasks, the calls and partial explanations, which had kept him busy until then.

Deb sat on the edge of the bed with a dark suit spread across her lap. Her fingertips ran back and forth over the jacket's satin lining. In the open closet in front of her, she stared at their son's thin, pressed dress clothes dangling from the plastic hangers. She had laid out a white shirt and a maroon tie and a pair of dark socks, and they sat in a careful pile beside her on the bed. Over the floor several small heaps of Grant's clothes still lay where he had left them.

"Deb?" She turned and Robert could see that she hadn't heard the door open. She looked as though he had just woken her, and he waited for her to come back to herself, her eyes focusing slowly. "Is that the one you want?" he asked.

She looked down at the suit in her hands. "Yes," she said. "He's got two, but I think this is the nicer of them. What do you think?"

Robert thought about the morning, when they had started to stir from whatever sleep each had found. It was barely dawn. Before he had a chance to say anything, Deb had quieted him with a hand against his mouth. "Don't talk yet," she had said, curling against his body. "Can't we have a second? Just one second where we pretend that everything is still the same? Please. Close your eyes." He did. "Now," she said. "Can't you hear them sleeping?"

He put his hand in her hair and she closed her eyes.

"I think that's a good one," he said. Deb reached up and hung her fingers over his wrist.

"I'm going to go over there now, I think," he said. "To Trapp's." She nodded her head and squeezed his hand as he took it from her neck.

Carefully, Robert lifted the suit off her lap and then picked the neat pile of Grant's other things up off the bed.

"Robert," she said when he was at the door. He turned around and she was watching him, her hands awkward and still on her lap without the suit to touch. She had begun to cry and she wiped the wetness from below her eyes. "Our son. He was beautiful, though. Wasn't he?"

"Yes," Robert said. "He was."

Wiping her cheeks again, she smiled.

Robert hung the suit on the rack beside the front door and slid his arms through the sleeves of his sports coat. Rachael stared at him from where she was curled up in the deep corner of the parlor sofa, watching television. He knew that she was waiting for him to say something, but he couldn't bring himself to look at her. Deb turned out of the room upstairs holding a pair of Grant's dress shoes and he looked up at the sound of her footsteps.

"My God," he said. "I would never have thought of those."

Deb nodded. "I know." At the bottom of the stairs she reached down and picked up her purse from the floor. "I'm coming with you."

"Okay," Robert said. He wouldn't have asked her, but he was thankful that she wanted to come, thankful that he wouldn't have to do it alone. He looked at the suit hanging in front of him and waited for a long second before picking it up again. "Rachael," he said. He turned, finally, to look at her. She had never taken her eyes off of him and her gaze, her face and breath, were so still it was as though her real self were somewhere else and she stood there, wherever it was, holding this other girl up. It was devastating for him, the unnatural silence this child had put on like Sunday clothes for her brother's death, and for a second he let himself look away. "We're going to go over to Mr. Trapp's," he said. He forced his eyes back. "You'll be all right here for a while?"

"Yeah," she breathed. "I'll be okay."

Outside, there was a small breeze and Robert closed his eyes and focused on the feeling of it across his skin. From the far crook

of the porch, he could hear the porch swing creak, and behind him
Deb's footsteps and the murmur of the television.

"Where are they?" Deb said beside him. "The reporters, the
vans. They've all gone."

"Earlier," Robert said, opening his eyes. "I went out and asked
them to go. It didn't seem right, them being here. Not now,
anyway."

She put her hand on his arm. "Robert, I know I haven't been—"
she said, stopping. "I don't know what I've been, actually. It's not
fair, though, is it? Expecting you to carry everything. But thank you
anyway." She nodded once. "I just need a little time, you know?"

"I do," he said.

They drove slowly over the side streets parallel to town. The
changing leaves were like small flags hung in the trees leaning above
them and the first of them to fall had already been pushed into the
rain gutters along the edges of the roads.

Robert turned and parked on the main street in front of the
wide, immaculate lawn of Trapp's funeral parlor. The few empty
storefronts peppered the antique stores and restaurants and hotels
like missing teeth, and, in groups along the sidewalk, teenagers stood
smoking cigarettes and tenderly trying to emulate the youth of cit-
ies they had never been to. Robert walked around the car and
helped Deb onto the curb, pulling the suit off the backseat hook
once she was out. The cement sidewalk was cracked and through
the empty spaces grass and weeds had grown tall enough to brush
against their ankles.

Looking up the five or six blocks of downtown, Robert said, "I remember when we had to put on our fresh clothes just to come get groceries." He smiled.

This was a different place, though, he reminded himself, than when he had been growing up. A place that he, if he was going to be honest, had had a small hand in changing, and the sidewalks were cracked now, and grass grew out of the cracks.

"It wouldn't have changed anything," Deb said softly. "The farm. If that's what your thinking of." She shook her head. "Not about town, anyway."

He looked at her, her fingers clinging to his elbow still. "Sure," he said. "I know."

Trapp's funeral home was an old mansion right on Main. Older even, Robert guessed, than his own house. They walked up the porch steps and Robert shifted the suit onto his arm.

"You ready for this?" he said.

"Honestly?" She took his hand. "I don't know."

Robert rang the doorbell. Through the old glass, he could see the hazy figure of Peter Trapp walking down the hallway. Dressed as he always was during work in an old-fashioned three-piece suit, he walked now with the quick, pointed steps that he had always believed made up for his shortness. Peter opened the door and looked consolingly into each of their eyes before taking a step back to let them in.

"Robert," he said. "Mrs. Shelley. I can't tell y'all how sorry Lilly and I are."

Peter Trapp looked altogether different from what one might think of as an average undertaker. He was small, with thinning, reddish-blond hair, and was round throughout. His red face glowed with a perpetual, delicate sheen of sweat, even in the dead of winter. Though he was around the same age as Robert, his skin was nearly unlined, the exception being a set of deep crow's-feet that spread from his eyes in the worn and practiced lines of sympathy. He had worn a heavy, well-groomed mustache since they had been little more than boys, which hung over his mouth in a long, red fringe and covered, Robert remembered looking at him now, the thin scar of a harelip.

"Thank you, Peter," Robert said.

Peter took another step back and stretched his arm out toward the parlor, where several antique chairs and sofas sat in the room's shade. "Won't y'all take a seat?" he said.

Robert looked at Deb, who remained where she was, still holding the shoes that she had brought from Grant's room tightly in her hands. The polished leather shone in small, bent puddles that collected around her fingers. Robert took her arm and led her to one of the sofas. Only as they sat down did he notice Peter's nephew standing in the shadows against the back wall. Peter and his wife, Lilly, had no children of their own and had more or less adopted this nephew years ago. Robert had always thought it must have been a natural choice, because, already, at twenty, the boy looked exactly as you'd imagine an undertaker to look. He was tall and pale, sallow, with a profound but unspecified sadness in the pale draw of his lips and the thin set of his light eyes. Peter sat down in a chair opposite them, and his belly rested, tight within the confines of his vest, over his lap.

"Now," he said. "I spoke with the mayor and the sheriff this morning, and they told me what needs to be done. So, all we need you to do is to sign a few forms for us and fill us in on a number of the details." His eyes fell down to the clothes Robert held in his hand. "Is that the suit that Grant'll be wearing?" Peter asked. His voice was soft and poignant and every word and inflection seemed purposefully designed to soothe.

"Yes," Robert said. "This is it."

"Okay," Peter said. He looked over his shoulder at the boy. "James here will take it for you." Robert handed the boy the suit delicately, and as he rested it with equal delicacy over his forearm, Robert felt slightly self-conscious, as if they had all agreed beforehand to indulge the ridiculous fantasy that these clothes were in fact his son.

Peter handed Robert a leather folder, propped open by a pen inside it.

"Robert, will the burial be in the same place as your father's?"

"Yes," Robert said. "In the Green Hill plot. I've already spoken to them."

"Perfect," Peter said. He took a small notebook from the pocket inside his jacket and made a note as Robert opened the folder.

"Now, my understanding is that the casket is being arranged for by the town," he said. "So this is just for the release. Any other bills incurred, we'll just send on after. If that'll be all right?"

"Yes," Robert said. "Of course." He let his eyes pass blindly over the three forms and then signed them.

The rooms that Robert could see from where he sat were all furnished with antiques from a period that he couldn't quite place but which gave the house a powerfully familiar feeling. The windows were cracked open despite the temperature and a light breeze brought the cool harvest-smell of early autumn into the room. At their edges, thin white curtains swayed almost imperceptibly. The room had a southwestern exposure that provided all the light he could see and beneath the tall windows the sun laid long, golden swaths over the floor and furniture. In the stillness, the quiet of the room, Robert remembered watching the older men in his family when he was a child, his first misunderstood impressions of the careful ease that comes before the harvest. The razor's edge they had stood on had seemed like peace, he remembered.

"Is my son here?" Deb said suddenly. Her voice lifted him from the dreamy, almost nostalgic feeling. "Now, I mean," she said. "Is he here right now?"

Peter looked at her steadily, trying, Robert thought, to get a feeling for what she was really asking. "Yes, Mrs. Shelley," he said. "He's downstairs."

Deb stood up and Robert could see her hands shaking at her sides. "I'd like to see him now, Mr. Trapp," she said.

Peter let his eyes move for a split second to Robert and then turned back to Deb. Both men stood up. "Mrs. Shelley," he said. He held his hands before him in the stiff, fleshy steeple of someone who wants you to understand that they pray. "In cases like these—in delicate cases, we don't advise the loved ones to view the deceased until they've been fully prepared."

"Love," Robert said. "I don't know that you want to see that." He touched her arm and her eyes flashed at him before returning to Peter. He took his hand away. Maybe she deserved that right, he thought, if she wanted it.

"I think I'll see my son now," she said. Peter looked at Robert and Robert nodded. "Yes, ma'am," he said. He bowed slightly and then turned and whispered something into the ear of his nephew, who walked quickly out of the room. They could hear his footsteps as he ran down the stairs and Peter gave them a quick, embarrassed smile before turning into the hallway. "Right this way," he said.

Three unlit Tiffany-style lamps stood like aberrant flowers on their small tables along the hallway. Peter turned down a set of narrow stairs, which must have originally led into a coal cellar, and Robert and Deb followed behind.

The stairs led into two small rooms that were tiled, floor and walls, in the small white tiles of an old butcher shop. The first room appeared far bigger than the other and at its far end, the thick, metal door of a cooler broke through the wall. Strong fluorescent lights hung head level throughout the room. The lights reflected a watery brightness over the polished tiles and shone against the damp skin of Peter's face as he looked nervously around.

"I apologize for making y'all come down here," he said. He shrugged his shoulders like someone who hadn't been expecting company and now stood in a messy house, resigning himself to simply not straightening up. "Normally, viewing takes place upstairs. But in this case, at this point—well, we just assumed."

Under several of the lights lay metal gurneys, the white sheets laid over them swollen with the bloated bodies underneath. Deb clutched her purse against her stomach and looked around the room. "Oh," she said.

"Yes," Peter said. "Well. I believe that Grant is in the other room."

The doorway between the two rooms was wide enough for one of the gurneys to pass easily through and directly below it the floors sloped into a wide, grated drain cut into the tiles. Their shoes cracked on the porcelain with each step and the smell of formaldehyde and other chemicals was potent and heady trapped in the small space. The walls of the smaller room were lined with surgical tables on which stood a number of large steel machines and a single light hung from the ceiling in the middle of the room, projecting their dim silhouettes over the tiles.

Beneath the light stood a single gurney and under its sheet lay, presumably, the body of their son. Robert felt nauseous in the fumes and the bright fluorescence, which seemed now too much like the emergency lights at the clearing. He tried to breathe through his nose and keep his face still, under the clear illusion that if he looked calm he might begin to feel that way. Peter said something softly to his nephew and the boy left the room. Robert tried to concentrate on the sound of his footsteps climbing the stairs behind them.

Peter stepped beside the body and looked up at them and without looking away from the gurney, Deb took Robert's hand. "Please," she said. Peter slowly folded the sheet down to Grant's waist and Robert could feel Deb shudder beside him. A thick, white handkerchief lay in a diamond over the boy's head, and below it his body had grown a light, uneven blue in the last days and looked bruised, a slightly heavier color tracing each of his ribs. The scratches that Robert remembered from the clearing fell from beneath the handkerchief in purple lines that crossed over one another like thick veins risen through the skin. Down the center of Grant's chest, shining black stitches held the incision of the autopsy together and empty, purple holes peppered his chest and shoulders where stray pellets of shot had been removed from the flesh.

After taking the sheet down, Peter had stepped back into the shadows that covered the far wall and lowered his eyes to the floor. Deb held her hand out over the body without letting it fall. Slowly she reached toward the handkerchief.

"Mrs. Shelley," Peter said quickly. "I'm really not sure—"

Robert looked to where he stood in the darkness, surprised that he was still there at all. Deb pulled the fabric off Grant's face and gasped. The white cloth ballooned in the still air for just a second before falling to the ground. They had cleaned off the blood and dirt and Robert stared down into the open skull and loose, hanging jaw of his son's face. He had the strange feeling of looking directly at the boy's ghost, as though without the earthly things that had muddled him in the dark clearing he was no longer real. Robert tried to breathe but he felt as though his chest were clamped.

"Mr. Trapp," Deb said, her voice even and calm, pleasant almost. "I'm sorry. That's not my son. I think you've got the wrong boy here."

Peter cleared his throat into his hand and walked out of the room without looking at either of them. Deb craned her neck to follow him. "Don't you ignore me, Peter," she yelled as he turned up the stairs. "I'm telling you, that there is not my son. It's not him, goddamn you." Her voice shot back and forth between the tiled walls before finally falling away.

"Deb," Robert said. She turned toward him.

"Who're you crying for?" she said. She had also begun to cry and she wiped her hand across her face. She pointed a finger at the body and her hand palsied above it. "Don't you cry, Robert. Don't you cry for this poor soul."

"It's him, baby," Robert said. "I saw him there the other night. The same."

"No," she yelled again, her eyes closed tight.

"It is," he said.

Robert reached out and pressed his hand onto her back. "That's not my son," Deb sobbed. "My son's beautiful. Remember?" She leaned down toward the body and rested her hand tentatively on Grant's ribs. "This is cold," she said. She looked up and her face was small and contorted. "This isn't beautiful at all."

Robert wrapped his arms around her and helped her straighten herself. "We'll go home now," he said. As he turned her away from the body, her hand reached back and swatted at it without force. "It's not beautiful at all," she said again. Robert didn't say anything as they walked slowly up the stairs together but just listened to her sounds fill the air, each one hovering, it seemed, in the tiny space around their bodies. "How could somebody do that?" she cried. "How could they do that to him?"

Peter waited in the hallway and walked before them to the door.

"I'm sorry, Robert," he said when they reached him. "Really, you have no idea."

"Thank you," Robert said. "And, please, forgive the—" He raised his hand in the air toward the inside of the house and shook his head.

Peter touched his shoulder. "Really," he said. "Not at all."

Robert helped Deb down the flagstone walkway. Heavy clouds had swallowed the ridgeline beyond town. They sat in the car but Robert didn't turn it on. Only now did he realize how unprepared he'd been to see Grant again. Deb was bent in her seat as if she were doubled over in pain and her fingers and hands lay haphazard over one another on her lap. Her face hung just above the curling fingers. She looked up at her husband and her eyes were terrible. "My soul," she said. She stared up at him. "It's like my soul was a whisper, Robert. And I can't hear it anymore."

	Past the last thinning houses and farms, past the open
4.	meadows outside of town and their scattered collec-
	tions of shining, riverside trailers, the woods became

thick again, collapsing against the road and hiding the river below

it. Two cars stood on the slim gravel shoulder and Hayden pulled

his truck in behind them. Stiff, pale leaves stretched over the wind-

shields, low branches leaning in an imperfect awning over the cars.

As the engine died, the sound of the tapping leaves pecked at the

silence. The day was warmer than the last few had been and tower-

ing white clouds sat motionless against the sky. The pavement was

dull and bright, and over the hoods and doors of the cars, the day

shone in pale streaks. Tall purple and green weeds grew along the

edge of the gravel and with the trees created a nearly solid curtain,

behind which Hayden could hear the sound of moving water.

Beyond the road, several hundred yards of loose woods de-

scended in a gentle slope to the river and its scatter of flat, gray boul-

ders, between which the brown water fell into the still pools and small, rushing arms that had once made it famous for trout. At the river's edge two small boys laid their simple poles on the ground and began skipping stones across the surface of a wide pool. They must have been no more than six or seven years old. Even from the distance of the road, Hayden could see the sharp points of their shoulder blades tent the fabric of their t-shirts as they threw the stones, elbow-heavy and sidearmed, in flat, bounding arcs.

Finally, Hayden found Evelyn sitting halfway down the hill. Her back faced the road and she hugged her legs against her chest. Curled up on herself in the shade, she became small, a part of the woods. She was watching the two boys and it seemed her whole body was focused on them. Hayden began walking down the hill and as he came close enough for her to hear him, she turned. Her cheeks were flushed from the day's warmth and she put a finger against her lips. Something about this, the dim, particulate shade and the open woods, the river and the numb, almost stoned feeling he'd had since the last time he'd seen her, reminded Hayden of the dreams he'd been having. His heart pounded and he tried to force himself to breathe.

"I don't want them to know we're here," she whispered as he sat down beside her. "I don't know why. It just seems better."

She turned back toward the river and the little boys. The ground was cool as he let himself down and though it wasn't, it felt almost wet. Evelyn didn't say anything and he sat there waiting for something to seem natural. He had thought of what he was going to say when he saw her, had had several things planned, long speeches that he had all but practiced, but he didn't say any of them. The river pushed slowly between the banks, willow trees leaning out above it and hanging their limp branches into the water. Tiny whirlpools spun behind the smooth stones. "I'm glad you called," he said. "After— when I dropped you off, I thought maybe I'd never see you again. Like nothing ever happened."

"Would you've rather?" she said without looking at him. "Like nothing ever happened."

"Please." he said. "Tell me how." He forced a kind of laugh and felt stupid hearing it.

She looked at him and almost smiled. Her fingers hidden in the sleeves of her sweatshirt, she pushed her hair back behind her ears. Through it Hayden could see the four bruises of Grant's fingertips on the pale skin of her neck.

"Aren't they amazing?" she said as she turned back to the river. "How easy they are. How perfect they seem here."

They were crouched down, the two boys, beside one another on one of the flat rocks, looking into the pool that had been trapped behind it. One of them pulled a stick from the bank behind them and pushed it slowly through the water at their feet. They started laughing, the thin bell sound rising up through the air and mixing lightly with the birdsong and the shaking sound of leaves in the high wind that followed the river. "They're kids," Hayden said.

"I know." She nodded. "I guess that's what I mean."

Hayden took a cigarette out of his pocket and lit it, staring down at his hand. "Evelyn, are you all right?"

She didn't say anything. She was still looking at the river, but there was something about her face, her expression, that felt tone-less, quiet, and it made her seem cold and steady and frightening.

She looked down at her feet. "Have you told anyone?" she said.

Hayden shook his head. "No."

She nodded and then looked at him. "Nobody can ever know what happened out there," she said. "Hayden, nobody can know about that. Right?"

It wasn't until she looked at him, really, that he understood it wasn't coldness or toughness at all, her expression. He remembered her when he took her from the clearing to the house, the begging, wordless sounds and her eyes so scared and empty as she dragged her palms across her thighs and between her legs, and though she had washed off the blood and the dirt there was no way to wash the rest.

Hayden looked upstream from where the boys were and through the trees he could see one of their fathers knee-deep in the water. The translucent motion of a fly rod whipped above him as he cast into a hole along the opposite bank. Hayden had tried to think about it all himself, before this. But he couldn't get past the rearing of the gun in his shoulder, the simple fact of seeing it all again in his head, the image mute, irreducible to any meaning, as though fear alone were saving him from what lay beyond it. He had hoped for something from her, he didn't know what, but something different. He watched the man reel his line in over the skin of the river and then cast again.

"I wonder if he knows the fish can't be eaten," he said.

"What?"

He nodded to the man. "The father," he said. "Over there. I wonder if he knows you can't eat the river fish anymore."

"Hayden," she said. "You're not going to tell anyone, are you?"

"No," he said. "I guess I can't, really. Can I?"

She touched his hand on the ground between them. "Thank you," she said.

They didn't say anything for a while and Hayden watched the man cast that same hole again and again. If he focused he could see the silverish whip of the line curling in the air above the water. Below the shadow of the fly, fish rose and broke its brown surface in perfect circles that lapped first against the rocks and then weakly against the far-off dirt.

"Would you want to be like them again?" Evelyn said. She sounded far away, her voice trembling, as though she had been think-ing about this through the silence, or maybe the whole time she had been sitting there, but was only now saying it out loud. "That young, I mean," she said. "Would you want that again?"

"Are we that different?" he said.

"Aren't we?"

Hayden looked at the ground between his feet and thought about what she was asking. The spines of old leaves stretched across the dirt, weaving through one another like a thin net thrown over the world. "I don't know," he said. He looked down again to where the two boys stood along the river. "If I were that age, my mother wouldn't even be sick yet."

"Your mother," she said. "She's dead, isn't she?"

"Yes," he said. "Seven years."

"I'm sorry," she said.

"You know what I keep thinking about? Since what happened?" he said. "She used to take me to church every Sunday when I was a little kid. I keep thinking about when we used to go to church, you know?" He looked up. She was watching him and he smiled. "The priest, and everything. And how everything was then. When we used to live in our old house and my father would make these big speeches about the Catholics when we got back home. How my mom would laugh at him. I used to feel like I disappeared there, in church. Not in a bad way, you know, but like you were nothing so specific as a person. You just were."

It is strange how saying any one thing leads to so many other things, how the mind webs between almost related moments that seem, in the second, suddenly the same, connected, as though they had stretched their hands right through you to grab hold of one another, and sometimes you can feel it, that reaching. "I've been having these dreams," Hayden said. He hadn't known he was about to say it. Evelyn wrapped her arms tighter around her legs beside him and he saw it out of the corner of his eye. "She's in them, my mother. Or they're about her or something. Being here reminds me of them. There's a river, but maybe it's not this one." He looked over at her and she didn't look back but stayed totally still. "They're all like the same dream, though," he said. "Or like each one keeps starting where the other finished. I'm following her through the woods, and I know the moon's big because everything has that strange blue light that the woods get when the moon is full."

Evelyn nodded. "I know what you mean."

"Right," Hayden said. "And she keeps on turning to say something to me but I can't hear it over the sound of the water. She doesn't look like I remember her, not sick, you know, but like she does in pictures. I'm trying to catch up to her, but I can't. Finally she stops and turns again, and I tell her, 'Mom, I didn't hear what you said. Back there, I couldn't hear it.' First, she just smiles. Then she leans near me. She's bleeding. In the dream, she's bleeding. And she says, 'I'll show you.' Really quiet. Just that. Then she turns around and all of a sudden she's far off again, and I'm running to catch her through the woods. But I can't get any closer. I can't get it out of my mind. You know? The feeling of it."

Evelyn just nodded again.

Over the floor of the woods, wide moths of sunlight beat their wings, folding in and out of sight as the leaves above them shifted.

"In the summers and falls when I was little, we used to come here," she said after a while. "To this place, I mean. There's good fishing on this part of the river, and there's almost never anyone here. We used to come all the time. My father taught me how to fish here, and my mom would swim around in the river so that we wouldn't ever catch anything. I never thought about it, but I guess she was kind of a hippie, you know, or at least an environmentalist or something. I think she used to smoke pot while my dad took me over to fish. My father used to say he was going to put a hook in her if she didn't get out of the water. And we would have picnics on those rocks down there."

She looked up at Hayden. "I can still remember how warm the stone would be on your bare legs in the sun. How it made everything feel better, that warmth through your shorts and on your skin. Back then, the road up there was just dirt. The whole place felt like a secret that was just for us. I still come here a lot, but my father doesn't really fish anymore. I don't know why."

"You should ask him to come," Hayden said.

"Maybe. I don't know what we'd say."

"Does it matter?"

"Sometimes," she said. "Sometimes it does."

She was looking at the boys again and the breeze carried her voice away from him toward the water, turned it distant and soft until it was almost just another part of the trees whistling and the birds, the padded chime of the water. The river was heavy and solid and only at the thin, gray edges could you see beneath the surface. The two boys had taken off their shoes and were rolling their pants up their thin calves. When they stood up again, their feet looked tiny and delicate against the churned surface of the rock, its rippling, millennial story of floods and currents.

One of them stepped off the stone and his feet were swallowed by the water before he jumped back, screaming. The other laughed. They went step for step with one another into the cold water until they couldn't take it anymore and they ran back to the safety of the stone. They were laughing so hard they had to hold on to one another simply not to fall down. Farther down the river Hayden could see the father looking toward the sound.

"Y'all didn't always live in that house?" Evelyn asked. "The one I was at."

"No." Hayden picked up a stick on the ground beside him and

ran it through the leaves at his feet. "My parents used to own a bookstore down on Main. We lived in that old neighborhood just up from downtown. Right near the Shelleys, actually."

Evelyn nodded and rested her chin against her knees. "I remember that store, I think," she said. "It was where all the old men used to sit in those rocking chairs, right?"

"Mm-hmm."

"Why'd they close it?" she asked.

"My father sold it," he said. "After my mother died. I think he just couldn't be there anymore. He didn't keep many of their friends after. I think he didn't really want to be the same person anymore without her. Maybe he didn't want to remind himself of her."

"Do you think you remind him of her?" A thin red line ran over Evelyn's bottom lip from where it had been broken and she worried the scab with her teeth.

"Sometimes, I think," Hayden said. "I think sometimes it's kind of hard for him. He says I look like her. Sometimes, I'll look over at him and he'll just be staring at me. He looks scared, like he would grab me and hold me wherever I was if he thought he could, if it was all right to. But I think there's something else, too. Like he thinks I'm a piece of her that he got to keep when she died. I mean, he never says anything like that. All he ever talks about is books, but maybe that's how he thinks." He ran the stick in a circle in front of his feet as he spoke. "She had a rosary," he said. He was watching the leaves and the stick, running it back and forth beneath them. "And after she died, my father hung it on the wall by the door. Every time he goes through the door, leaving or coming in, he touches it. Really soft, you know, like it's a part of her and she can still feel it. I don't even know if he knows he's doing it anymore, but he does it every time.

"Maybe it's kind of like that for him with me. I mean, sometimes he looks at that rosary so sad, but other times he looks at it like maybe it means everything in the world to him. I guess that's kind of funny. That something Catholic would be so important for him. But then again, so was she."

"Why?" Evelyn asked. "Why would it be funny?"

"Oh. He used to make fun of Catholics all the time. He used to say it was like a sleight of hand religion. That only people with hangovers and landlords could ever really understand it. When we'd go, he'd always say, 'Off to the four-H club?'"

"What?" she said.

"The hideous harbinger of the homosexual histories," Hayden said, smiling. "That's what he called it, the Church."

"Weird."

"I didn't even understand what he meant until so many years later. But I guess you have to know him. He's kind of weird. Really, all he does is read these old books all the time," Hayden said. "But, maybe that's not even it, because he's not like he was. Maybe you would have had to know him then. Before. He was funny, then."

"Oh," she said.

Hayden felt sort of empty, talking about all this like it wasn't his life at all but some sort of distant past. He realized how long it had been since he had talked about his mother and he knew he wasn't saying any of it right and he wondered if he had begun to lose her, her memory, without knowing it.

"Dad, look," one of the boys shrieked. Hayden and Evelyn both jumped at the sound, which was amplified and made sharper by the acoustics of the slopes rising up from where he stood at the water's edge. Six or seven tiny goldfinches rose from a high bush down the hill and hung suspended for a shrill second just above it, their small wings furious and invisible before they disappeared again. The two boys were hunched over a log just back from the riverbank. Downstream the man walked into the water and looked toward them. One of them reached down under the log and pulled something out in his hands. He walked carefully into the water and held it up in the air for his father to see. He looked, standing in the brown water, like some tiny angel knee-deep in the mess before creation.

"What is that?" Evelyn asked.

Hayden looked at the little darkness behind the boy's fingers. "I think it's a rabbit," he said.

"But it's so small."

"It must be young," Hayden said. "I bet that's the burrow he pulled it from." The other boy stood on the bank and stared up at his friend's lifted hands. "I hope its mother doesn't leave it because of their smell," Hayden said.

Evelyn looked at him and her mouth hung open for a second. "Do rabbits do that?" she said. "Like birds?"

"I don't know," Hayden said.

"Go on," the boy's father yelled from the water. "Put it back, now."

They watched as the boy walked slowly back to his friend. He reached his hands gently into the log and the two boys stepped back and stared into the hole. It seemed that neither of them moved at all. Their father walked down the river to a new pool and when he started to cast again his line caught the light from a different angle and spun a goldish aura over the water.

"You know they're closing school for the funeral," Evelyn said.

"Yeah," Hayden said. "My father told me."

"My parents are making me go," she said. "My father said something about what makes communities strong. They think death scares me, that I can't face it." She pulled her hair back again, collecting the strings that had fallen loose over her face. "If they had any idea how little I could face it," she said.

Her eyes were fixed on the boys and Hayden looked at them, too, because he didn't want to look at her then. They were still standing at the log looking into the burrow where the rabbits lay. While Hayden watched them, one of the boys reached out and took the other's hand. They didn't look at one another and they didn't seem to say anything, but just stood there, staring and holding hands.

"I didn't have to shoot him," Hayden said. "Evelyn, I didn't have to kill him, did I?"

From all around them, Hayden could feel the hush of the woods. The air had gotten cooler as the afternoon passed and now the cold lay against his back.

"I want to be like them, again," Evelyn said softly. Hayden

thought she might be crying but he didn't look. "They're beautiful," she said.

She lay back on the ground. Hayden heard a splash as the man began to reel in a fish. He looked over and the big trout jumped out of the water and splashed down again. Its body was slick and taut and its colored belly flashed. When the father pulled it out, Hayden thought how strange the fish seemed curling its muscled, shining body against the man's hand, how beautiful and blinding, even from this distance, it became within the tightening knot of sunlight that held it. The man pulled the fly delicately from its mouth and then slowly pushed the fish back into the water, guiding it away with his hand. Hayden felt relieved as the fish fell away, as it disappeared, strangely colorless now, into the muddied water beneath the surface, and he closed his eyes. He didn't know why exactly, but he thought he couldn't have stood to look at it any longer.

"Hayden," Evelyn said beside him. Her voice was so soft that he almost didn't hear it, and he knew when he did that she was crying. "Hayden," she said again. "Will you touch me?"

The Children of God

My hands lay across my chest and I remember only a few years back when it was still flat, just nothing there. There's something terrifying about that, I think, about the body, not so much a piece of you as an instrument of time.

The morning is gorgeous and seems somehow misplaced in March. The sun's a solid thing draped over my bedroom. Mama's on the porch with some of the civic committee ladies. They're drinking iced tea. Saying what a nice spring it's going to be for all this year's events. They're here today to talk about the cotillion, I think. Twenty minutes after waking up and I'm still just lying in bed, their voices floating up to my window with the brand-new spring smell of the day, all flowers and cut grass. I pull in a big breath, the smell outside so familiar it hurts, try to let it take me back to when I was a kid, me and my brother running around the yard throwing handfuls of the cut grass all over each other.

I try to drown out their voices, concentrate on my breath like the Buddhists say to do. But the sound of my mother's voice keeps breaking through. I hate that they can be so petty now. That they can think about all these fairs and venues, about girls and their dresses, when there are boys coming home in boxes. When, half a world away, there are deserts, hotter than anything, that are swallowing boys whole. My brother, Randall, hasn't been buried for six months. I know the world has to go on and all that. I don't know what else I want from them, from anyone, but it just seems like a lie to talk like that now.

I pick my jeans up off the floor. They're Mama's old skin-tight bell-bottoms from the seventies so I have to jump up and down a few times before they slide over my butt, but when they do, boy, look out. In the bathroom off my room, I brush my teeth, run my fingers through my hair until it falls right.

I stop for a minute as I walk back through my room. It's still filled with all my little girl things, a pile of ragged stuffed animals lying in one corner, pressed after years into the outline of my body. I can't bring myself to get rid of them. All their arms and legs, the tiny, warm bodies that seem to grab hold of me when I lay back against them, that special smell that comes up when I press my face down and close my eyes, like I can smell my whole life coming out of them. It makes me feel something. Safe, I guess, protected by all those years I loved them. I look at the picture of Randall, framed, on my dresser. It's his high school graduation picture. He's still a boy in it, just a beautiful boy, looking like he just conquered the world. All teeth and eyes, his hair a little long, he looks like he could be the poster boy for America. I keep thinking that he's going to be just downstairs, or sprawled out on the lawn with his friends, casually flirting with the old women that come to see Mama. I can't get my mind around it.

I have another picture of him, too. A later one, taken just outside Fallujah, I think, that I keep in a drawer. He sent it to me in a letter. Randall sent all of us our own letters. In that picture he looks different, not quite a boy anymore. But not all the way a man, either. He looks like an animal that's got backed into a corner. It's of him and a friend, arms around each other. They aren't smiling, though, like you'd imagine two friends would be in that pose. No, they're serious as a plague. Randall's face is dirty, mud or sand smeared across it, and gaunt. His eyes are popping out at you. Neither have shirts on. Their ribs shine through the skin, they're sweating so hard. With their free hands, they're holding guns. On the back of the picture it says, *This is my friend Jordan. We came up together.* I don't like to look at that picture. But I keep it anyway.

I slip my cigs in my back pocket, walk down the stairs to the kitchen. The light pops on in the fridge and I just look into it. I don't want anything, really, but it's nice to see all that stuff there, so close. I let the cold reach my skin. From the door I grab a Coke, pop the top, and listen to it hiss. It's so sweet I don't want to swallow.

When I open the screen door, Mama and the other ladies, sitting in their big wicker rocking chairs, stop talking. The morning sun isn't hitting the porch straight on, but it's laying across the yard like a quilt. For a second I think I'm going to run right past Mama and her friends and out into it. Just fall right onto the ground and let it cover me up. But if I didn't stop and say hello, Mama would never let me borrow her car, which is what I'm shooting for.

"Well, Josephine Anne," Mama says. "Nice to see you among the living."

I smile. Sometimes you see Mama's old brightness come out, her smile that makes everything funny.

"Morning, Mama." I lean in to give her a kiss.

"You can say hello to Mrs. Blancheaux and Mrs. Jackson, can't you?" she says.

"Oh, leave that girl alone," Mrs. Blancheaux says. She and Mama have known each other since they were little girls. Apparently, she was wild when they were young. A hippie, I guess. The day after they graduated high school, Mama says she hitchhiked down to New Orleans with the older brother of a girl in their class. Apparently, the way Mama tells it, she came back four years later with a gorgeous, long-haired husband who wanted to grow dope and build a commune in the hills. They're pretty normal now, though. Mr. Blancheaux has this sexy, kind of growly accent and builds subdivisions all over Virginia for people who drive into D.C. and Richmond.

I know subdivisions don't count as communes, but still, she's my favorite of my parents' friends. She still smokes pot, too. I only know that because I once caught her smoking a joint in our backyard at a party, which made her laugh to no end and elicit promises of silence upon pain of death. Sometimes, at parties you can find her and Mr. Blancheaux drunk as skunks, making out in a corner. All Mama's friends say you can't blame them because of how they were when they were young. I think it's romantic, though.

"Hi, Mrs. Blancheaux, Mrs. Jackson," I say. My Coke has started to sweat a little, and I take a long sip.

"Hi, honey," Mrs. Jackson says.

"What y'all talking about?" I ask. I already know, but they love to talk about this stuff, so I let them.

"Oh, we're just talking about this year's ball, honey," Mama says. "Getting some of our final planning together."

"Oh," I say.

"You must be excited," Mrs. Jackson says. "What with your mother on the committee and all." Mrs. Jackson's part of that old Virginia society that always seems nostalgic for the time when it was still all right to be nostalgic for the time before the Civil War. Not that she's a racist or anything. But just that she's got that kind of daft look that some rich ladies have here, as if they woke up one morning and all the ways of being they learned as little girls had suddenly become artifacts. I guess she's nice enough, though. She's known them since they were all little, too, Mama and Mrs. Blancheaux.

"We have an appointment to get her dress fitted tomorrow," Mama says.

I have never heard about this. "Huh?" I say.

"Didn't I tell you?" Mama says, as if it must have just slipped her mind. "I got them to squeeze us in tomorrow morning."

"I've been thinking that I'm not going to the cotillion, at all," I tell Mrs. Jackson. "In protest of the war."

Mama looks down at her hands in her lap. Mrs. Jackson's staring at me like I'm one of those old crazy ladies screaming at the bushes in the supermarket parking lot. Mrs. Blancheaux kind of smiles, but I can barely see it. And I'm looking.

"Christ, Jo Anne," Mama says. I start to feel a little bad. I always do, I guess, when I say things like that to her. I think if she had her way, she would never hear of the war again. Also, she talks about it like it was something magical, when she and the others had their ball, like it's the only purely lovely thing she can recall anymore. I sometimes wonder if in her mind that's the last memory she has that's only hers, that isn't touched somehow by my brother. It makes me feel like I'm taking something away from her, when I tell her what I think. Anyway, it's become a big thing for her, me coming out. It's all she seems to think about.

"A joke," I say. Even though it wasn't. "Where's Daddy?"

"Oh, he had to go to the office for a few hours this morning," she says.

"On Saturday?"

"You know your father," she says. Her eyes go soft for a second, locked with mine, and then blank. "Some big case."

"Uh-huh," I say. "Um, Mama, could I borrow your car for the afternoon?"

"Why?" she says. "Where you going?"

"Just over to Missy's."

"All right," Mama says. "But, Jo—"

"Yes?" I say.

"Don't you think you might want to, I don't know, put something on under that t-shirt?" You can just tell she thinks this is so funny. "You might be some kind of a road hazard looking like that," she says. She can barely contain her laugh long enough to get it out.

"God, Mama," I say. But I'm smiling, too.

"Oh, honey, I wish I still had it like that," Mrs. Blancheaux says.

Mrs. Jackson gives her a sideways look, says, "You wish you ever had it like that." Mrs. Jackson almost never says anything close to funny, so that's it, they all start cracking up.

"Okay," Mama says. "Go on. My keys are in my purse in the kitchen."

"Thanks, Mama," I say. When I come back out I don't even stop, just yell back, "Bye, Mama. Bye, Mrs. Blancheaux, Mrs. Jackson," the sunlight closing in over top of me.

"Bye, Jo," they all say. "Be home for supper," Mama calls to me. From the car I can hear her say, "That girl, I swear." And Mrs. Blancheaux say, "baby, baby," like she was a rapper, though where she heard that I can't imagine, and they all start laughing again.

Missy's my best friend, hands down. We were babies together. Her folks have a stretch of land just outside of town. It's been in their family forever, used to be a big working plantation farm, but now it's just wide-open land. It's on the other side of town from the hills. Missy's got a few horses, and every Miles Davis album ever made, including bootlegs, most of them on vinyl. She just won a place in a painting course in New York City for the summer, which is killing me, that she's going to leave. She's sort of brilliant, and to be honest, she's got be the prettiest girl you've ever seen, which would be unfair if she wasn't just Missy. But she is, so. After we graduate, she says she's moving to Greenwich Village. But I read in a magazine that you can't even get a closet in Greenwich Village for less than two thousand dollars a month, so I don't know about that.

At Missy's I say a quick hello to her mom and dad, run upstairs to her room. I'm like family here, so there's not much ceremony. Missy's lying on her floor reading one of those massive art books. She's got a picture there, too. I recognize it the second I see it. It's a picture of her and me and Randall and two of his friends at a barbeque my parents had a couple of months before he left. When I walk in she slides it under the book.

I lie down next to her. She sits up. She's got three blue streaks in her hair and her grandfather's fedora on. Scraps of paint stain her fingers like rings. We don't say anything. She puts a record on. I listen for a while. It's *Sketches of Spain,* I think. If you're going to be friends with Missy, it helps to be conversational in the atmosphere she lives in, which album is which, who painted in what style. When she first started getting into jazz, I didn't get it, but now I think maybe I do. It seems like it's always saying, there's this empty place in life, right? Some nameless thing you miss without ever having known. Well, listen up. Here's what it sounds like.

I push open her window and light a smoke, which she takes halfway through and then gives back. When we're done, I push it into the secret ashtray she keeps under the desk, lie down again. From where I'm lying, I can see out her window, the sky so blue it doesn't seem real, clouds moving feathery and slow across it.

"So," Missy says. "I showed Steve the De Kooning book the other day." Steve is the boy she's started dating, and that book, whose every last page I've had to more or less memorize, has become like a test for her. I wait to hear how it went. "He's so dense," she finally says. She starts laughing before she even gets it out. "It's like the boy doesn't have eyes, or something." And poor Steve just got bumped to the temporary list.

Then she starts talking about the Woman series, one of which she's made me drive all the way to Washington to see—that, I'm not sure I got; Missy called it visceral, but who in the hell knows what that means—and how they're not really misogynistic like she once read at all, but maybe the opposite. He's releasing women from the constraints of the beautiful form, she says. Or the form, beautiful. I'm not really listening. She's been developing this thought for a few weeks, so I know when to say, uh-huh, and when to act interested. I'm thinking about my father. How I know he wasn't working, but just went to his office to sit and be alone.

You see, here's the problem—this isn't the Sixties, nobody's getting drafted. Randall volunteered to go to Iraq, if you can imagine such a thing. He was strange like that, though. I don't know that I can bring myself to call it poetic, but he always did the things you'd least expect. He said if this was going to be the moment that defined his time, he wanted to be there for it.

I was never scared, I don't know why. We covered it all with crepe-paper drama, acting like it was maybe important but kind of a lark, too. If something can even be both important and a lark, I don't know. But not Mama. No, she didn't think any such thing as that. I thought she was going to lose her mind when Randall told her.

We were eating dinner.

At some point he said, "Why should only the poor people go? Are they worth less? What, war is all fine and good as long as only poor boys go?"

"Oh, Randall," she said. She was crying by now. "You don't risk your life because the world is unfair, darling."

"You don't?" I remember him saying. It gave me shivers almost. "What do you risk your life for, then, Mama?"

"Nothing," was all Mama said. But there was something about the way she said it, because if Daddy was smiling before, he wasn't after.

"You're not listening," Missy says.

"No. I am," I say. The clouds are passing through the window faster now. I can hear the wind against the glass. "I'm listening."

I think my father was ambivalent about Randall going, truthfully. He felt there was something happening in the Middle East that we were going to need to face eventually, especially after those towers in New York. But he certainly wasn't one of those people who thought a war was the only, or even the right, way to face it. He had been too young for Vietnam, but his father had been in World War II, and maybe there was a secret part of him, of all those men his age, that felt the brutal idiocy of Vietnam had stolen something from them, maybe from the world, some cyclic tempering of the generations by a righteous fire, by a worthy cause, that made him hesitate. Maybe he was even jealous, caught up somehow in the Pearl Harbor rhetoric that was going on then. It's impossibly stupid, being jealous of a war. But men have their own mythologies, don't they, that are separate from us. I mean, World War II and blonde pinup girls with big tatas and motorcycles and all that. And besides, he told Mama, remember the first Gulf War. Nobody dies anymore in these kinds of wars.

Maybe it seemed to him like an adventure. I will never know.

But here's the thing, in the end: Daddy hadn't told him not to go. That's what it boils down to, doesn't it? At first he had scoffed a little at Mama, but he started looking at her different, his eyes softer, drawn down a bit more at the corners, later, as the letters from Randall began to come from Iraq. It was strange, he just stopped smiling. When the call came last year, it was just the last thing.

Once, I snuck into Daddy's study while he was still at work and looked for one of Randall's letters. I wanted to see what could make him change like that. I only read a little of the first one I found, just the end, but it was enough.

Dad, it said. I remember it almost word for word.

I take back what I said about the waiting, about how the waiting was the worst part. I dream of the waiting, now. How could I have known? How could I have known what this war would be like, what it could do? I'm one of the youngest, but still we're so many of us just kids, really. How come no one told us how bad this gets. The killing is so much, so hard for anyone to imagine what it's like to see, much less . . . But, maybe the seeing is the worst. When I close my eyes, I can't stop it. It just crawls through me, what I've seen. I wonder if I can ever get away from all that I've seen now. I don't even want to say it, any of it.

The sand is terrible. It grates your skin down raw and climbs into you like some kind of an animal, a parasite. It sticks to your face if you've been crying. It goes unsaid, somehow, that none of us mention the crying. You try to step away from the others, but there's not always someplace to go. Everyone just turns their backs. It's the only thing you can do. I guess that wouldn't seem generous, normally, would it?

I can't sleep anymore. Not really. I wake up shaking, sweating. I just try to remember what I was like before this. I try to hold on to it, but sometimes I wonder if when I get back I'll even be a person anymore. I wonder if I deserve to be. I love you and Mama and Jo so much. I think about you all all the time. Pray for us, please.

your son, Randall

I never read another one of Randall's letters to Daddy.

All of a sudden the sky outside Missy's window seems so empty. So big and empty, I can't look at it anymore.

I turn to Missy, who's still talking. She's changed topics now, but I didn't notice.

"I'm going to go," she says.

"What?" I say.

"To the dance," she says. "The cotillion."

I don't say anything for a minute. We've been working this out together, our positions on it.

"I don't know," I say. "Doesn't it feel just like one of those horse shows your father goes to? I'm afraid I'll be all dressed up, trying to have fun, and the whole time I won't be able to stop wondering how long before they grease me up and give me the bit."

I'm as much a feminist as anybody, but this isn't the real problem, and I know it. There was a time when we were excited for all this, any excuse to get dressed up and drunk, to have a party and make out with some boy, when the absurd parade of it all was the point, and Missy knows it, too.

She looks at me for a long second and then leans back against the wall.

"No," Missy says. "No, I've been thinking about it a lot. I've been thinking maybe it's important for us to go. They all say it's some first grand moment in our lives as women. And maybe they're right, you know? But not for why they think, not because suddenly we're available for marrying or some arcane thing like that. Maybe it's symbolic, though. For us. Maybe it'll be like saying good-bye to being children. Because what we'll be doing, it's something a kid could never even understand."

"What?" I say. "Dancing?"

"No," she says. Her face says I'm being dense on purpose and she knows it and doesn't care for it one bit. "Acquiescing," she says. "We'll be acquiescing."

"Didn't we already take the SATs?"

"I'm serious," she says. "You of all people know this. I mean, you of all people understand this. Right?"

"What?" I say, hoping it's nothing like what I think she's trying to say. "I'm not sure that I understand anything."

Her eyes slide half over the book, the picture I know is still underneath it, as though she is trying to decide whether to pull it out, whether to remind me of all the things I know. Thank God she doesn't, but when she starts talking again, her voice is almost too soft to bear. "Nothing's what you want it to be. The world isn't perfect," she says. "Not anymore, maybe not ever. But you're in it anyway."

I don't say anything. Of course, she's right. The world is not so simple as I'd like it to be, and maybe it never was. But, why do I have to acquiesce? It's a stupid question, I know, but why does the world I've lived in all my life suddenly get to change?

"C'mon," she says. She tries to smile but it can't shake what's in her voice. I don't want to look. "We'll get dressed up like sad Renoir girls and get twirled around in the streetlights by insufferable bores." She reaches over and touches my leg.

"Let's go riding," I say.

Daddy's car is in the drive when I get home. Mrs. Blancheaux and Mrs. Jackson have gone. Mama's cooking. When I open the front door, the smells of the food wrap around me. Peppers and chili powder with that tangy sweetness, vegetables in their sauce, buttery as a kiss. I kick my tennis shoes off at the door and walk to Daddy's study. He's sitting behind his big wooden desk reading a magazine, an old country singer on the CD player. The drink on the desk next to him looks steamy behind its glass.

"Hi, Daddy," I say.

He puts down the magazine, looks back at me. His blond hair is ashy now, but you can still see those blue eyes a mile off. People say we have the same eyes, but I don't think mine have ever shined quite like that. He stands up slow, out of his chair, turns toward me. Then he bends forward, reaches out his hand. I put mine in his, and we start dancing to the slow music, swaying together, turning around the room. He does stuff like this sometimes, out of nowhere just surprises you with something so sweet. But now, this dance, it's almost tragic. When the song finishes, he leans down and gives me a kiss on the cheek.

"Hello, beautiful," he says. "You ready for supper?"

"Uh-huh," I say. I almost can't say anything else. I'm thinking about that letter, what it must have been like to read it, what his face must have looked like when he imagined Randall in hell. The thought that maybe he sent him there. But then I look into those eyes and the smile that comes with them, and he's just Daddy.

"I'm starved," I say.

"Well, your mother's been cooking something up," he says. "Should be ready soon. I've been dying smelling it for the last half hour." He's trying to bring back the man that was here before. I can hear it sometimes when he's talking to me, the effort. And he's close, I think. Getting closer, anyway.

He laughs and I'm a little girl again, just like that. That's all it takes.

I walk into the kitchen and see Mama standing over the stove, almost bathing in the steam. She has a cigarette burning in the ashtray and a blood-red cocktail within arm's reach.

"Hey, honey," she says. "How is little Ms. Missy?" Mama has called Missy this since I can remember and it has never failed to put a smile on her face whenever she says it out loud.

"Fine," I say. "Obsessed." I sit down on a stool at the counter.

"Who now?" she says.

"De Kooning," I say.

"De who?" she says. "I can never keep up."

"Abstract expressionist," I say.

"Like, ah, like what's his name," she says. "The one who splatters the paint everywhere."

"Pollock," I say.

"Right, right." My parents have two of Missy's paintings hanging in their house, both sort of abstract landscapes of the valley just on the other side of the hills. She says she did them both from memory, and there's something wistful about both of them that I love, like they're of a dream more than a place.

"What you cooking?" I say. "Smells good."

"Chicken in some kind of Cajun sauce. Mrs. Blancheaux gave me the recipe today," she says. "Thought I'd give it a try. What do you think?" She blows on a big spoonful of sauce and reaches it out for me to taste.

"Mmm, Mama. That's good," I say. "Spicy." It's the kind of food Randall liked, spicy food.

"Oh, good," she says, stirs the sauce up.

"I wish Randall were here," I say, before I even think that maybe I shouldn't have. She looks up at me.

"Yes," she says. Tears web in her mascara. From the way she stares at me, I know she's been sitting here thinking of him the whole time she's been cooking this. I start to say something else, but she just holds up her hand. "Please," she says, whispering almost. It's strange to think of your mother pleading with you, begging, but that's what it is. She tries to smile. It's enough to break you heart, the whole thing.

I wish I could reach out and grab her, just to touch her. I wish I could walk her upstairs and lay down with her, just close our eyes and not say a word about any of this together. But how do you say something like that; what is it exactly that you're offering? And by the time I even think any of this, she's already stirring again, the shaking cigarette in her hand the only thing that would tell you anything had ever been said.

After supper, Daddy and I are washing dishes when Richard, my kind-of, sometimes boyfriend rings the doorbell. Mama's upstairs getting ready. That's one thing I love about my parents, every Saturday night, rain or shine, they have a party with their friends. I kiss Daddy and yell, "Bye, Mama," as I grab a jacket in the front hall and open the door. The night hits me right in the face, the breeze making curlicues over my skin. And there's Richard, just as goofy as you please, standing with his hands in his back pockets, not a clue in the world of what to do with himself. He's cute, but more like a puppy than a rock star. I close the door, and he leans in to kiss me on the mouth. I let him, but then I push him away.

"Right on my parent's front porch and everything," I say. "God, Richard." I can barely keep myself from laughing.

"Oh," he says. But then as he turns to go down the stairs, I reach out and grab his butt.

"Shit, Jo," he says. But he's smiling from here to Missy's. You really have to feel sorry for boys sometimes.

We get into Richard's car, which looks like it got washed today, the streetlights reflecting in mirrorhouse squiggles over the dark paint. We live in the cradle of the hills, just outside the valley, and as he turns onto the road out of town, it's like the entire world opens up around us. The hills are just a darkness behind us and out in front is the dark, wide-open farmland and eventually, somewhere, the ocean, and above it all the stars are everywhere. Richard drives fast enough to make me feel like we're running away from something, which is kind of sexy, or headlong into something, which is less so. I turn on the radio. A guitar wails right through the car and out the windows to the whole world.

"Y'all get beer?" I ask. That's the boys' job. We just have to show up.

"Yeah, Steve's brother got us some," he says.

"Nice," I say.

Richard keeps looking at me from the corner of his eye as he drives. I know he says he's in love with me, but that doesn't mean anything. The problem with the boys I know is that they don't even see you. Not really. You're something else to them, I don't know, some kind of possibility, an emblem: Girl.

He starts talking about something. The football game they're going to play tomorrow. I don't listen. I just look up through the open window at the sky, so many stars. God, it's amazing.

When we get to Missy's, the four boys bicker about the best way to make a fire. We sit around them drinking beer, passing a cig between us. The ground is getting cold. We pull our knees up to our chins, hold ourselves tight between sips and drags. When the fire catches the boys sit down beside us. They talk to one another.

They talk about the football game tomorrow, the cars they want to buy, colleges they may or may not go to. The girls talk, too. Missy tries to relate whatever it is they're saying to something nobody else knows anything about, which is a problem she has. She's saying something about Picasso, I think. She says his children are always blind and beautiful, always looking away.

I watch the fire as it grows, burning up the air above it. I wish it would go right up to the sky, like it does in the Bible. But it doesn't.

Eventually, after a few beers, the couples start to wander past the firelight into the tall grass around us. This is the way it happens. Richard reaches for my hand, gives me a look. I stand up. His hand is sweaty and soft in mine. We walk into the darkness of the grass. We walk a while, but not too far. I watch the tops of the grass sway in the wind, all together. It seems like a long, slow dance the world does.

When we've walked far enough, Richard turns, faces me. He says something stupid, like, "To me you're more beautiful than all these stars put together," his hands on my hips. I don't hear the words. I'm waiting for him to kiss me, biting my lip so he knows I want him to, and then he leans in and does. I love these kisses. The first soft ones that send shivers all the way to your toes. It's my favorite part, those shivers. I wouldn't mind feeling that forever.

We kiss like that, standing up, our bodies pushing together at all the important places, for a while. Then Richard kind of drops to his knee, but still kissing me. Which is weird and makes me want to laugh. But I go to my knees, too, and then we're lying down. He's half on top of me. His kisses come harder once we're on the ground. I want to tell him to keep it slow. But he wouldn't understand. I guess for boys it's the harder the better. He sticks his tongue all the way into my mouth, and I feel my lips cracking, I'm opening them so wide.

He slides his hands up my shirt, pushes and grabs until my breasts begin to sort of ache. I don't know if this is supposed to feel sexy or not, but the pressure is strong, and that's something. The pressure, at least, is a feeling. You know somebody is here with you. You know they're grasping for something, even if it might not really be you. Sometimes I think that we have to let them figure it out. That our bodies are like a battlefield on which they become men.

While he tries to unbutton my pants, Richard licks my neck, his breath heavy as cloth on my skin. I look up into the stars, let my eyes lose focus so they're just light. Nothing particular, just a sheer light hanging in the darkness. For some reason, I wonder what the night sky looks like in Iraq. I start to think about Randall, whether he ever got to just lay and look at the stars over there, what it was like at night. I wonder if it was ever quiet, if there was somebody to just hold on to if he needed it. I wonder if it's beautiful over there, and if there are the same stars or if they're in a different hemisphere or something. I can't believe I don't know, but I hope that at least it was beautiful.

Richard puts his hand into my underwear, which sometimes feels good, and sometimes feels like you're getting poked with a stick. I close my eyes, feel something like space open up inside me. Something almost like pleasure. I can feel him hard against my thigh, and suddenly I want to suck him, which is a thing I've only done once and never with him. But for a second it's so strong, the urge, I can barely breathe. I want to put him as far as he can go inside me, want to gag on him. I don't know why, and it's not particularly sexy. I just want to swallow this stupid boy whole. And I want to slap him for some reason, too, to beat his head and neck and shoulders pressing down on top of me, but instead I just grab a handful of the grass, bite my lip so these strange sounds grow quieter. It takes me a while to catch my breath again and my eyes tear up anyway, as though I were gagging, when I haven't even done anything.

After a while, he stops. He's been watching me and he has this dummy proud smile on his face like he just won a prize. He thinks I came, I'm guessing. Our breath is heavy against the cool air. He lays his head on my shoulder. I like it now, how it is at this moment. The weight of him and the silence between us resting on my skin, covering me. He kisses my neck and the bones that rise out of my chest. He rests his hand on my belly and I can feel the wet on his finger. After a while he picks his head up.

"So, Jo," he says. That silly grin still on his face. "Are you going to ask me to this dance, or what?"

"Fuck, Richard," I say.

"What?"

"How romantic." Though the problem's not how he says it.

"Well," he says. "I was just wondering, anyway."

"I don't want to talk about it," I say. "Not right now."

He puts his head back down, lets out a long breath. "You never want to talk about it," he says softly, into my chest. He says it so I almost can't hear, but I do. For some reason, it's like the saddest thing.

We lie like that for another minute. Then he rolls over onto his back. We both lie there just looking up at the sky.

"We should go back," he says.

"Okay."

He stands up, restless with his hands. He is all pent-up energy in this soft leaning grass. I wonder what sex with him would be like, what sex would be like, and if it would be like that feeling a minute ago. I hope not. I wonder if we will do it together. I sit up, button my pants and run my fingers through my hair. As I stand up, Richard takes my hand and we push through the pasture toward the air that glows orange up ahead.

Missy and I sit with our backs to the fire, just out of its light. We have beers cold between our legs and a joint that we're passing between us. She finishes it, slides it under her shoe. Behind us, I can hear the boys shotgunning beers, cheering each other on. The girls are starting to talk about the ball. I concentrate on the wind until I can't hear any of it. You can almost hear the air rushing down from the valley behind us, and above and in front of us, the darkness of the world goes on forever and ever until the world doesn't even exist, just the darkness. I look over at Missy and think, right now we're like astronauts. Right now we are two girls lost in space.

I let myself fall back so I'm lying down. Missy looks over at me.

"Hey, Jo," she says. "Can I ask you something? I mean, you don't have to answer if you don't want to."

"Sure," I say. "Shoot." I imagine us in our space capsule, nothing but time.

"Why don't you ever talk about Randall?" she says. "I mean, how you felt, you know, when he died. How you feel now. You never talk about that."

I sit up. I know that Missy and Randall had something serious between them, that she was in love with him. It's strange, but it was never something we talked about. Maybe because I was jealous, I don't know, or maybe it hadn't happened all the way yet, or maybe just because it was something between them, something private. But I saw the way they looked at each other. Everyone did. I know that she has been hurting about it. I know that she wants to talk about it but doesn't because I haven't.

It's almost funny, though, how the tears come into my eyes, like out of nowhere. "I don't know," I say, which is not true. I pull my beer up, feel its cold absence between my legs. I'm not being fair, and even I don't understand why.

"Oh," she says.

We sit there, not saying anything. We look out into the world, so big it's hard not to run the other way. I am crying now, quietly, the tears just rolling down.

"It hurts," I say. The tears start to come so hard I can't see.

I say, "All the time. It's like the world suddenly decided to become something different, to scream, and it's just screaming and screaming and I'm going deaf hearing it. I'm going blind seeing it. That's how I feel. You know?"

I look over at her and even in the dark I can tell she's crying, too. I can hear her breathing.

"He loved you," I say. When I say it, I know it, know it's the truest thing I could say.

Missy's crying harder now but she stays perfectly still for a long time. Then, slowly, she takes my hand and lifts it to her mouth. She kisses it. It seems like the most beautiful thing anyone has ever done, and I know it doesn't make anything different, but still, for a second, it's like the rest of the world, the boys and all their trouble, doesn't even exist. For one, almost real second, it's just us, as we always were.

Eden

5. Dressed in a dark suit of his father's, Hayden stood in the hallway without making a sound, his shallow breath exhaled softly, carefully, from just behind the doorway. In the cabin, the kitchen and the big main room were separated only by a long, waist-high counter, and behind it, his father leaned against the stove, staring out the small window above the sink. His arms were crossed over his chest and a steaming mug sat cradled by one of his hands in the crook of his arm. On the counter, water trapped between the hotplate and the glass coffee pot hissed and then stopped. The cuffs of his father's dress shirt were rolled up and the starched white cotton made his corded forearms look even darker and stronger than they were. His long, gray bangs were combed back off his forehead and his collar was still unbuttoned and his tie hung loose below it. Hayden watched his slow breath rise and fall against the stiff shirt. The morning sun pressed through the window just in front of him and then fell away, swallowed in the electric light of the room.

Along the wall, between the kitchen and the fireplace, stood the tall gun cabinet. It was old and behind its ancient, uneven glass, the long rifles stood in dark, buckling columns and Hayden tried not to look at them. His father turned as he walked into the room.

"How's the suit?" his father asked. He took off his glasses and wiped the lenses with a handkerchief.

"It's good," Hayden said. He buttoned the jacket and the lapels buckled, angling off his chest. "A little tight."

"No." His father smiled. "You look sharp. Want some coffee?"

"Please."

He handed Hayden a cup and then let his weight fall back against the stove again. Hayden held the coffee with both hands and loose steam spilled over the lip of the cup. The dog, Sam, lay stretched out over the floor, his huge skull pressed against the warm exhaust vent of the refrigerator. A bloodhound, he was almost fifteen years old, and milky, blue-white cataracts covered his eyes and made him look, with the wrinkled, folding skin of his face, more and more like a man.

Hayden's father pulled a pack of cigarettes from his shirt pocket and knocked one out of the open hole in the top of the pack. He held it out to Hayden.

"No thanks," Hayden said. His father looked back to the window as he struck a match and the light trapped the spinning smoke he exhaled against the windowpane.

"We probably have to go soon, huh?" Hayden said. "If we're going to go." He looked down into his coffee. Small, oily rainbows floated over the top.

"Yeah," his father said. "Pretty soon." He picked a fleck of loose tobacco off his tongue but didn't move. "Why?" he said. "You don't want to go?"

"No," Hayden said. "Not really."

His father nodded. His mouth turned down, deep lines creasing the skin between his brows as he smoked. He didn't say anything more and Hayden wished he had taken a cigarette because suddenly this silence seemed bigger than the house that held it. "We should, anyway," his father said. "It's important. I've known the Shelleys a long time. And besides," he said. He tried to force a smile but then looked away again. "Now we're all dressed up." He knocked the last hanging ash of his cigarette into the sink.

"Will it be like Mom's?" Hayden said after a while. "Do you think?"

"No," his father said. He turned the faucet on and let the water soak through his cigarette before tossing the butt into the trash beside him. "Look." He reached into the pocket of his pants and brought his fist out and held it between them. "I thought you might want to carry these," he said. He looked down into his hand as he opened it. "Just for the services today, you know. I don't know why, really. I just thought you might like to have them."

Hayden's mother's rosary lay in a tangled ball in his father's hand.

"It's Mom's?" Hayden asked. He looked behind him at the front door and the rosary was gone from the wall.

"It's your mother's," his father said. "Yes."

Hayden picked up the rosary and let the chain fall loose from his fingers. The beads were still warm from his father's pocket and below his hand, the small cross snapped taut and swung back and forth as it settled. "You sure?" Hayden said.

"Just put them back after," his father said.

"I will."

"Make sure you do."

"Okay," Hayden said. "Thank you."

His father set his mug in the sink and began to walk out of the kitchen but stopped just beside Hayden. "This death," he said. He shook his head, lifting his glasses to rub his eyes beneath them. "This kind of death, I mean, here, with nothing to explain it. I know you knew him. Grant. It must be hard. I suppose it doesn't even matter if you liked him or not. When it was your mother, I sort of hoped that you were still too young. You know, to fully understand it. Not that she was gone obviously, but just death, the soul of the thing. How brutal it is. But now, at your age, you see it, don't you? All of it." Hayden watched him as he let his glasses rest again on his nose. He stared at the far wall and then he looked at Hayden. For a second they stood like that, just looking at each other.

"You said it was important," Hayden said. "That we go. Why? Why is it important?"

His father looked toward the wall again. "*Antigone*," he said. "Think of *Antigone*."

"I don't get it," Hayden said.

"The play?"

Hayden shook his head and his father looked at him again. "What are we, Hayden," he said. "What are we when we can't even put away our dead?"

His father squeezed Hayden's shoulder and then walked to the table where his jacket hung over a chair. He unrolled his cuffs slowly, pausing with his head down while he held the jacket in his hands. Standing there, still, his free hand resting inside the jacket, several loose, gray clumps of hair fell over his veined temples and freshly shaved cheeks. For some reason it made him look gaunt, which he wasn't; the wide curl of his iron hair, the hard set of his face seen from the angle Hayden watched him made him look grieved, as if this were all more personal for him than it should have been. Finally, though, he pulled the jacket over his shoulders and walked out of the house.

Hayden turned to look at the rosary hanging from his fingers. He wondered how hard it was for his father to release it, even for so short a time. The quick sounds of his father's footsteps over the wood floor snapped behind him and the dog lifted his head as the screen door shut, waving his nose slowly in the air at Hayden's feet. He finished his coffee and put the rosary into his jacket pocket.

The air was cold and Hayden could see his breath as he closed the front door behind him. The line of trees that edged the far side of the gravel driveway cast their shadows almost to the foot of the house. His father stood just inside the sunlight that spilled across the wide garden, his face turned up to a small, metal flask that shone in his hand. When he was done, he screwed the cap back on and slid it into the back pocket of his pants, nodding at the valley sprawling below him. Small tongues of blue mist curled out of the blue-red woods along the far ridge and the morning dew still lay in a gauzy sheen over the vegetables and grass in front of the house. The late rows of tomatoes they had planted glistened wet in the sun like small, bloody hearts.

"Okay," Hayden said behind him. "You ready?"

"Yeah." His father turned and nodded, watching him come down the stairs and across the grass to the garden. "This time of year," he said when Hayden had reached him. His voice was soft. "It's the most perfect time."

"It's pretty," Hayden said.

"Yeah. It is." His father pushed his hands through his hair and took a deep breath. "Okay," he said. "We can take my truck if you like."

The line at the edge of the driveway where the sun and shadow met was sharp and seemed to separate two different mornings, one bright and clean and the other musty, dark, though both felt cold as winter. Hayden stopped just before the line and turned back toward the house to let the sun warm his face. The dog stood on his hind legs at one of the front windows with his face pushed into the glass as though he could still see. Hayden held his hand up to wave good-bye and felt embarrassed, standing with his hand raised to a blind dog. It was one of those rare moments, though, when a person sees exactly where he stands in time, and Hayden could almost feel it beneath him, the line between being a boy and being a man, the raising of his hand and the awareness of its stupidity each present, separated by a line as sharp as the line of the sun. Behind him the engine of his father's truck turned over.

As Hayden lifted himself onto the vinyl seat, his father let out the clutch and the truck eased slowly forward over the gravel.

Inside the cab the air was cold and the engine coughed as his father put it into second gear.

"You should read some of those I books I give you," his father said. "What're you going to do when you finally go to college and all you've read is what they gave you in that high school?"

"I know," Hayden said. He leaned into the window and each time the truck bounced he could feel the cold coming off the glass.

His father looked at him. "I'm sorry," he said. "Don't listen to me."

"The winter's coming early, huh?" Hayden said. "Look at the grass, it's already going." Along the hump between the tire ruts in the road, what remained of the summer grass was limp and browned, already slumping into the dirt.

"Maybe," his father said. "It could be like this for months, though. Or it could snow next week and then be warm till January."

"That'd be nice," Hayden said.

"No kidding." His father smiled.

At the edges of the road, the smaller trees held their shadows close against the slanting morning light, while the tallest leaned into a loosely stitched archway above. Hayden's father put a tape in and then turned the music down to a hum. Ahead, the dirt road emptied out into the highway, gravel strewn over the perfect black-top in a brackish spray.

"It'll be bigger than your mother's, I'm assuming," Hayden's father said as he slowed the truck at the intersection. "The funeral, I mean. It's not in a church, and a lot of people in town will come because of how it happened, so—"

The truth was that Hayden barely remembered his mother's funeral. All he could remember now was a picture of the priest bent over the altar and the distant, whispered sound of the prayers carrying through the church. What he remembered more, though, was the burial, but even then his memories were a piecemeal of scattered images. He remembered the way the day made the polished marble headstones look wet, and the coffin, the rails, and the grim, slow machine cranking it down as he and his father stood beside the open grave; and he remembered specifically the backs of these particular women, how in the wind their thin dresses clung to their calves as they made their way through the stones, leaving.

"It's not outside, is it?" Hayden asked.

"No, we won't go to the burial," his father said. "That's a thing just for the family." Something about the way he said this made Hayden think that he, too, had just been thinking of the burial and the thought was comforting, even if it wasn't true. He nodded and turned back to the window.

The morning seemed to explode over them as they came out of the trees and the valley opened up beneath the highway. The sun rested on every shining thing in a paper-thin confetti, and for a second before the road descended, the whole of it was laid out without any distinction, a single quilted skin of field and forest sewn together by the twisting, gray-brown seams of rivers and roads. Hayden's father downshifted and held the truck tight against the curves as the road switched back down the face of the hill.

In the wide, open fields, thin cattle huddled in groups of twos and threes against the cold, and where they stood close to the road, their wet eyes and dark, wet muzzles followed the truck as it passed. Large cylinders of hay that had yet to be brought in for the winter sat in sparse rows over the freshly turned pastures and along the roadside the ancient, gray and weathered split-rail fences were shadowed by new rungs of barbed wire. Behind them all the dusty and ancient barns and farmhouses stood, nostalgic and lovely beneath the clear sky. Most of those in the valley who had farms like these couldn't make their living from them anymore but wouldn't give them up either, and they looked exactly like that, resistant and, finally, lost.

Between the fences of the farmland, small lots held mobile homes, the rusted frames of old cars and toys scattered over their lawns. Gardens and sleeping dogs lay like dreams fenced in beside the trailers. As they passed by one of them, a thin, hard-faced man looked up from under the open hood of a hot rod and held a beer can up in the air.

Closer to town the old farms and private lots fell away and the long, manicured flats of corporate farms stretched their arms out to the horizon. The low, prefabricated metal outbuildings huddled between the fields, blistering in the sunshine. The highway went right into town and became one of the two main streets and Hayden could see down its length to the low, hazy skyline of the town's storefronts, cars stalled and stopped along all four sides of the intersection on their way to the service.

His father turned onto a small road that skirted the main intersection and passed through the tiny black neighborhood of town. School had been canceled. Young children playing in the street slowly parted and stood to the side of the road as the truck passed. Their small, brown faces and round bellies turned like watch hands as they followed the windows, staring. The old people sat on their porches and watched the children and watched the truck.

Behind the houses, old, broken gravestones of family plots rose out of the grass in the yards. This had always been the black section of town and they were the graves of those who had died when blacks weren't allowed in town lots or those who were poor enough that the change hadn't mattered. Where the small road met the main street, a ruined, abandoned chapel had been boarded up years ago. Hayden looked up at the steeple, which showed, more dramatically than the rest of it, the distance the church had fallen when part of its foundation crumbled. Tall, wild grass had grown up around the walls and curled, smoky, over the still-white front steps.

Two old black men had brought a folding table into the church-yard and now sat playing dominoes and watching the traffic, occasionally sipping two beers that sat on the table. Their faces were enormously lined beneath the close-cropped silver hair and their long, graying fingers moved slowly over the table, flipping and pushing the small tiles into place absently as they talked.

Hayden's father pulled into the line of cars inching along Main Street toward the high school. He turned off the tape at first and then turned it back on. Neither of them had spoken through most of the ride and his father sucked in a long breath to break the silence.

"You know, you were baptized Catholic," he said. "Did you know that? Your mother, she did it when you were a baby. I didn't know, but she told me about it before she died."

"I know," Hayden said.

"She said she asked the priest to do it spur of the moment one day. She said that if they existed, she wanted the angels to know you were there. Don't ask me how that makes any damn sense. But maybe that's why I gave you the rosary," he said. "Which doesn't make any sense, either. Damn, she's got me doing her voodoo from the grave."

Hayden looked at him and his father pulled a cigarette from his pocket and lit it. "Shit," he said to himself. "That doesn't have anything to do with anything."

"What?"

"That's not why I wanted to give it to you. There's something more," his father said. "I mean, I have something else for you. Maybe I was even trying to convince myself that I didn't need to give it to you."

"Dad," Hayden said. "What are you talking about?"

The cars in their rows hulked forward like some great herd of colored animals, and in the new cold, the exhaust was solid, visible, as though they were all breathing, all trudging forward together into the fall.

"Your mother wrote a number of letters for you. Near the end. She said she wanted to be there when you were older. So she wrote these letters and gave them to me to give you when I thought was best." He looked over at Hayden. His hand rose up and rested over his breast pocket and Hayden could make out the outline of the letters in his jacket.

"I've been thinking I should give them to you for a long time, now. Years, really. But I didn't. You deserve to have them, though, and this is probably a better time than most." He reached inside the jacket and took a bundle of yellowing envelopes from it and let them rest on his lap. "Before I give them to you, I want to tell you that I'm sorry," he said. His hand lay on top of the envelopes and his middle finger ran gently over the edges. "That it's taken me this long. It's hard for me, you know. I've had them for a long time now. It's not right, and I know that, but it's been hard for me to give them to you." He handed the letters to Hayden.

Hayden touched them only delicately. He didn't know how to feel. He leafed through them and they were all opened; the glue yellowed their frayed edges where it had been wet and sealed so many years ago. His father was watching him and Hayden held up one of the envelopes and propped the back up with his thumb. His father nodded.

"I've read them," he said. "I'm sorry."

Hayden looked out the window. Through the tears in his eyes, he tried to focus on the radio tower rising in the distance behind town, the single red light flashing inside its crossed antennas.

"What're they like?" he said.

"Well," his father said. "How much do you remember from right before she died?"

"A lot, I guess. I don't know."

"Do you remember how quick it came at the end? How hard it was for her to keep it together in the last weeks? She wasn't very coherent then."

Hayden remembered. He remembered the morning when his

mother couldn't recognize him and he had stared at her, gaunt and yellowed, trying to will her to remember, and maybe she did eventually recognize him before she closed her eyes. He had always told himself that, anyway. "Yeah," he said. "I remember."

"They're like that, some of them," his father said. "Some of them are like that. All about God, you know, whether he was there with her, at the end. Whether He's here with us at all, I suppose."

They had almost come to the high school, and above all the cars, over the wide lawn, its huge flag hung at half-mast, snapping in the silent wind, rolling and snapping, hanging just inches, really, above the ground. Hayden looked away from it, back through the window at the old, crumbling storefronts and the new, plastic gas stations and banks on the corners.

He wasn't thinking about anything, not the letters, their thin, dry, papery feel against his fingertips, not about his father keeping them all this time, nor what long, unimaginable moments he must have spent with them. He wasn't thinking about where they were going, not about Grant, or Evelyn, or any of it. All he could think about was the flag, hanging out there in the cold, so huge, so thin you could almost see through it.

"It's all right to cry," his father said. He put his hand on the back of Hayden's neck and the weight of it felt enormous. "It's okay to cry now," he said.

He lay his head against his hands. The letters, they smelled like smoke.

6. Cheap, plastic turf had been tied to the rail beside the coffin and hid the darkness of the grave below it. Above, a canvas tent formed a small ceiling staked into the ground on long poles that leaned in the wind and lay a heavy, twitching shade down over Robert and Deb and Rachael, the minister, and the massive coffin in front of them.

People stood in the sunlight just beyond its edges, their bodies shielding the casket and its flowers from the wind. Locks of the women's long hair would rise and dance, suspended in the breeze for just a second before their hands could find them and tuck them away again. They kept their eyes down mostly, these mourners, locking the family into a shallow privacy around the grave. Beside him, Robert could hear the minister speaking, but he paid no attention to what he said.

Large, ornamental oak trees were scattered over the careful green cemetery lawns and lay pools of shadow across the white and gray stones huddled beneath them. Standing alone, their brief flashes of autumnal color brought an unexpected vastness to the twin mono-chromes of the lawn and sky. Robert couldn't feel the wind that had risen through the afternoon, but he saw it in everything, the women's hair and dresses, the sway of the tent and the suit jackets flapping along the edges of the crowd. From the trees it stripped leaves and spun them over the rolling grass until they disappeared in the distance. He could hear it, too, the wind, clapping the fringed edges of the tent into an unsteady rhythm.

Against the back of his knees pressed one of the folding chairs that had been set out behind him and Deb and Rachael in case they needed to sit during the service. And Robert did want to sit down. He wanted a moment to simply account for this, to cut through the daze and find something, any one thing, to focus on. But he didn't. He forced himself to stand, to at least seem solid, stable, as though the figment of strength were even relevant here. But maybe this was the only thing, he thought, this willful abstraction, this mythology of men, of little boys' heroes, that he could hold up now and say, this, this will make it better. And even if it wouldn't, still he reached for it, because whatever else, it was something, something to hold on to, and maybe that's the most we're given in the end, a dream we can hold on to.

Without turning, Robert looked at his wife and daughter, the heels of their shoes pressing into the carpet laid over the grass, their exposed ankles and calves. They were each lost in their own thoughts, and he realized that at least they were all together in that. The thin-stemmed white roses they held teetered between their fingers and their dresses, thin black sheaths, both of them. Everyone at the service had been given a flower to throw onto the coffin at the end of the ceremony, and while the others had carnations, he and Deb and Rachael had been given these roses. He ran the pad of his thumb over a silky thorn and wondered if anyone really expected this thing, this simple flower, to stand in for something as impossible as good-bye. Or was it like the suit at the funeral parlor, every symbol suddenly stunted in the face of what was true, reduced to a silly grasping just when you needed their full breadth most.

The minister was repeating the psalm, *lo, though I walk through the valley of the shadow of death,* and Robert tried not to listen. He reached between them until his hand found Deb's, but the gesture felt forced, affected, because, at least in this second, they shared none of this, and he let his hand drop beside him again. She was so still, Robert wondered if she had noticed the touch at all. It took him a minute after that to realize that the minister had stopped talking. The song of his voice had fallen away and all that was left was the awkward rhythm of the tent snapping and the distant whistling of the wind against the gravestones. Slowly, the people raised their eyes. The sunlight pressed down on their faces and bleached their features. He remembered, of course, what he'd been told to do, but he couldn't believe that the service had passed so quickly. It took the minister's hand on his shoulder to finally convince him that it was over. He nodded and the hand fell lightly away.

Robert took a deep breath and walked to the coffin in front of him. He felt stupid and angry, walking forward and putting his flower down in front of all these people like a good mourning father, pantomiming the grief he didn't even understand for them. Between the bodies of the crowd he could just make out his father's gravestone. The polished marble was brilliant in the daylight that slipped through their bodies. He tried to remember his father's funeral, what he felt during it and then after, but he couldn't.

Standing over the casket, the glossy wood seemed somehow liquid, bright despite the lack of any actual light. He felt nauseous, empty, not torn apart inside like he might have expected, but distant and small beside the heavy wood. Only now, directly above it, could Robert see the darkness and the earth below the casket, the strange mechanical arms that held it up above the empty space. It was supposed to be his grave, the one he stood beside now, the one beside his father, and he had the brief, irrational urge to throw himself inside of it—fuck these pretty symbols. But to push the casket aside and drown himself in that darkness, let these people see that. He would take his rightful place as though the past were something that could be forced, contrived or colluded with, tricked into never having happened. But then he remembered the clearing out in the woods, what he had seen there, and he thought that it was that place, not this, not this hole, that his son would never come back from.

He leaned down and pressed his hand against the coffin. An ornate arrangement of flowers lay on top of it and the tangled net of stems seemed to clutter the thin lace cloth beneath them. The wood was cold at first, but slowly warmed under his hand. The pungent and thick smell of the flowers stuck in the back of Robert's throat and reminded him of the smell of his son's body in the clearing, that viscous, almost living taste of something dying, dead. He gagged and then held his throat tight so it didn't happen again. As his weight shifted, the coffin moved slightly and the translucent petals of the flowers trembled against one another and seemed, in that second, almost tender.

He had been expecting something from the contact of his hand with the coffin, some sort of revelation or rupture, but whatever it was, it didn't come. His mind refused to grow deep and think of something that would make this moment important, and he was left just standing there, the smell of the flowers the only thing he could think about. This thing, he thought, it's just a box. He lifted his hand off the wood. Just a box.

Outside the tent, Robert waited for Deb and Rachael. The sun was stronger than he had imagined and the day was nearly warm beneath it and from where he stood now, the shade under the tent seemed too much, the kitsch of an unnecessary prop. Deb was slow making her way to the casket. Cupped lightly in her hands, the rose seemed thicker, fleshier pressed against the dark belly of her dress. With the exception of her face, she was totally still after she dropped it onto the other flowers, her hands held out above them for a long moment until she brought her fingers to her mouth. Her face simply collapsed. It was an expression that, given the circumstances, must have seemed unremarkable to everyone else who was watching her. But to Robert it was frightening, because he had seen this expression already. It was as if this grief were an infinite stairway that she was descending, carefully, one step at a time.

She turned from the casket and began to walk toward him. Her eyes were glassed and dull, the blind antechambers of actual consciousness. When she stepped off the felt carpet, the sharp heels of her shoes sank slightly into the earth and she pitched forward, swaying slowly until she balanced herself. Robert raised his hand in front of her but didn't touch her. He wanted to grab hold of her, to pull her somehow out of all this, but he was afraid to also, afraid for a second to even touch her. He forced himself to slide his arm around her, though, anyway, and her body leaned limp against his chest as she sobbed.

He could smell her skin this close, and the mixed fragrances of her body and soap and perfume hit inside him a distinct note that brought him back again, back to her, to the actual woman, and it was like a nostalgia, as if someone had just shown him a photograph of a world in which they were more than just vessels for this unbearable sadness. "What can I say?" he asked. He wanted to reassure her, but as soon as he heard himself say it, he knew it was more selfish than that, more pleading. "This is our family, Deb," he said. "We still have that left here." He wanted her to help him, that's what it was. Show me, help me, that's what he was really saying, he realized, and he felt weak, lacking, because it was he that was supposed to show them.

She looked up and her bloodshot eyes searched his face. Shaking her head, she said, "Stop. There's nothing to say. Don't you understand that, Robert? Nothing can be said."

He turned away from her, her stare, the bleeding, wet witness of it, which he suddenly couldn't stand. They both watched Rachael walk toward the coffin, her arms held at slight angles from her body to balance her on the unpracticed heels of her new shoes. She raised the flower in her hand but didn't drop it immediately. She looked at Robert and Deb and then back. Stretching her neck, she looked down on the coffin and the flowers, the motion carving the exposed hollows above her collarbones even deeper than they were, providing the shade caught inside them the illusion of density. She dropped the flower and began to walk toward them before it had even settled.

Rachael walked between them and Robert's arm lay over Deb's along her shoulders. A hundred yards off, the cemetery was split in half by a road that divided the old, wooded graveyard from this newer addition, itself nearly three-quarters of a century old, and all along the road's length the low forms of cars seemed to cower. Robert thought the curving road looked like a river, the perfect, shining pavement showing a false depth where the sun broke through the shade trees above it. A long, black limousine waited for them, the daylight etching white rivulets over its skin. The driver stepped out of the car and opened the door. His ancient, black uniform, his back straight and head bowed, the black visor of his cap covering his eyes, it all made him look terrible, like some kind of gruesome Percival, a vestige of the world that had survived through its changing.

Rachael's heavy, stuttering breaths were the only sound as they made their way through the stones. The sun warmed Robert's dark suit and through it his back. The driver took a half-step away from the door as they walked up and he bowed slightly and nodded as

Deb put Rachael into it. It was dark inside the car, consoling. "Ma'am," he said as Deb folded herself in after.

Robert looked into the car where Rachael and Deb had all but disappeared and then turned back to the grave. The last of the people were just now crowding around the coffin to place their flowers down, and over the dark wood they rose in a formless pile, and all around it, the fallen and shredded petals littered the green carpet with color. Beyond them the horizon arched in the shapes of the hills all around, which, turned small with distance, seemed as dangerous and quick as the bent backs of circling animals.

Amidst the people walking toward the road and their cars, Robert saw Dan send his family on and begin to head toward him. He nodded when he saw Robert looking at him and Robert walked to meet him on the grass. Heavy bags hung under Dan's eyes and his wide belly pushed the open front of his suit coat out with each step. Before they reached one another, Dan pulled a cigarette from his pocket and lit it, and as they shook hands, he pushed the smoke out of the side of his mouth where it was carried up into the air.

He held up the cigarette and looked back to where his wife and daughters were walking. "Not supposed to be smoking anymore," he said. He huffed out a short, faltering laugh. Robert nodded.

"How're you doing?"

"All right," Robert said. His voice caught slightly, and he realized then how little he had spoken today. "I'm all right, I guess. Thanks for coming."

Dan nodded. "Of course," he said. "How's Deb?"

Robert looked back to where the limousine sat waiting. "I don't know," he said. "It's tough, you know. At Peter's she saw him. Grant. She asked to see the body."

"Jesus."

Dan took a long drag off the cigarette and his eyes squinted and sent deep lines into his cheeks. People walked in silent, sparse groups through the cemetery all around them, their squat, dense shadows carried at their feet.

Dan looked down at Robert's hand, and Robert followed his eyes, only then realizing that he still held the white rose he had been given. He could see, in the sunlight, the small, delicate veins that ran through its petals. He held it up.

"I thought I had put it down," he said. "I can almost remember dropping it."

Dan nodded.

"I don't know what's wrong with me," Robert said.

"Listen," Dan said. "You can't expect too much. Not yet, not from any of you."

"I just hope," he said. "I just hope that I have enough for this, for them."

"Enough what, Robert?"

"Strength?" he said. "Love? I don't know what. Maybe that's what scares me. But this, all this here." He looked over the cemetery, but he was thinking about the clearing, the tall grass moving in small eddies around him as he kneeled beside Grant's body, the random sections he had noticed that had been threshed by bone or shot. "This can't be the end for me, Dan. I thought maybe it could. For a second, I thought I wouldn't care about any of the rest of it.

The why, the how. It would all just be eclipsed, you know, by the fact. But it isn't, is it?"

"What can I say?" Dan said.

"Tell me something," Robert said. "Tell me anything."

Dan put his hand on Robert's shoulder and let out a long, smoky breath.

"I know," Robert said. He nodded. "I'll see you at the house."

They shook hands and Robert watched Dan walk toward the road for a second before heading back to the limousine. The driver still stood beside the car and he didn't say anything as Robert lowered himself into the back.

Rachael lay against her mother's breast, crying, and Deb held her with one of her arms. The child's tears had soaked the fabric of Deb's dress and the stain reminded Robert of when she had been breast-feeding. Her face was turned toward the window. Robert followed her eyes. Across the road, through the knotted tree trunks and low, sprawling branches, the crypts and ancient, powdery stones of the old cemetery had begun to sink back into the ground after so many years, leaning now in dull, pious angles to the weedy sunlight.

Through the tinted window the sun took on a dense sepia-tone. Robert watched Deb but she didn't notice. He wanted her to be different now, easier, to feel the catharsis of the funeral in the way he didn't. In this light, it seemed as though grief, the simple, brutal strength of it, had made her more beautiful than Robert thought would have been possible.

He leaned forward and took her hand from where it lay on her knee and kissed it. Without looking at him, she caressed his cheek as though he were another child. And it made him feel like a child, the touch, contemptuous and needy. He lifted his hands over his face and he felt the stem of the rose he had forgotten again bending over his skull. Such a stupid, delicate thing.

The Children of God

 I wanted to stop suddenly, to just stand beneath the simple, opening sky with eyes closed and face turned upward, while the rest of the world ran past me. But I could already see the yellow lights of the bar on the corner, so I just kept on running from eave to eave instead. The rain had been coming down off and on all day, the gutters turned into tiny, ashen rivers spilling over the sidewalks. As the air darkened into evening, the streetlights had flickered on and now soaked the wet, uneven pavement in wide swaths. At the end of the street, I could see the courthouse where I worked rising above the roofs, its gilt, uplit dome radiating even in the rain. It would have been nice, though, to stop for a second anyway, just to get wet and not care.

Inside, the bar was warm, the air steaming with damp, clothed bodies and cigarette smoke, and from within its lights, what had seemed like twilight outside became pitch dark. I wiped my face as the sounds swirled around me, the soft tenor of young, boozy voices and music. I was glad to be there, glad to be around people who were, frankly, exactly like me.

I tried to soak it all up instantly, as though I were a sponge of carelessness. Hoping that the giggles and the whispers, the old Tom Waits song on the jukebox and the faint sound of the pretty girl, already drunk in the corner, singing along had the power to turn me thoughtless, to beat out of me the conversation I had just had with my mother. Her voice always sounded so far away over the phone, so tired now with reports of my father's health, with telling me how much it would mean if I came home. I sometimes thought that her voice itself had simply grown sad enough, weak enough with grief, that it could no longer make the trip over those hills to the rest of the world. But it could also have been me. Maybe I just couldn't hear it anymore.

I lit a cigarette, rolled my head around my neck. The warm flush and perfumed, appley smell of the girls' skin, the big smiles and shining hair, the wide, flat oxford shirts of the guys, they were quietly comforting, and I was lifted a bit, I think, by the nonchalant narcissism that can only be achieved by someone looking at their own. We were all around twenty-five, fresh and important with our first grownup jobs and grownup lovers, death so far away, it seemed, we could hardly remember the word. Everyone was laughing, all of us.

I noticed Ted, the friend I was meeting, sitting at the bar, his jacket thrown over an empty stool on his left, a lovely looking rocks glass in front of him. I made my way over, tossed my cigarettes and lighter on the bar from behind him.

"Didn't I ever tell you the story about the whore?" Ted said without looking up from his drink. I pulled out the empty stool. His hair, thin and blond, had dried from the rain and now hung haphazard over his eyes. I wondered how he'd known it was me standing behind him.

"No," I said. "I don't think so."

I slipped my jacket off and slung it around the back of the stool. Ted picked up the drink in front of him, the watery oak of whiskey that's been sitting a while, thin skipping stones of melted ice floating along the top. As he looked over at me, a limp, heavy smile on his face, I could tell that he was halfway to drunk and probably feeling more sentimental than I might have liked.

"Glad you came out," he said.

I hadn't been coming out much lately. Things had been weighing on me, and I had mostly been getting drunk in my apartment, ordering Chinese, passing out with my clothes and the lights still on.

"Thanks," I said. "Me, too."

Ted took a sip of the whiskey he was holding up, and I motioned for the bartender.

"Scotch," I said when he came over. "Rocks. Macallan, if you have it." I read somewhere, once, that a man should be able to order his drink in three words.

He nodded, looked at Ted. "You want another?" he said. "Bourbon, right?"

"Please."

He nodded again, grabbed two glasses, and turned around. Ted reached over and pulled out one of my cigarettes, lit it.

"There's this new thing," I said. "It's called a machine. You don't even have to wait for the girl to come around anymore."

Ted smiled. "If you put on one of those cute little dresses, though," he said. "I've got a shiny fifty cent piece for you."

I had moved to town, the state capital, almost a year before, when I took a job as a clerk at the district appellate court. Ted was fresh out of journalism school, splitting time between the obituaries and the city desk of the paper. Sometimes I gave him tips, and he had gotten me invited to a few good poker games. We became friendly that way, kept helping each other as we donned the stiff, new gowns of competence and adulthood. I dated his twin sister, Emma, for about three months, until she broke it off.

She said she couldn't watch another boy run away from things, drink until he forgot, and I thought that was fair. She said I was too much like Ted. I wasn't sure, but I might have loved her.

When the bartender brought our drinks, I laid down enough money for both.

"Thanks," I said.

I waved the change away, felt the dry burn of the first sip slide down.

"So," I said. "How's Emma?"

She had been with me when I found out about my father, the tumors growing through his lymph nodes. She had curled up around me, immediately sensing, in that frightening female way, what was going on, or at least how bad it would be, while I tried to keep my voice steady on the phone with my mother.

Ted looked up, his expression sort of out of focus, sympathetic. I tried not to talk about her that much. But I guess I did, anyway.

"You know," he said.

"Yeah," I said. I did know, not how she was but what he meant. He didn't know. They were close in a way, but only in a way. It was strange, watching as you got to know them, disarming, like those rare moments when it suddenly dawns on you that everything in your reflection is backward.

She was the prettiest girl I had ever slept with. I took another sip of my drink so that I wouldn't say anything else.

"She dating anyone?" I said, mouth full of whiskey.

Ted looked up at me again, his eyes slow as two moons.

"I can't believe I never told you that story," he said. "The one about the whore. Really?"

I breathed out. "Okay," I said, swallowing. I could understand. "Tell me the story about the whore."

"All right," he said. He took a deep breath, ashed the cigarette in his hand.

"I've been thinking about it all night. No idea why," he said. "It was a few years ago. Early in the summer after I graduated from college. I had barely slipped through my last finals. I mean, barely. My father had died a few months before. Emma was really broken up. I guess we all kind of were, in our own ways. I was getting pretty wild. Doing a lot of coke, drinking, like, nonstop. None of my friends had jobs for the summer yet, so we would start drinking about noon. By eight we had picked up a bunch of blow, so we could keep going, you know? Strictly maintenance. Then out all night."

"Listen," I said. I stretched my hand over my eyes, touched my temples. "No offense, but I'm not sure I can handle this kind of thing right this second, you know? I mean, some kind of comparison thing. Some kind of don't go down the dark path thing. I already heard that shit from Emma. And anyways, maybe I like the dark path, maybe the dark fucking path looks like Disneyland to me right now, slushies and trippy lights and seven free rides with Snow White and a dwarf up my ass. And so what if it does?"

I stubbed my cigarette out, wondering where the hell that had come from.

"Relax, man," Ted said. "What do you think this is? Oprah? You're not going to jump up on the stool or anything, are you? Listen, I don't give a shit about healing the wounds your inner child got jerking off. I'm not Emma. I'm just telling you a story. This is just context. And, besides, I like you just the way you are—drunk, smart, ugly, and evasive. Winning combo, man. Don't change a thing for me."

I shrugged my shoulders, picked up my drink.

"Okay," I said. "Sorry."

"No problem. But it was completely crazy, that's all I'm trying to say. I don't even remember it all that well. Patchy, how shit gets sometimes, you know?"

I nodded. I knew something about times like that. And Emma

had told me some things about this time in their family. Told me about Ted, how he had almost killed himself mixing booze and some kind of prescription pills after their father died, how it was the saddest thing she had ever seen, watching him throw up in the emergency room through a tube.

"You think I'm ugly?" I said.

He looked over. "No, but if I hadn't thrown that in there it would have gone to your head and you wouldn't have listened to a thing I'm telling you. And this is a good story." He looked down at his drink. "I don't know, real."

"Fair enough," I said. "Continue."

"Anyway, Emma was hating me," Ted went on. "She said I was running away from human connections, that I had intimacy issues. She was reading a lot of books, you know, self-help shit. Stuff about grief."

I nodded. She wielded these kinds of accusations like a chef's knife, and they were not totally unfamiliar to me.

"And our mother, she was like a zombie. She would just sit in the kitchen all day in her bathrobe listening to the preachers on the radio. It was weird, but it was all right, too. You know? I felt like I needed to be completely alone. I had my own way of dealing. Seven dwarves dancing a waltz on my prostate and all that." He smiled and slanted a single blue iris over at me without turning his head.

"Right, right. Of course," I said, "there's something to that," nodding my head.

Ted looked at me.

My glass was empty. He motioned for the bartender to bring two more and swallowed the rest of the whiskey in his glass. He dropped enough money for both drinks on the bar. I lit another cigarette.

"Can I get another?" Ted said. I pulled one out for him, and he lit it, pausing.

"I thought there was a whore in this story?" I said after the bartender had brought our drinks.

The whiskey was making me feel heavy, and so far Ted wasn't helping. I wanted him to move away from the context, the stream of events, which were unappealingly, but distinctly, familiar, like seeing a picture of yourself on drugs.

Moreover, I wanted the feeling in my gut to go away, the one that I got every time I talked to my mother, the one that felt like someone had just pulled a drawstring on my insides. There were too many things it pulled tight. Of course, there was Emma walking out my door, crying, that last time, and the look on the judge's face when he pointed out, the other day, that I had vomit on the pant legs of my suit. But really these were just stand-ins for the real memory, the one where I stared out the window, the only time I'd visited my father's hospital room, at the clinging, early morning mist and the light fingering the hills where I had spent my childhood not so long ago, while he described, in the gravely whisper his voice made before the morphine had had a chance to smooth it out, how humiliated he felt, shitting himself in front of a nurse after his operation. I couldn't even look at him, all those tubes worming under the skin.

What I mean is that I was sort of looking forward, now, to hearing a story that didn't have anything to do with me, and I wanted it to move on.

"I'm getting to that," Ted said. "This night, the one I'm talking about, was just like any other during that time. It was raining, I remember that. One of those insane spring storms, you know?" He nodded his head to the window of the bar still muted into antique glass by the rain.

"Because I remember someone saying something about streets of gold while we walked into town. We were all constantly trying to be ironic. But, actually, it was really pretty.

"But before that there was nothing special. I mean, nothing particular happened during the day. I went over to my mom's house in the morning, when I woke up. Emma was there, cooking breakfast for her, and she was just sitting there, dazed, listening to that fucking Bible radio. I swear I thought that voice was going to drive me crazy every time I went over there. And Emma's just acting like nothing's wrong, like everything is just cool, you know, while my mother's sitting there in her underwear, this old, ratty robe hanging open, intense as hell, like the radio is going to save us all. I walked right in and right out again. Didn't say a word. It was just too weird."

"Did they see you?" I asked. Emma had never mentioned the radio when she talked about that time, never mentioned her mother in a bathrobe, empty-eyed or undressed. She was the kind of girl who neatly clipped out the ugly memories as if she were making a collage of pictures for later in life, and I had sometimes wondered what hadn't made it, what images had ended up lying facedown on the floor, waiting to be swept away. Ted had never talked to me about the time after his father died at all, except when I told him my father was sick. Then he had given me a hug, said, "It's hard as shit." At the time, it had seemed like enough.

"I don't think my mom even noticed," Ted said. "But Emma did. I heard about it later."

"I can imagine," I said.

"But, anyway, this was late, what I'm talking about now," he said. "I was walking home by myself. Maybe that's why I remember the streets so well, because they looked like that when I started walking home, too. Everybody else was still partying, or had gone home with some girl, or something. I was walking out of downtown, and it started raining again. In less than a minute, I was totally soaked."

I pulled two more cigarettes out of my pack, put one in my mouth and one on the bar. I pushed the cigarette on the bar over to Ted and watched it roll across the wood, slowly, until it lay against his arm. He didn't even look. I could tell he was at the point in the story where he was entering it all again, the time, the place of it, feeling that night around him through the simple, total force of remembering. It was interesting, like a promise he was silently making: his eyes lost, roaming through another time, freed from the tyranny of actually seeing to be instruments purely of expression, his mouth slack with the weight of words about to form.

"I was about halfway home," he said, finally. "Walking down that end part of Lincoln, you know?"

I nodded. I knew the neighborhood he was talking about. It wasn't exactly bad, but it wasn't good, either. You know, weathered shotgun houses with sagging porches and flaking paint, dogs on chains. Tucked between the student neighborhoods and downtown, it was the type of place your mother would read on the Internet that people got mugged, which was just a slightly less overt way, when you got down to it, to warn that black people lived there, too.

"It had gotten a little cooler," Ted was saying, "with the rain, and I remember holding my jacket together at the collar. I guess I was trying to stay dry, though I was pretty far beyond that by then. I had been smoking a cigarette, but the rain took it right off the filter. So I was just trying to get home, quick. I heard somebody yell, 'Hey.' I figured they weren't talking to me, but I stopped and looked around anyway. I don't know. I was wasted so I stopped and looked to see who was yelling. There was this woman standing on the porch of one of the houses next to me, watching me. She must have been there the whole time, but I hadn't noticed her at all. I hadn't noticed that anyone was out.

"She was standing just under the porch light, so I couldn't really see her. Not well. She was kind of backlit, you know? Even though the light was above her. She was all shadowy, her face, and I couldn't make it out. She was wearing this tiny pink negligee-type robe thing, and she had it pulled really tight around her, the same way I was doing with my jacket, even though she was under the porch roof. All I could think was, she must be cold. She must be really cold."

Ted picked up the cigarette that was resting against his arm. I watched as he sucked the flame in, the paper burning back in small, stuttery patches.

"I thought this was in the spring?" I said. I motioned for the bartender to bring two more drinks. "Why would she have been so cold?"

"It was spring, but it was cold," he said through the smoke. "I was cold, anyway. But then, I was wet and she wasn't. And the robe, there was something about the robe. I don't know; it's irrelevant, anyway. Whether she was actually cold. It's just what I thought."

"Okay," I said.

"There was another woman, too," he said. "Leaning against the doorway. I couldn't really see her, just her shape behind the first one. The one who had yelled, she just smiled. She reached out her hand and said, 'Baby, come on out of the rain.' Those exact words."

The bartender had brought our drinks, and I laid down the money for them. I stubbed out my cigarette while Ted kept talking.

"I was standing in the middle of the street," he was saying. "In this crazy storm, you know? Even drunk, I knew she was a whore. I had never even spoken to a prostitute before. I mean, I'm not the kind of guy who goes to whores. But I just walked up the steps. I didn't even think about it. Nothing. I just walked up and took her hand. The strangest thing was, I don't even think I looked at her. Not until later anyway. I just took her hand, and walked into the house. She had bare feet. I remember that. She didn't have any shoes on."

"Were you scared?" I asked. I don't know why I asked him this, except that I thought I might be scared. I had never been near a prostitute outside of the court, and I guess I thought it might be scary. I come from an Irish Catholic family. Not that this explains it exactly, but it seemed to me, right then, as I wondered at my prudishness, that maybe it did. You see, sex itself, the silken heart racing, the strange alchemy of creation and transgression that still remains a generation or two after real shame has fallen away, it's frightening enough to me, much less bringing money into it. Money is a sort of dirty thing already among the Irish Catholics I've known, to be spent as quickly as possible, best of all in profligacy, just to show how little you think of it. I don't know, it's a cultural thing, I suppose. Involving money in sex feels a little like robbing a bank and then sitting in your car to smoke a joint before you go. You've kind of forgone the option of leniency, haven't you? Maybe the poverty of our history has turned sin, or at least ours, into a kind of socialist endeavor, each one compounded exponentially by the weight of the change in your pocket at the time.

Ted thought about my question for a while, though, as if it wasn't simply neurosis. He took a last pull off his cigarette, while the filter smoldered black at the edges, turning in on itself.

"No," he said. "I don't think so. Not then, anyway. I wasn't really thinking. Not about anything. Not enough to be scared or excited or anything. I just kind of went."

He stubbed the dead butt out in the ashtray, took a sip of his drink. I did, too.

"We walked past the other woman," he said, "as we went into the house. She was smoking and she smiled at me and her teeth were crooked and the smoke came out of her nose when she smiled. You could tell that she was young, but she didn't look young."

He shook his head. "Anyway, we passed a bunch of doors that were closed and some that were open, and in one was this old lady, really fat, in an orange dress, smoking a cigarette. She nodded at us as we walked by, and I remember thinking, I know what's going on here. I know what's about to happen."

"Of course," I said.

"No," he said. "But, see, that's the funny thing. I didn't really, you know? I didn't really know what was happening. I mean, I thought the words, but not the concept. What I was really thinking was how small her feet were. I remember that they looked almost like a little girl's feet, they were so small. They seemed totally misplaced in the situation.

"She stopped at the end of the hall by this stairway and turned around. It was the first time that I really looked at her, that we were really face to face. She was old. I couldn't believe it, how old she was. She must have been in her fifties. Or at least close. She was still holding my hand, and I thought, God, she's so ugly. She wasn't; she was just older. But that's what I thought. She's so ugly."

I picked up my glass, but didn't take a sip. We had been going pretty fast and the three whiskeys were seeping through me thick as sap. I held it there in front of me, though, and felt the cold condensation against my hand, listened to the tinkle of the ice. For some reason I was thinking about Emma, how last summer's tan line clung to her hip like something hungry.

"She looked at me. She stared at me in the eyes," Ted went on after taking a sip of his drink. His words were coming slower now, the pauses longer as he slipped farther away from the bar into this other thing. "She was smiling. Our hands still hung between us. And with her other hand, she opened her robe. So gently, though. She slid her hand down her body, and the robe just opened.

"She was standing there basically naked. Her breasts were big and heavy, not like any girl I had been with. They hung off her. And she had these stretch marks across her belly, but none of that mattered. All I could think about was her hand coming down her robe. She barely touched it, you know, as if it were priceless.

'We'll go upstairs,' she said. And I couldn't say anything. I just nodded. Really, it was all like that dream feeling, like you're there, and you know it's you, but you're kind of also just watching. Like you have no control?"

"Sure," I said.

"Right, so it was like that. One second I'm standing there looking at her, and the next we're walking up the stairs. Just like that. I mean there was more to it than that, I guess. I remember thinking that I might throw up. I remember that. Thinking, if I don't have another drink soon, I'm going to throw up. But that was kind of an aside. Part of the running commentary that comes into your head and then goes."

"Right," I said.

Ted crunched a piece of ice between his teeth. I watched the people in the bar through the mirror behind the bottles, watched as they smoked cigarettes and talked like us. I was wondering, I guess,

if life was really all that different for any of us, or were we all just
sort of standing together in the surf here, ankle deep and waiting
for the water to calm.

"She took me to this room just at the top of the staircase, on the
left. The light inside it was kind of deep, and her little robe became
more sheer, nearly transparent, and I could see her body through it
like an outline, moving as she breathed.

"There was a bed in the room, and a small dresser in the corner, a bedside table, and a sink against the wall with a rag hanging
over the side. I remember wondering about the rag. It was kind of
unsexy, you know, a rag? All the light in the room came from this
small lamp on the dresser with a red or purple scarf thrown over
the shade, and everything in the room had these long, slanting shadows. I looked at our shadows, hers and mine, and they fell all the
way across the floor to the opposite wall, and I thought they seemed
huge. I almost laughed. I don't know why. It wasn't funny.

"There was a window, too. It had these thick drapes over it, but
I could hear the rain still pounding against the glass outside. I
thought, oh my God, this is real. It's funny, but the rain was the
only thing that made me think that. When she turned around, I
could see the blue under her eyes through her makeup. Her lipstick
was cracked. She took my hand and brought it up to one of her
breasts. It was so heavy. I just held it. She looked at me and said, 'I
need sixty bucks, baby.'"

The bartender brought two more drinks over, even though
neither of us had finished ours, which were, by this time, mostly
water from the ice that had melted in the heat of our hands.

"This round's on me," he said as he dumped the ashtray in front of us, wiping it with a napkin.

"Thanks," Ted said.

I pulled out another smoke, lit it, passed one to Ted and lit that one, too. Both of us breathed out at the same time, these long, white breaths.

"This part was strange, you know?" Ted said. "I mean, I hadn't really spoken to her yet, and it kind of took me by surprise, the business of it, the fact of the transaction. Somewhere, of course, I knew it would get there, to that conversation, but I hadn't really expected it. I kind of fumbled. I remember feeling myself blush, my ears ringing softly like they always do when I blush. Does that happen to you? I thought about how much money I had, and I knew that I had at least sixty on me.

"I asked her, 'For what?' and she smiled. 'It's okay,' she said. She must have seen how nervous I got. She stepped toward me, and took my hand, the one that wasn't on her breast, by the wrist. She lifted it up, and brushed my fingers against her lips, opened them a little, just enough for the tip of my finger to run over her tongue. It was warm. Have you ever had your finger sucked? Not like a full-on thing, but just a little?"

I thought about it, and though I was sure I must have, I couldn't remember a single time. I shook my head.

"It sends shivers all the way through you. Anyway. She told me, 'There.' Then she pulled my hand down her body, between her legs. 'And there,' she said. And the whole time my other hand is holding her breast, and it seems so heavy. I mean, crazy heavy.

"Everything was different, then. I was sobering up, and I started getting turned on. But not like you'd think. At first, I was thinking, all right, this is one of my mother's friends, or, you know, like a professor who was seducing me in her office, or something. All these crazy fantasies about older women I'd had since I was a kid. But then it was different. It was just the plain fact of it, of us. That kind of detailed fantasy fell away, and it was just the feeling of this situation. Looking at her, touching her, I felt she was kind of debased or something, you know, tragic."

Ted took a sip of his drink, his eyes on the bar. As the whiskey lay in his mouth, he shook his head softly, as if to taste it all, before he swallowed.

"She was this totally broken person," he said. "That's what I was thinking then, when my fingers were almost inside her. And maybe it wasn't even true, probably not, but that's what it felt like. And I was suddenly getting off on that, and not in some kind of an ephemeral, fantasy way, but for real. It seemed—I don't know."

"That's deep," I said. Not sarcastic, like it might sound, but seriously, and I felt stupid for saying it, for being so simple, so cliché. I wanted to say something else, but I didn't know what.

"No, it was, man," Ted said, still looking into his distance. Then he looked at me. "That's it exactly. It was deep."

I poured the tan water from my glass into the new whiskey in front of me. For some reason I didn't want to look at Ted. I lit another cigarette. My throat hurt from the ones before, and I didn't really want it, but I felt like I wanted something and this would have to do.

"I gave her the money," Ted said. "She told me to undress and lay down on the bed. I was still soaking wet, and I had to pull my clothes off my skin. It took me a minute. As I lay on the bed, she got some things out of one of the drawers. The rain was so loud against the window. I was trying to make it into a rhythm in my mind, trying to concentrate on something, anything, other than what was about to happen.

"She crawled on the bed, between my legs, with her hands on my thighs. She looked up at me and asked me if I had any sores. I shook my head. I watched her at first: how the wrinkles in her face changed as she moved, as she pulled in her cheeks. The blue under her eyes looked like bruises from that angle. I remember her lipstick turned the condom pink in her mouth. Then I closed my eyes.

"It's funny, but from that part of it, you know, when she was going down on me, with all the good feeling, what I remember most is her hands on my thighs, how tight she held them. That's what I remember when I think about it now.

"The next thing I knew, she was lying next to me. I thought, maybe we'll just lie here. But she pulled me over her, on top of her. I was still cold from the rain, so it was a shock, how warm she was. She made the rhythm with her legs. Her hands pressed on my back, and I can still remember her fingernails. I don't know why, but I couldn't hear the sounds she was making. I could feel them, though, in my ear and along my neck."

Ted stopped, took a sip of his drink. I knew that feeling, when all the sound is gone. When skin becomes the only tool of communication. But I didn't want to break him away, didn't want to be broken away myself, from where he was, so I didn't say anything about it.

"I didn't know when I had started," Ted said, quiet. "But after I came, I realized that I was crying. Not tearing up; sobbing. Isn't that funny? I could count the number of times I had cried, as an adult, on a hand. But I was bawling.

"She just held on to me, too. She just kept rocking, like we were still fucking. All I could feel was her heat, how hot she was, and I could feel my tears on the pillow under my face.

"'Shhh,' that's what she kept saying. Just, 'shhhh.'"

Ted was still holding his drink up in front of him, and I don't know why but I tried to remember when he picked it up, how long it had been there in his hands. I lit my last cigarette, crushed the pack, and took a drag. Then I offered it to him. He took it and just watched the smoke rise off the end.

"I guess I was lying," he said through the smoke after he had finally taken a drag. "When I said I didn't believe I hadn't told you that story before. I've never told anyone that before."

He passed the cigarette back. I took it, nodded slowly to the bottles shimmering in the lights behind the bar.

"I hardly ever think about it, that time," he said. "But you know what's crazy?"

"No, what?"

"That was the best sex of my life," he said. "That's fucked up, huh?"

I don't know how it connected or why it seemed relevant, but I suddenly wanted to tell him that for the first time in my life I had begun to have an inkling of what life could be, how complicated it could become. I wanted to tell him I felt so careful I could hardly breathe. But I didn't say it.

"Yeah," is what I said. I nodded. "Fucked up."

Ted leaned over to the people sitting next to him and asked to bum two cigarettes. He turned back to me and held one out.

He was smiling. "Yep," he said.

Eden

7. Again, my eyes open when the house begins to move, the old wood expanding and creaking as the dawn comes down on us. Every morning it comes later. I know how the seasons are, how the year moves, and I know soon enough we'll have to get up in the dark, but still it surprises me. At the edges of the windows, where the curtains don't quite reach, is the dull, muck light of the day. The light hurts my eyes, they're so dry.

The air from the fan above the bed pushes against my face. It lies down and squirms on the pillow beside my head like the tiny body of an infant. I turn so I don't have to feel it, pull my night-gown down around my hips from where it twisted up in the night. As soon as I do it, I wish I hadn't. Robert's up. I can feel him beside me in the bed, the tension like a heat rising off of him. I try to stay as still as I can so he just thinks I was tossing in my sleep, but it doesn't work. He rolls over toward me. He lays his heavy hand down on my hip and his fingers curl over the bone there like four question marks.

He wants to be inside me, now. I can tell by the way the touch is, soft but pulling, too, like a weight tied around my middle by a silk ribbon. He wants to fuck everything away. He has that man's need to survive, blindly, to survive no matter what the price. What's almost funny is that that is exactly what ruins them in the end, men, what makes them so much weaker, and what makes them pure, in a way. The pure and the ruined, they're always men. But what men never really understand, it seems to me, is what survival is—simply the accumulation of pain, until, in the end, even the worst is only one more thing.

He wants to fuck the world away, and I'd like to let him. Believe me. But he can't do it, and I can't let him. My body is wooden, a chest of things that are tucked inside. I don't even feel him.

I sit up and his hand falls off me. As I walk to the bathroom, I don't look at him lying there in our bed. I want to, trust me. But I don't. That's how it is for me now. We buried our son two days ago, but it feels like I bore him the day before that. Years are just ashes floating behind me.

"Fuck," he says. It's just loud enough that I hear it. The word is spit out, like gristle. I've known him so long, this husband. I know that he says it like that, hard, because he's about to cry and he doesn't want to, not now, not in front of me.

From the bathroom window, I can see the dawn about to rip the sky apart. The wet mist is gray, thick. Above the long, dripping hills, the clouds hang in the sky like old sheets thrown over the furniture. Lights in the houses all over the valley are flickering on, and suddenly I want to know if anybody is standing in those windows looking back at me. I am still as a ghost behind the glass, searching the other windows. But then, just as suddenly, I don't want to know.

I turn on the water and splash it over my face. The cold sends its fingers—tick, tick, tick—down my spine. Brushing my teeth, I try to count off two minutes like I used to when I was a little girl. Forty-three, forty-four, forty-five. I remember being a little girl. The tiny hands and skinny legs. The flush of it all, the way the world seems big as you like. One hundred and four, one hundred and five, one hundred and six. Rachael reminds me of that sometimes, though she's a different kind of girl than I was. Far-off and small as a burnt piece of paper caught in the wind, a single car is driving down the old highway. The windshield glows orange with the sun as if it were actually on fire. It's beautiful. One hundred and twenty. White spit hangs from my lips like blood in the movies. I wrap my bathrobe tight as I can around me. The cold, though, is still there, tighter than that.

Robert's still lying on the bed, his arms crossed over his face. I walk to the door. I'm almost there when he says my name. I look over, but it's as though my eyes go soft, out of focus. I love him, I tell myself. Somewhere, I know that's true, and I tell myself so.

I look at the floor between us. "I've got to go get Rachael up," I say.

"Baby," he says. "C'mon. Please."

I don't need to see his eyes to know how they look. There's a million things I'd like to say, but how, that's what I'd like to know. I know it's not a fair thing. I know that it was probably worse, all that he's had to see. That night. I know it's not his fault. But my hands are shaking even now. There is a part of me that wants to lean over his soft, tired face, wants to scream, over and over again, what kind of man lets this happen, until we are both deaf from hearing it, all the stupid, angry questions that have no words piling up until we are both buried under the ones that will have to stand in.

I nod. "I'll go get Rachael," I say. I want to be different than this, I do.

"Deb," he says as I walk out.

I open Rachael's door just enough to push my head through. Her shades are open and the light lies on her skin like so many thin and shining kisses, this little girl. Her mouth and eyes are half-open in sleep and her fingers curl loose over the edge of her blanket. "Rachael," I whisper. It's too soft. I could go and sit with her, wake her gently, touch her head and cheeks.

"Rachael," I say louder.

I remember the way I found her the other night, all wrapped up in his blankets, lying in her underwear in that other bed. I couldn't stand to see it for some reason and still it makes me shudder now just to think.

Her eyelids stutter as if they were just learning how to do this, how to open. It makes her seem delicate and new. They are soft and grayish in the dusty Light; Lord, are they careful looking. They look just like two little dusty moth wings, moving so softly. But when they finally open, her eyes are big and dark and frightening as caves. She stares at me. She doesn't so much as blink.

"It's time to get ready for school," I say as I begin to pull my head back from the door.

"Okay, Mama," she says. I look at her again. Her elbows are little knots as she stretches her arms out above her, her hands as delicate as two flowers opening up. She hasn't called me that in years.

She was always the stronger.

At the bottom of the stairs, the light that floods through the windows is still partial, not the bright of day yet but still colored with its coming. Already, though, it's warmer than the dark. The clouds are golden now and swim through the perfect blue as though angels were really that big and just as slow as whales. I hear the pipes shudder above me as Robert starts the shower. Walk into the kitchen, I think, start a pot of coffee. I don't drink it, but Robert does, and I am still, no matter what else I am or might become, a wife, and he is going to work today. Yesterday, he told me he wouldn't if I didn't want him to, but I told him to go. Go! Go! Go!

I appreciate how hard he's trying. I do.

I walk into the pantry, where the walls are lined with cans and boxes, the small and cold bodies of things. There's a stool here that I brought from the kitchen and I sit on it and close the door. The darkness is complete. When I close my eyes, I am just another thing inside of it. I don't know what made me think to sit here. I mean how the idea came to me first, a few days ago. All I know is that it's small here, and close, cool and silent. It feels easier somehow. I've heard that dogs prefer confined spaces. I can understand that.

I don't know how long I'm sitting here before I hear the footsteps on the stairs. From how they come, so light and quick, I know it's Rachael. I wipe my eyes once and open the pantry door. Compared to the dark, the light in the window is a terrible thing. The day is full now, dawn fallen off the world in just these few minutes like some blanket pulled away. I go to the window. The fat sun sits above the ridge and I just stare out at it. When I close my eyes again, the most lovely and violent colors float across the dark.

Rachael gets to the bottom of the stairs and her footsteps disappear. Even with that huge backpack on, she is quiet as a dream. I keep my eyes open just long enough for the sun to burn them. Then I close them again. Behind me, in the dining room, Rachael rests the bag on the floor softly, as though someone is sleeping. She is a careful girl. She always has been.

I hear her come into the kitchen. I should open my eyes. It's strange not to. I know that. But I just can't let go of those colors yet. They're so perfect and whole, like the petals of some terribly strange flower. If I open my eyes, I'll lose them.

"Mom?" Rachael says behind me. I'm opening my eyes already when she says it but she says it first. She's dressed in jeans and a t-shirt to go to school. They don't have to wear anything specific. They don't do that anymore. I try to smile. But my face is made of tin and wires. I just look at her standing there. She's so dark and gentle, like the wind would tear her apart. But pretty. Oh my Lord, this girl is so pretty it takes your breath away. I watch her eyes crawl over the kitchen, stop on the open pantry door and the stool inside it. Then she looks back at me. It's me that turns away. It's not fair, the concern that turns her eyes into wells. She is just a child. That's what I keep thinking.

"You all right, Mama?" she says.

She doesn't have this in her, smart and strong as she is. Who has this in them? That's what I'd like to know.

I nod. "What do you want for breakfast, little girl?" I say. I can feel myself sinking into the earth.

"Cereal," she says.

"Okay. Go sit down." I want her to go away, to take her sad, steel eyes off of me. It's horrible. A mother shouldn't think things like that, but that's what I want. And when she does turn back to the dining room, I feel lighter, like I can breathe again.

I take out a bowl and fill it with the kind of cereal she likes. I pour milk over top of it, and the white, the perfect, thick white, fills all the cracks. I pour her a glass of juice, too, and then I walk them both, careful, to the table. When I set it down, she stares into the bowl like it was a crystal ball that she could see the future in.

"Can I have the other kind?" she says, soft as a whisper. She doesn't look up, and I don't know why, but I almost smack her small, pretty face.

"This one's poured already," I say. I lay the spoon down beside her hand and it shines like a razor.

All Robert likes before work is coffee. He's got one of those fancy half-thermoses from the Starbucks that just opened in town that he takes with him. It's slick as polished chrome. When I pour the coffee into it, the steam rises out as though the shine of the metal simply continued on up into the air.

When Robert comes down, he's cheerful. It's a show he's putting on for Rachael and as I hear his voice, I cover my mouth so I don't make a noise. So big and phony, I almost run out and hug him for it. "You ready, angel?" he says. I can hear the smile that makes the words round in his mouth.

Rachael stares up at him. I can stand to look at her like this, from behind. The tiny cups of her spine fall down the back of her neck where her hair parts over her shoulders. She favors Robert's mother, stunning and silent. You could never tell what that woman felt, with her dark hair and eyes. I always thought she might have Indian blood, but you could never ask her a thing like that. She was a country woman, lived and died on the farm Robert grew up on, and she was brutal and strong like they are. Robert has purple skin that cuts across his calf from the edge of a yardstick, but I saw her wash her husband's body after he died. I saw her prepare him. And you have never, in your whole life, seen anything as tender as that. Rachael is like that, too. She'd've been good at that kind of life.

From the sliver of her face I can see as she turns to look up at her daddy, she reminds me of one of those angels who must've woken up in hell wondering how they got lumped in.

My fingertips are pressed against my mouth still when Robert walks into the kitchen. I wipe my eyes, quickly, and point to the coffee I've poured. He walks toward me and I start nodding. I'm holding my breath. He leans close to me and runs his fingers through my hair. I'm nodding and shaking my head all at the same time, and his fingers run shivers over my neck. I will love him. I will love them all again.

But when he leans in to kiss me, I turn my head away. It's not that I don't want it, it's something else. I am made of paper is what it feels like, and they, they are made of flame. He nods his head, says, "Thanks for making the coffee." He's got purple tears of flesh under his eyes. I want to say something, something that will explain this, something that will make it all right. But there is nothing like that. I want everything to be different, but it isn't. He turns and goes back to Rachael.

He blows onto his coffee and little bunches of steam rise up on either side of his face. He slides his hand onto the back of Rachael's neck and something about it seems sexy, inappropriate, and for one gross, horrible second, I'm jealous of my daughter. His fingers slide into the notches of her spine like she was a knife handle.

"Let's go," he says.

Rachael looks back at me as she stands up and when I see her, I don't feel any of that anymore. Just my heart breaking. As they walk to the parlor, I feel like I can't swallow. I follow them quickly to the front door. Robert's already out on the porch, waiting for Rachael to get her bag over her shoulders. I smile, but as she goes to step out of the house, I grab hold of her arms. I don't know why. She looks back and I want to say something but my mouth doesn't even open. Beyond them, past their bodies, there is only sky. The houses, the trees and buildings, they're nothing compared to that sky. My mouth is dry, dry silence grabbing me by the throat.

"Deb," Robert says.

I look down. My fingers disappear into the arm of her coat and I can feel her tiny arm beneath, the hard, tiny bones.

"Bye, Mama," she says. "I love you."

"Yes," I say. "Yes." I'm sure it's not the right thing to say, but slowly I let her go. She rolls down the window of Robert's Mercedes and waves as they disappear down the street.

I'm still standing there when the mailman walks up to the front gate. I don't know how much time has passed. He's young and I don't recognize him, so I figure he must be new. He's about to put the mail into the metal box at the front of the walk when he sees me. Then he nods and begins to walk up to the porch. He can't be more than nineteen, I think. His face is broad and strangely beautiful. Shallow pockmarks trace the lines of his cheekbones. He might have black blood, I think, mixed, and lovely like they are. I don't even notice when he holds out the mail. He looks down at the letters and bills in his hand. When he looks up again, he's embarrassed that I'm still looking at him.

"Ma'am," he says. It's only then that I realize I'm still in my nightgown and bathrobe.

"Yes," I say. "I'm sorry." I take the mail from him and he smiles. His eyes are almonds.

I watch him walk away. His broad back and taut, strong legs move easily, as though the body itself was sure, as only a child's, only a boy-child's ever is. The air is so cold and thin it seems to shake. In the house, I look around. I don't know what I'm supposed to do anymore. I walk to the kitchen and all the dishes from yesterday have already been done.

I take all my cleaning stuff out from under the sink. Rubber gloves and spray bottles, sponges and rags. What I do first is the windows. I want them so clean they disappear. I spray them all over, wipe at every mark until my arms hurt. Outside, I watch the dull, bleached sunlight drag across the world. White silos stand out of the earth around distant farms like giant gravestones scattered over the valley. I rub a spot that won't go away, spray and rub, spray and rub. It takes me minutes to realize that it's moving. A single bird high over the fields, circling.

It's some time before they're all done. The silence of the house is like a clock ticking. After the windows, I straighten everything up. There are doors I don't open. I fix the pillows on the couches. Then, when I walk back through, I fix them again. Only the windows seem right. I oil all the wood until it shines with the blunt gleam of water. The rag I used has dark gray streaks across it from the dust. You never even see it until you wipe it away, the dirt of living. When I turn the vacuum on, the sound is like a blessing. But when I'm finished, everything looks flat. The house looks like one of those model houses you walk through to see if you want to buy one just like it.

I go up and collect the dirty clothes to put in a load of wash. The washer and dryer are in the garage. I open the door and inside it's dark as night. The light trickles on, gray and dishwater thin. It seems like one of those Egyptian tombs in a *National Geographic*. This is the scatter of our lives in here. In the corner an old set of weights stands propped against the wall, skinny and absent as a skeleton, a shroud of shadow wrapped around the bones. I don't look at that as I dump an armful of clothes on top of the dryer.

Behind me, my car sits big and still as some dumb and shining animal. Everything in that car is so soft you feel underwater when you're in it. It's a BMW station wagon that Robert bought me a few years back after he had made a small fortune breaking apart some farm. Sometimes I look at these cars, this big house, and I think this isn't us, this rich, fancy life. When I met Robert, he wasn't much more than a farm boy. I mean cultured, educated, but country, too. After his father made him promise to sell their farm when his mother died is when he started this other thing.

I know it's hard on him, what he does. I know it wasn't what he imagined. But he says that what he's doing might be the only good living left in the valley, and when that's done no one will be able to live here anymore, and maybe that's right. But I've been to some of those farms with him and I've never seen anything harder than a man giving up his land because he can't live off it anymore. I remember when I watched Robert do it. God, we were so young then. I don't think I understood it. I don't think I understood what he was giving up. Sacrifice, it's not a word you understand that early, is it?

A bunch of coins fall out of one of Robert's pants pockets when I turn them up. They are the dead, worn gray of gunmetal. Even with the light above, they don't shine at all. The washer begins to fill up and then rocks back and forth as it starts to spin. I leave it to run. But back inside, all I can see is how clean everything is, like it's someone else's house and I'm afraid to sit down. I walk up the stairs. My feet sink a little with each step into the softness. When I get to the top, I can see my footprints in the freshly vacuumed carpet, darker shapes like small pieces of myself that I've left behind.

I don't know these sounds, I think. These ones coming out of me now.

In our room the ceiling fan turns its wide leaves above the old bed, shaking, gently, on its stem. I go into the bathroom and turn the shower on. Almost immediately, steam fills the small room. It's like looking through a wedding veil, only heavier. My bathrobe and nightgown are a puddle of soft colors on the floor at my feet. I am naked.

The water is almost scalding and turns my heavy, dimpled flesh into glass. This body doesn't even look like me, with its big, round shape, the thick tangle of hair that's nearly lost now between my thighs and belly. These fat breasts like weights pulling me down, their strange, brown nipples tough as river stones after breastfeeding. I want to go down to my knees, but what good would that do? God doesn't come. It's not that easy anymore.

When I turn off the water, I can almost still feel it pounding on me. I've read that amputees still feel cramps in their missing limbs. I wonder if it's anything like this. The tiles drip long tears of condensation. I walk out of the bathroom and the cold tightens my skin as the water drips off it. I don't stop. I keep walking right out of the room into the hallway. I put my arms up on the doorframe, but they won't hold me. My wet palms keep sliding down the painted wood. I can't hold on tight enough.

I open the door and the room is still exactly the same. My knees sink into the carpet. My naked thighs buckle in tiny ripples and my stomach and breasts fold into one another as I lean into the mattress. My hands are in the sheets, swimming, like fish, like starving fishes. My hair clumps against my face, caught in the wetness. I lay myself down against the bed. Maybe I'm screaming.

But what I'm thinking is this, this is where my son sleeps. Grant. The little boy with tousled blond hair hanging down in curls over his forehead, big eyes staring out at me, waiting for me to explain everything to you. My child, how can I explain this?

You're just a boy.

No, you're dead.

| 8. | The chassis shuddered as the engine labored down until finally the truck was still and silent beneath them. |

The headlights bleached the arced zebra grass and tall wildflowers barely swaying over the top of the hill before Hayden turned them off also. Without their pewter fingers, the world fell away in a darkness that was simple at first, complete, until the night stepped forward, its features articulated slowly, cradled by each scrap of light in the distance. It was always the wholeness of it that struck Hayden from up on this hill, the level of degree in which dark grows discernable from dark that made him think now of a boat drifting through the ocean in the middle of the night, only the momentary and fleeting, moon-drenched whitecaps to offer perspective.

Beside him, Evelyn rolled the window down and the glass scraped a long, dull whistle against the inside of the door. Holding on to the edge of the roof, she pulled herself out and lay back and the cold rushed down her body into the truck. Her shirt rose above her jeans, exposing a thin ribbon of white skin below her navel and the matted edge of purple silk at the top of her underwear. She smiled and held on to the truck as though it were a spinning carnival ride, the tendons of her hands hard as wires through the skin.

"This place is amazing," she yelled.

Hayden looked over his shoulder to the rusted metal gate that stood open still, leaning out on its loose hinges. "Yeah," he said. "It's cool, right?"

"Wow," she said as she slid back into the truck. "Did you see that moon? I didn't even notice it before."

"I saw it when I was coming into town," Hayden said. He leaned forward to look at the low crescent again through the windshield. "Harvest moon, I guess."

Just a half hour ago, when he was coming to pick her up, the moon had been huge and red and hanging belly down in the east low enough that it seemed to teeter on the ridgeline. But in the time since, it had risen off the hills into the sky and grown smaller, the color bled out of it until it was only the pale, dusky orange that he saw now. "It's pretty, though," he said.

"Uh-huh," she nodded.

Her face was flushed from the cold outside. She turned around on the seat and leaned her back against him and lifted his arm over her shoulder. The cold radiated off her jacket onto his stomach and her fingers were cold and dry as she ran them lightly over his hand.

"What is this place?" she asked.

He had brought her to a wide, fenced hill about fifteen miles from town that stood higher than almost everything except the ridgeline and the water tower hovering in the glow of town. Hayden had found it several years ago, the gate held shut by a rusted piece of wire looped around the fence rail and the ruts of a car path overgrown by years of wild grass and flowers. It wasn't obviously connected to any property and he had decided to drive up and see what it was. From the top you could see the whole valley sprawling out around you, the connected veins of pavement crossing and recrossing the hills and falling finally into the distant towns, the gray-brown river and yellow and brown creeks parceling out the woods with their complicated maze of arms and fingers.

"I don't know," he said. "Probably it was grazing land once, but I've never seen any animals or anybody on it. It's kind of like that place by the river is for you. I come here sometimes, just to think, or whatever, when I want to be alone.

"Sometimes, it looks totally different from how it does now. Like in the beginning of summer, the whole thing is covered with daylilies. You can come and lay over there and watch the sun set. It's amazing. Every little hollow in the valley fills with the color, and it's like they're all burning, and with the flowers, you know, the color of the lilies, it's like the fire is coming right up around you."

"That sounds kind of amazing," Evelyn said.

"It is. My father, he always talks about how the valley burned, you know, during the Civil War, and I know it's not what he means, but it always reminds me of that, sitting here in the summer. He would probably think that was callous or something, but it seems it must have been kind of beautiful. It makes the idea of the burning different, somehow."

"I don't know," she said first. Then, "Isn't everything kind of like that, though? I mean, there's nothing that's so simple, right? Even things like that, even the bad things, they're not so simple. Otherwise, what's the point?"

She lifted her head up a little and they looked at each other for a second. "You know?" she said.

Laying her head back on his shoulder, Evelyn ran her fingertips absently over his ribs, each of her nails sending small, nervous armies across his body. "But," he said. "I like this place more how it looks now, anyway, in the fall. When the lilies die, all this Queen Anne's lace and hemlock and goldenrod that you hadn't even seen before is still there. Like it was stronger all the time, but you just couldn't see it for the colors of the lilies. They cover the whole field over like it is now. A million little silver Christmas ornaments, you know, where no one is even there to look. It seems like there's something cool about that."

"It's like if you can just get far enough out," she said. "Maybe it's just you and the world all alone again."

"Right."

"Who owns it? This place, I mean?"

"I don't know," Hayden said. "Maybe nobody, anymore."

"No way," she said. She was smiling as she turned up to face him and she pushed against him to steady herself. She raised her eyebrows and below them her eyes grew wide. "We're trespassing," she laughed.

Hayden smiled. "Maybe," he said. He could feel his heart

beating in his chest and he wondered if she could feel it, too, leaning against him.

"Thank you," she said. "For bringing me here." She pushed herself up and kissed him quickly on the mouth and then let herself sink back against his chest. Though it wasn't exactly that kind of kiss, Hayden could still feel it shoot through him and his crotch tightened and he told himself not to think about it. "I think I needed it," she said. "I'm going crazy in my house. It's like all of a sudden I can't stand being there anymore. I can't talk to my parents. I hate even being in my room." She looked up at him again and this close he could see the green in her eyes, as though he were looking at one of those stones you see at the bottom of the river, mossy and shivering beneath the water. "I used to love my room," she said. She smiled and Hayden looked away.

As his eyes had adjusted to the dark, the stars in the west had crowded more and more intimately together, and below them the small and scattered lights of houses had taken shape and shimmered now against the velvet hills. "I saw you at the funeral," he said. "At the school." She had been sitting with her parents in the middle of the gym when he walked in. He had wanted to go up to her until he had seen her face, a still, white thing that scared him. She looked like a different girl now, which, if he thought about it, was frightening in its own way.

"I know," she said. "I saw you, too. That's your dad that you were with?"

"Uh-huh." Wide, sparse clouds had come into the valley and

reflected the moon in shallow, milky patches along their bellies as they passed through the sky.

She nodded against his chest. He could feel her shivering against him.

"You cold?" he asked.

"A little," she said. She had left the window open and Hayden reached over her to close it, but she stopped him. "No," she said. "I like it."

As Hayden breathed, her head rose on his chest. He could feel the cold in his lungs, a thin, clean pressure.

"Is this weird?" he said. "Right now, being like we are. We're on some kind of date or something, aren't we? Do you feel weird about this?"

"Do you?"

"I don't know," he said. "I mean, this is crazy, right?"

She pushed herself up and turned around to face him. Her knees sank into the seat of the truck and she balanced herself on his thighs. "Why?" she said. "Why does this have to be crazy?" Reaching up, she touched his face. "We're going to be normal again, Hayden," she said. "You and me, we're going to be normal again."

She leaned into him and started to kiss him. With her it was different from any other kiss he had had, as though it were specifically theirs, as though their bodies had already set all this down, had already gone through the period when you figure this out. He remembered it from the river. He remembered the guilt, too, though, as though it were wrong to touch her, wrong after what had happened in the clearing and wrong, too, after what he had seen, as though she weren't a girl anymore, and that wasn't fair, was it. If she could be changed so easily, then he could be, too. And if that was true, then what had he become?

And maybe that's what she meant, anyway. That it was up to them. He wanted her to be right, to be right about both of them, and he didn't want to feel wrong for touching her, for wanting to touch her. He didn't want to change. He closed his eyes as she pulled him out from under the steering wheel and crawled on top of him.

The kiss grew harder and their lips and teeth seemed like thin obstacles to the fast begging of their tongues and their hands and fingers found holds on one another's body in the dark. She pulled his hand beneath her shirt and flinched from the cold of his skin. But when he tried to pull it back, she stopped him. "No," she said, dragging his hand up her ribs. Pushing him against her breast, he could feel whatever was under the skin, the round and separate gland. "Like that," she said.

She leaned back and pulled her jacket off quickly and let it drop down on the floorboard behind her and then she pulled her shirt off. The moon had lost all of its earlier color and it pushed a clean, almost white light through the glass of the window behind him and lit the small translucent hairs all over her body as though she were covered in tiny filaments, silver and electric. He watched her skin tighten in the cold, pinpricks raising up and texturing the flesh and turning her nipples hard and small. Her hair had been swept across her face when she took her shirt off and it made her look breathless.

Hayden pulled his shirt off, too, and the vinyl seat was cold and hard against his back.

They sat like that, staring at each other, their mouths half-open, their lips slack and swollen. Their chests and bellies moved, rising and now falling with their breath. He put his hand flat against her breastbone, between the thicker flesh, and it was ridged and jagged, rough-hewn as though her body were seamed together imperfectly. He could hear her breath shaking. Suddenly, Hayden felt frightened by looking at her like this, her naked torso shockingly so like the barely covered skeleton it in fact was.

He didn't want to look anymore, didn't want anymore time to think about this, and he pulled her toward him. Her hair covered their faces in dark curtains. She reached around to the back of his head to balance herself as she lifted her body up onto her knees. With her other hand she reached down between them and pressed her weight onto his crotch. He began to unbutton her pants and then he stopped. He thought about her in the clearing, the blood for some reason coming to his mind that had hung between her open lips. His heart crashed against his ribs and bones like he carried a larger animal's heart inside him, too huge and strong for the tiny shelter of his body. He pulled back from her and she followed him so her lips were still on his.

"Do you—" he said. "Is this all right?"

She leaned harder against him, and he could feel her lips making the words. "Please," she said. "Please don't ask me." They kissed again, quick, almost savage, and then she rolled herself off him so they were sitting beside one another on the truck's seat. They both pushed their feet into the floorboard and lifted their hips as they unbuttoned their jeans and pulled them down over their feet. It was awkward, but they did it quickly, and this was like a courage, Hayden felt, though he didn't know toward what, but it seemed to make the moment more immediate and less embarrassing, this thought that they were fighting for it, whatever was left to be saved.

He looked over at her when they had both finished. Her body was slight, slighter even than he remembered from the clearing, and the pale skin seemed to fall, all of it, her whole body, into the crux of dark between her legs. She reached out and let her hand hover over his middle, and above him, her hand shook as if she were afraid to touch him. Hayden thought his penis looked ridiculous standing like some toy figure in the dark and he was relieved when she let her hand come down on him. She wrapped her fingers around him and held him tight enough that it hurt. The vinyl was cold and unnerving against his bare thighs, but her hand was warm and tight and he concentrated on that.

Slowly, Evelyn lifted herself up and pushed her leg over him again so she was hovering several inches above his body. Her pubic hair hung down in two short, mossy, silhouetted fingers between her open legs. Hayden's hips rose, almost of their own accord, and he felt the wet on her pubic hair, the rough, soft steel wool that had none of the wetness but just carried it. She stayed where she was, though, above him, and just stared down at them.

Finally, she reached down and opened herself and began to lower her body onto his. Both of them let out their breath as he pushed inside of her, surprised almost, as you always are, by the feeling, by how quick it comes. First, he could just feel the wetness, and then he felt the heat, the almost unbearable heat of her insides like something pulsing, as though it got hotter and cooler as her heart pushed the blood through her, and then he didn't feel either thing, not the heat, not the wetness, not exactly, but just the movement, the slick dragging as she pushed her hips around him.

They tried to kiss again, but her body was moving too high and they stopped and she pressed her mouth against his ear. He could hear the breathy, wet sounds as her tongue moved against her cheeks and her teeth. Hayden thought about the first time he had sex. He was fourteen and it was with his twelve-year-old cousin's best friend. About how tender and soft and fumbling they were, and about how hard he had to push and she with her hands on his hips, first pulling and then pushing and then her little cry as he slipped in. They had snuck together into the barn, and he remembered that he didn't get past the wetness, but what he mostly remembered was the wet, green smell of the fresh-cut hay, and how when he stood up after, his penis was covered in a stiff purple skin of her blood. He thought, too, about the last time he had had sex. It was with a girl that he barely knew and they had both been drunk at a party and had stumbled into a bedroom together. When they woke up, the night still dark outside the windows, she told him they didn't have sex and he didn't argue. But after, he left and drove around for hours with the hungry feeling of being alone in his belly.

Evelyn pulled back a little and he looked at her face. Whimpering sounds trickled out of her mouth as she pushed against him, and her eyes were held closed so tight that deep lines had cut into her skin all around them. He had the feeling of what it might be to look at her as an older woman. He knew that what was happening inside her was different than what was happening inside him, the feelings, the way the body struggles to meet pleasure and the way the mind finds a language for it, but still it was frightening to watch. She looked somewhere between pleasure and pain, not so simple as either feeling exactly, but as though she were trying to get somewhere, her eyes fighting behind the tight, insistent purple slips of their lids.

Hayden closed his eyes and leaned into her and her breast changed, molded to meet him. Her nipple was hard, as though the skin had focused all its tension there. He took it in his mouth and she gasped and rocked his head in her hand. "Yes," she said against the side of his face. His hands reached around her and pulled her harder into him. Her spine was a line of unshelled walnuts in his hands and he ran the hard ball of his palm up and down them. He sucked hard on her breast and there was something profound in it, as though the act alone were salvific, the immersion in a memory you hold so deep in your body it has no image, no words or smells attached, a memory with no place, no time, without even you.

"Oh, fuck," she said.

Underneath him, the truck seat creaked and whispered. Hayden tried to move with her but their bodies were too close and he just blindly raised his hips against her instead, like some dumb animal whose thoughts are limited to closer, deeper. Her whole body shuddered as the thick bones in their pelvises clapped dully together.

Images careened in his head. He thought of his father the other morning, standing outside the cabin, the flask shining in his hand, glowing white-hot in the sunlight like some kind of religious thing before he slipped it into his back pocket. And about her, Evelyn, laying in the grass, becoming a part of it. And then about his mother, a photograph and the dreams where she is leading him to the river.

And then he didn't think about anything anymore.

He could feel everything pushing inside of him, up through that place deep inside his middle, that place that feels the fear and all the rest of it, that thing that throbs, that drops and pulls, and he felt it pushing up through him, aching now, almost breaking. He tried to stop moving, but she didn't. "Evelyn," he said, hoarse, throaty, and quick. "What do you want me to do?" he asked. He could smell her as he pulled back, her skin, the sweat from under her arm, briny and sour and soft, and the sex smells rising up from between them, like nothing else, like only sex. She pushed her whole body up against him, leaning him into the back of the seat and pulling his head into her.

"It's okay," she said into his ear. "You can come inside me." He tried to push off of her, to look at her, but she was too close. Her legs were tensed over him, controlling the way she moved now, curling her hips so that she followed him all the way to the bottom. The light from the outside caught on her thigh and the corded muscles cut her flesh in gaunt and glowing, ribboned sections. "It's all right," she said. She pressed her mouth against his ear. "I don't bleed."

He could feel everything now, hot and fleshy and human, and it all crawled across his body and up through the bottom of his spine. She began to push again, faster, and the bones inside them clapped out a rhythm, stulted and quick and desperate. Tears rushed into his eyes and when he opened them again everything was blurred and shining. He could smell the sex again, as though it had changed as they moved faster against each other, and he thought maybe it was like something else after all, like the sea maybe, like the nastiest and most living part of the sea, the red part, the part that glows when you touch it.

They rocked together, still faster now, and easier, like they were made for it, and she rose and fell over him like some gross and hot piston, as if they, their bodies, were the machinery of creation, which, when he thought of it, they were. Her sounds were getting louder now, too, and he could feel the pressure changing inside him, moving up. Every muscle in her arms and shoulders was taut, tensed, and it made her body look strong and spare. She pressed her fingernails into the back of his neck and the snowy, white crescents of pain almost made him laugh.

It was different than when he masturbated, where the pressure was more like a release. This was a slow thing, a thing that promised to break you up inside with how long it waited, with how long it could possibly go on. She gasped and ground her hips into his and he pulled her against him and pushed into her and then a thick, unexpected blindness fell between him and the world as though he were some small bird in a cage and this was the perfect silence, the shining dark of a silk slip, and on the other side there was nothing.

When he could hear again, he could hear his own noise, a growling, violent, hungry sound and he pushed his face against her chest and he could feel again the small bulbs and crevices of the bones there. She rocked his body against hers, and he could hear what she was saying.

"It's all right," she said, softly. "It's all right now."

He hadn't noticed it before, but his skin was sticking to the vinyl of the seat. He didn't know whether it had been three minutes or thirty. For a second the world had fallen away but now it came rushing back to him, all its sticky, vinyl details grabbing hold of him again, time contracting again until you could feel all its ticking seconds on your skin, and the feeling, the physical feeling, of being lost spread like some great set of wings, some shadow, over him. What about this is normal? he thought. What about us is normal, now?

"Evelyn—" she covered his mouth with her hand and rocked on top of him as he grew small inside her. He looked up at her and she was staring out the back window, the moon cutting white sweeps of brilliance into her face where the tears slid down.

Hayden looked past her shoulder out the windshield. He held his arms tightly around her back and he could feel the heat between their bodies, pressing its face against him, the smell of them beginning to fade already.

"See," she sobbed, almost laughing. "We're all right."

The Children of God

It's the dogs I see out in the woods, their eyes reflecting. It's strange. At first you barely see them, only that sharp green-yellow flash of their eyes. Then you can make them out better. They're walking slow, in a line, through the tall, old trees, deer pathing the heavy rhododendron. Normally they run everywhere, especially home. It puts a feeling in my stomach. Seeing them walk like that.

It's Sonia that's leading them up. She's a good dog. Part malamute, part akita. Big like a malamute, but darker, thicker, like an akita. I've had her about six years. She's the kind of dog pulls fifty or sixty pounds behind her when you're going up in the mountains. She hauls all her food and some of my gear, too. She never seems to mind. You have to love a dog for a thing like that.

After her come Caleb's two dogs. Caleb is my nephew. We're not even four years apart though, so we were raised more like brothers. He's got a setter and a wolfhound, both male. Beautiful dogs. About five years apiece. The wolfhound is big as a pony, and fast as hell. The setter's that perfect copper color they can be. He could be a show dog. He's got the papers. It's the setter coming right behind Sonia. Then the wolfhound. Those three are something. I've seen them take a full-grown buck like he was newborn. Just took his throat out. It wasn't the season, when it happened, but we took him home anyway.

Then comes my pup. He was the biggest of a litter Sonia had a little less than six months ago. He's already near as big as his mama. Though he doesn't know what to do with it yet. He stumbles over his legs. She wasn't bred, which is to say I didn't breed her. I took her out west with me, to Yellowstone, and soon after we got back she was getting fat. Must have found a male somewhere out there. From the size and look of the pups, I think he may have been wolf. But I don't talk about it. Hybrids are illegal all through Virginia and North Carolina. We live just below the border. In a year or so, he'll be one hell of a dog though. Sonia's teaching him. For now, he's just funny to watch. But you can see it in him already.

Behind those four a ways is the basset hound. He has some trouble keeping up with the big dogs. But he tries real hard. We trained him on scents, and he can track just about anything as far as it can go, trail or no. You don't lose a thing if he's there. He needs heart to keep up with the rest of them, and he's got it. Brother, has he got it.

Seeing them come like that, so slow, I wonder if they hadn't gotten into a scrap in the woods. I wonder if they're hurt. It's rough out here for dogs. They get hurt from time to time. It's not nice. These mountains can rip a dog to pieces.

I hear the door open behind me.

"Uncle John?"

It's Caleb's little girl, Summer, behind me. I'm watching her for the day. Her voice snaps me out of a haze. Watching dogs will do that to you. Take you away from yourself. It's all nature'll do that to you. Sometimes it's exactly what you need.

"Huh?" I say.

I turn from the woods and look at her. She's a beautiful little girl. Just about six, in dirty pink corduroy overalls, and bare feet, even though it's starting to get colder in the evenings. She's a handful. But sweet as anything. She's got these ratty blond curls and these big blue eyes. You almost can't stand to look into them. Watch out when she's older, I sometimes joke with Caleb. You'll have every kid in the county coming around here, I say. I guess I joke like that less now.

"Where's Sad Dog?" she says. That's the basset, Sad Dog. Caleb gave him to Summer a few years back for her birthday. She was too young to come up with a proper name for him, so she called him Sad Dog on account of his eyes and face being droopy the way bassets' are. She cried for near a week about it, how sad he was. She thought he didn't like her. It took us a long time to convince her that that's the way all hounds look, even when they're happy. We had to show her six other dogs before she would believe us. She'll still tell people, "His name is Sad Dog, but he's not really sad." Then she'll lean in a little, "He just looks that way," she'll tell them like it's a secret, "all hound dogs do."

"He's coming down just now," I say. "See." I point to where the dogs are coming through the woods, though it's almost dark now.

She follows my finger and says, "Oh, good. I was afraid he would be lonely without me."

"I'm sure he was, sweetness," I say. "But he likes to play with the other dogs, too. Doesn't he?"

"Uh-huh," she says. But I can tell she is already thinking about something else.

"Why isn't Daddy home yet?" she says.

"He's still in the city with your mama," I say. I almost say, *at the doctor's*. But then I don't.

"Oh," she says. She looks down at her little toes against the porch slats. Then she turns and walks slow back toward the house. I want to say something, because you can tell that even if she doesn't know, she understands. She goes into the house. I start to gathering the kindling for a fire later, look back for the dogs in the last of the light.

When I was about sixteen—he would have been thirteen—Caleb wrecked an ATV real bad. We were out riding around together. He came on some loose gravel on the side of a hill, and tried to pull a spin. The machine turned over. It rolled about fifteen feet down the face of the hill, and Caleb went with it. His leg had gotten caught somewhere in the process. By the time it stopped, Caleb's leg had broken bad.

The bones were clear through his skin. When I got to him he wasn't conscious, and the blood was coming fast. I tied his leg as well as I could, but I couldn't stop the bleeding. I picked him up and carried him to my four-wheeler. I took the steadiest way home I knew.

It took ten minutes for me to get him home. When we got there, there was blood everywhere. All over me, and the machine, and Caleb's whole bottom half was dripping. There was a trail on the ground the whole way back. I picked him up and took him in to his mother. It wasn't pretty. She smacked his face to get him awake. She was screaming. And crying. There was a lot of screaming. She wrapped his leg in towels and I carried him to her car.

She turned around and slapped me across the face. I remember feeling cold because of the blood on me, how it wasn't warm anymore.

She said, "What'd you do to my boy, John? What'd you do?"

I didn't know what to say. She just got into the truck. It could have happened to anyone, though, was the truth. He hadn't done anything we all hadn't done a hundred times.

She drove him to the hospital. She said she was going a hundred the whole way there. She was worried he was going to lose the leg. But when she got there, they said it was just in time.

They took him into surgery, and she called to tell us. They were pumping him full of new blood. They were putting his leg back together, with pins in it. She apologized to me for what she had said at the house, told me, "This wasn't your fault. I know that. I was just scared," she said. I could understand that.

He didn't wake up for two days after that. When he finally woke up the whole family went to see him. His folks hadn't left the hospital since it happened. Caleb said it hurt, but not all the time. He said he didn't remember anything after the four-wheeler rolled that first time. A day or two later he was back home. Six months after that, the cast came off. We didn't think about it much again.

Then about two and a half years ago, Caleb got sick. AIDS. He was twenty-three. Summer was three. It was the blood all those years back had it. It was before they were screening for that type of thing. The doctors said he had had it for a long time. Caleb sued the hospital, and they gave him half a million dollars and free medical care for the rest of his life. That's how he bought the land we live on. The valley where we had grown up had gotten too expensive for what he was looking for, so we started looking south down the ridge until we came upon the mountains proper. When you've grown up among hills, it can take a while to get used to the mountains. But we both came to love them, actually. The way a person might love God. They become the thing you balance yourself against.

Anyway, he took two hundred thousand of it and bought a hundred acres of the most beautiful land you ever saw. All through this hollow and up the mountains on either side. We slept in tents while we cleared a road to the heart of the land. Then we built two A-frame houses about a hundred yards apart, and cleared out most of the woods between them. He put the other three hundred thousand away for Summer and her mama, Kelly, for when he's gone.

The year Caleb got sick, he, Kelly, and Summer were all going to the city every six weeks or so, to the doctor's. Summer was young enough that she doesn't remember much of that time now. It's probably better. Neither her nor her mama ever got it. It was a miracle. And I'm thankful every day for it. I just don't think I could watch that little girl die.

The dogs have been back for some time. Sad Dog, the hound, is in Caleb's house with Summer. She is watching the television. I can see her silhouette against the flickering light. I'm sitting out on Caleb's porch, drinking a beer. The time for sitting outside is too short not to use it. The pup is sprawled out at my feet, sleeping. The rest of them are lying around the clearing in front of the house. Not a scratch on any of them.

The night has opened up clear and fine, stars everywhere. I'm just sitting here, staring up at poor, hunched Orion, when the dogs jump. I see the lights on the road a second later. It's Caleb's truck. I finish my cigarette, drop the butt in an empty can. I wait for them to come. Their headlights flood the clearing. I stand up and walk down the three steps of the porch. I still can't get that bad feeling out of my gut, the one from watching the dogs walk through the woods, but I'm trying not to think about it.

I walk toward the car as they open their doors and get out. Kelly's eyes, in the light coming from the moon and the house, look swollen and red. Her cheeks are streaked from where she has been dragging her hands against them. Summer runs right by me to the truck, yelling the whole way, and Caleb takes her up in his arms. She wraps every part of herself around him. "Hey, my darling girl," he says. He puts her down and Kelly is there to take her hand.

"Let's go in," she says.

"Let's wait for Daddy, too," Summer says, watching as Caleb walks into the clearing between the houses. He stands there, kicking ash into the fire pit. Kelly starts Summer toward the house.

"I think Daddy wants to talk to Uncle John for a minute," Kelly says. She's looking at me as she says it, and then she looks down at Summer. "Okay, baby?" She calls Caleb that, too—baby.

"Hey, John," she says. She gives me a kiss on the cheek, and presses against my back with her hand. She looks at Caleb in the darkness. This close I can see the wetness still in her eyes.

I walk behind them to the porch and grab two beers from the cooler. I slip them in my jacket pockets. Then I take some firewood from next to the door. The dogs are playing in the clearing around Caleb. The pup's waiting for me at the bottom steps. He thinks it's time to play.

I walk over to where Caleb is standing, drop the wood on the ground next to me. The smells of the dogs and the earth and the wood rise up together and become a single thing, as though it were an ocean lying at our feet. I pull out the beers one at a time. I crack the tab on the first one and hand it to him. He takes a sip, breathes out deep. I pull out the second one and take a sip. Even though it's not warm outside, the cold of it feels good going down. We stand this way for a while. Caleb runs his thumb up and down the watery beer can, feeling it.

The pup's joined the rest of the dogs. He's getting tossed around by the wolfhound. He keeps coming, though. He's learning, I think. He'll need to know this.

"Bad?" I say.

"Uh-huh," Caleb says.

We sip our beers. We don't say anything for a while. We stand there looking into the woods.

"What is it?" I say.

"My T cells."

"How low?" I say. I've read what I could.

He looks down, says, "Twenty-two." We both know what this means.

"The new pills?"

"They're not working," he says.

I don't say anything, and he looks up. He tries to smile. "Hell," he says. "Someone in Mexico gets a scratch, I'm getting the infection."

I smile.

"They want me to start going to a group," he says. "For patients."

"What do you think?" I say.

"I don't know." His thumb keeps working that beer can. "I guess I'd rather be spending my time here," he says.

"Yeah."

I put my hand on his back. I squeeze his shoulder.

"I'm scared, John," he says. "I'm so scared about Summer," he says.

All of a sudden, I want to start the fire, want to turn the dark into something solid around us.

I bend down and put my beer on the dirt. I throw some dry leaves from the ground into the fire pit. Then I grab some kindling and a few of the logs and put them on top of the leaves. I pull out my lighter and light the leaves. I watch as the kindling catches. And then the logs. I watch as the light spreads. Then I light a cigarette. I look up at Caleb. He wipes at his face, the lines that glow orange now, reflecting. He tries to smile.

I stand up. I put my arm around him. He breathes in deep. Then out. The light jumps back and forth on the trees and our bodies.

"That's nice," he says. He kicks his foot toward the fire. "That feels nice," he says.

Kelly opens the door. She steps out onto the porch and looks at us. She has to squint. Against the firelight we're just shadows. "You guys want to come in for dinner now?" she says. "It's ready."

"Yeah, we'll just be a second," Caleb says.

"Okay," she says. She leaves the door open. Inside, I can hear her talking to Summer. "Look at all this good food," she says. "They'll be in in a sec, baby," she says.

Caleb wipes his face one more time with his sleeve. He touches my hand on his shoulder, turns toward the house. I put two more logs on the fire before I turn to go in. I want it to keep burning. I want it to be burning when we come out again. The dogs have stopped playing. They lick each other's fur. Lying around the fire, calm in the heat.

Caleb and I walk to the house. We leave our empty beers on the porch, and grab two new ones. The dinner is good. Kelly has the table laid out like a flower. It's steak and asparagus and potatoes. Kelly says Caleb needs the protein now. Summer asks, "What's protein?" I say, "It makes you strong." She says, "Oh." She tells everyone to eat a lot.

We are quiet as we eat. Summer talks. She talks about everything that comes into her mind. About the frog she saw in the creek, about the cartoons she watched, about Sad Dog. She says he misses them when Caleb and Kelly are gone. I wonder if she knows how much we all need her voice right now. I wonder if this is why she talks so much, or whether it's just because she's a kid. I don't care though. I am thankful either way.

When dinner is finished, Kelly stands up and begins to clear the plates. She washes each one slowly. She says she and Summer will read for a while, before Summer goes to bed. Summer goes to pick a book. She likes fairy tales. But only the ones where people have to fight. The ones where there's a dragon, and a hero. She says, "A girl can be the hero, too, right, Mom? I could kill a dragon," she says lifting up her arms. She thinks this world is full of magic.

Caleb nods to me and we go outside. We bring the beers with us, and some more firewood. We sit on big logs at the edge of the fire pit. A while back, we cut them from an old-growth tree that had fallen. We sit on the moss that grew on the tree. We open two beers, watch the fire. Caleb lights a cigarette. Of course he shouldn't be smoking, but I don't say anything. He blows the smoke out. I watch it fade into the air. Then I light one, too.

"Can I tell you something?" he says.

"'Course," I say.

"I don't know why I want to talk about this," he says. "I just can't get it out of my head."

"Just talk, man," I say. "It's me." I look over at him as he sips his beer.

"I know," he says. He flicks the second half of his cigarette into the fire. I look into the fire and wait. I watch the flames jumping into the air. I watch them disappear, replaced by new ones. I take a deep sip of my beer.

"The other night," he says. "Summer was asleep, in bed. And Kelly and I were getting in bed. You know. Messing around, whatever."

"Uh-huh," I say. We don't talk about this kind of thing often. But every once in a while it comes up. We spoke about it some when Caleb got sick. How it was going to change. That type of thing.

"And it started to get more and more serious. And it's been hard for me lately. I don't feel so attractive, or whatever. And I'm so tired and all, all the time. So, anyway, this was nice, that it was happening. It was exciting. She was excited. So we started to get more into it. Taking our clothes off and all. And then it came time to, you know, to get down. And I was so excited, and I almost just started, but then she stopped to get a condom." He stops to take a sip of his beer and to light a cigarette. His hand is shaking.

"Uh-huh," I say.

"So she unwraps it, and goes to put it on. And I just go limp, man. Just like that," he says.

"Caleb," I say. "That isn't nothing, man. Shit—"

"No, John," he says. "That's not it," he says. "I started crying. I couldn't stop. I was just crying, and crying, like a baby. The same way. Just lying there, shaking, and crying. Just holding on to her. I couldn't stop, man."

I look down, take a sip of my beer. The pup is lying at my feet, and I reach down and rub his neck. Watch the shadows play across his face.

"Then she picks up my head, and looks at me, right in my eyes. She says, 'We don't have to use it, baby. If you don't want to, we don't have to use it.'" He looks over at me. "I almost lost it," he says. "I swear to God."

"Jesus," I say.

"Because that isn't even what it was. I mean, using a rubber with your woman, with your little girl's mama, it isn't nice, but, fuck, I'm not stupid. I know where we are. I know what we have to do. I can deal with it. But that wasn't even it. Or at least not the whole thing. It was something else. Something more than that." He stares over the fire as he tells me this, into the firelit dark woods, into something else. He takes a sip of his beer, but doesn't move his eyes even a bit. I don't say anything. I bend down and throw some more wood into the fire. I don't know anything to say. The setter nuzzles Caleb's hand, and he looks down at the dog, half-smiles.

"I lay there, on top of her, for a while," he says. "And when she thought I was asleep, she got up, out of bed. She went to the bathroom. I listened to her cry for about a half hour before I fell asleep. Then, in the morning, when I woke up, she was already awake. She was just looking at me. And when I opened my eyes, she kissed me. She just kissed me. And that was it. We haven't talked about it again."

I reach my hand over and rest it on his leg. Caleb looks over at me. I tighten my hand, then take it away. He looks back toward the dark woods. The fire's light is a ghost in the trees. We sit there. We don't talk. We drink our beers and think. I wish there was anything that was enough to save him.

I am lost in the fire, in the woods around us. Somewhere between the darkness and the light. We've drunk a couple of beers, when Caleb finally says something.

"Huh?" I say.

"There's something else," he says. "Something more I want to say."

"Okay," I say.

He looks down. "About Kelly," he says. "If when I'm gone," he says. "If you two ever want to—"

"Caleb," I say. I shake my head. "Don't."

He looks over at me again. "That would be all right," he says, and then he doesn't say anything more. The firelight slips over his eyes as he nods, and I look away. I can feel him still looking at me. I don't know if he's asking something or telling something, but I don't want to think about it either way, not any of it.

"We should go in," he says after a long while. "I want to be with Summer before she goes to bed."

"All right," I say. We get up, stretch our legs out. We pick up our beer cans, and leave the fire to burn out on its own. Before we reach the house, I stop. Caleb stops, too. We look at each other again. I want to say something to him. But the words aren't there. I want to say everything will be all right. But there is a time when you have to stop telling yourself that, even if you're not ready to. There is a time when not saying that is the only way you can survive it. Caleb looks at me. He nods. We walk into the house.

Kelly and Summer are sitting on the couch. Kelly is reading. Every now and again Summer jumps in with a word or a sentence that she can either read or knows by heart. When we walk in, she looks up. "Daddy," she says. "This is the best part." Caleb sits down on the couch next to her and she curls up against him. I sit on a chair next to the couch. Sad Dog and the pup are crying at the door. I get up and let them into the house. Kelly gives me a look, but doesn't say anything. Summer brings Sad Dog up into her lap. She talks into his ear. She is catching him up on the story. There is a princess who is waiting to be saved. There is a dragon who just might eat her if someone doesn't do something fast. This is what she tells him. He licks her face, and then rests his head on her lap, like he's waiting to hear the rest of the story. I love that fucking dog.

I stand up to get some beers. The pup, who's lying next to my chair, looks up to make sure everything is all right. I look out the window at the other dogs. They are sitting around the dying fire, watching the woods. They look like they are remembering some-thing, something animal, something better than words. I look at them for a while. Summer's what gets me back.

"Uncle John," she says. "You're going to miss everything."

I hadn't realized she had stopped the story. "No, girl," I say, "I'm listening."

My voice is choked a little.

"Come on," she says. "Sit down." I walk over. I put the three beers I got on the table, and sit down. The pup nuzzles my leg, shows me his teeth. Kelly starts to read again. Caleb and I grab two of the beers off of the table. We all sit there and wait for the story to be done.

When Kelly closes the book, Summer is already yawning, eyes heavy. Kelly gets up. She looks at Summer. "All right, little girl, it's almost bedtime," she says.

"Uhn-uh," Summer says. She curls against Caleb as if for protection from sleep. "Not yet," she says. You can see her trying to push her eyes open. She is so scared to miss anything. She is right to be, I think. She'll need these things later. Kelly must be thinking something like that, too, because she doesn't say anything more about it. Kelly goes to put the book away. Summer crawls into Caleb's lap. She throws her arms around his neck and looks at him. She makes the face she's seen adults do. She is trying to be serious.

"I love you forever and ever, Daddy," she says.

Kelly covers her mouth behind them. She looks like she is trying to save her breath from falling.

"I love you, too, little girl," Caleb says.

"For ever and ever?" Summer says. She wants to get to the bottom of this.

Kelly turns toward the window.

"Forever and ever," Caleb says.

Eden

9. Hayden looked back before the door closed behind him. The dampened echo of his last step still fluttered through the silence like a bird caught in the rafters. Finally, it was like everything when compared to memory, smaller, more dense, the simple claustrophobia of all those tiny details that make a thing real and that the mind never cares for, preferring instead the vast specters of our more moving nostalgias. At his feet the frail shadow of his body tumbled down the aisle toward the lace-hooded altar and those stunning windows, their colored tongues lapping at the gloaming of the churchlight, before it was swallowed finally as the door fell shut.

Even this late in the afternoon, the stale, charred smoke of the censer mingled with the air inside, and the cold evening felt clean and easier in his lungs. About to set somewhere behind the church, the sun pressed a gasping, cold, and naked glare over everything. Hayden looked back and forth between the church and the old man he had followed out. Its face eclipsed, the flagstone wall was little more than a dark, topographical shadow, as if water had settled in the recessed mortar fittings. From the outside, the beautiful glass windows were flat and dull as paper. The shadow of the church itself, though, sprawled over the ground in front of him and lent the building the massive and stable feeling he had remembered. The one thing about it all that was the same was the stillness, the strange feeling perfectly held in the low painting of heaven that stretched over the cathedral ceiling, a faded gilt and pastel thing too poor for restoration left now with only leprous angels lying across their lucent clouds, handlessly reaching for God and one another.

Hayden hadn't understood why all the old people were in the church this late until he had seen the man walk out of the confessional. But once he had, the time he had spent sitting there seemed to fall down around him, to crumble within the sweet residue of incense too thick to pass anymore for air, and when the man stood up from his prayers, Hayden stood, too.

Outside now, he thought about going back into the church, trying to figure out again why he had come here, but he didn't. He just watched the old man walk across the parking lot to his car. He looked tired under the weight of the heavy coat and scarf he had worn even inside the church, and he seemed, Hayden thought, like an old fighter, his heavy, gnarled hands swinging at his sides, each chalky finger twisted into a bulb at the knuckle. His wide shoulders hunched as he shuffled forward, giving him the look of someone who agrees with death, someone who has decided, finally, to meet death halfway, so that when it comes it will be easier, less painful even than what it takes you from.

The headlights of the man's town car flashed on and passed over Hayden as he pulled out of the parking lot and disappeared. Hayden walked over to his truck and lifted himself onto the hood. He could see the sun from here, standing just in those seconds before it will be consumed by red.

Already, though, the air was growing bluish, thickening, the low, mustard-colored clouds rouged with the pinkish bellies of fishes. A tall row of evergreens edged the church land and between them you could make out the first houses of the neighborhoods beyond, their lawns turned blue in the deep and ragged eastern shadows, aluminum siding shining still on the southern sides. Throughout the churchyard, bright yellow and red trees stood like hungry foreigners against the darkening air and the dark pines and firs, and beyond them all, a flock of sparrows suddenly lifted, weightless.

Hayden thought about the last dream he'd had of his mother, in which he'd watched her walk into that river, her back glistening black blood, her bloodied clothes soaked to dripping; small swirls of red twisting paisley downriver. It still made him shiver. He wondered if that's really why he had come here, to fix her finally outside of the dreams, as if memory were something that could be controlled so easily, called forth or held down by the simple weight of a building, perhaps even discarded inside it. Now that he was here, though, he knew it wasn't that easy.

Around him, he could watch the air getting darker, measure each shade that it fell, and with each one, it grew a little colder. No matter how cold the day is in the sun, it's colder still without it. He got into his truck and turned it out of the parking lot, the street-lights snapping on all around him as he climbed the hills.

Once on the gravel road, though, it was dark again and the cabin glowed between the trees like a small, still fire in the distance. The headlights bleached the wide poplar beams of the house as they spilled across it while Hayden pulled the truck in beside his father's and then turned it off. Without the lights, the trees that surrounded the cabin looked flat and dark and their leaves reached trembling into the breezes above them.

The house exhaled its warm breath as he opened the door. Sam, the dog, stood just in the hallway, waving his pink nose from side to side in front of him. Smelling Hayden, he thumped his tail against the wall once before turning away and hobbling back into the hallway toward Hayden's father's study.

In the far corner of the room, the embers of the season's first fire glowed, red cylinders of ash and wood shifting over one another behind the glass door of the iron woodstove. The pipe that carried the smoke up to the roof hissed and popped, settling only slowly after so many months into the heat. Through the hallway, Hayden could hear the muted sound of a jazz singer coming from the radio of his father's study. The voice strained and whined, tinny on the poor speakers. The sound was too low for him to place the song.

As he turned and began to untie his boots, the gun cabinet stood against the wall just in front of him. Hayden stared at it, al-most surprised to see it there, where it had always been. The cabinet had been in his father's family for generations. An ornate pattern was carved into the wood and in the low places the red-brown stain grew darker, almost black. Hayden remembered running his finger through it as a child, being convinced that it never ended, that design. The two cabinet doors were still sectioned in their original, hand-tempered, thick and hallucinatory glass, and behind them the rifles and shotguns became like ghosts of themselves. Shorn of all the solidity of their real bodies, they were not delicate enough to become unreal but only surreal, unstable as objects behind waves of heat. They looked terrifying, these things that Hayden knew so well, had grown up with, and he couldn't take his eyes away. He followed the line of the second from the right, up and down. Up. Down.

"Hayden?" his father said behind him. "You all right?"

He had frozen in the middle of taking off one of his boots. He straightened himself and turned around, kicking it off with the toe of his other foot. "Uh-huh," he said. "Yeah." He tried to sound easy, casual, but he didn't believe himself.

His father stood half in the study and half in the hallway, holding on to the door frame with one hand. "You in for the night?" he asked.

"I guess so," Hayden said. "Yeah."

His father nodded again. "Why don't you grab a glass and a bowl of ice and come sit for a while?" he said. "If you want. I'd like to talk to you." He looked back into the study. As he turned his head, the warm glow of the room spread over his face. His shirt was open at the collar and Hayden saw his lit Adam's apple rise in his throat.

"Okay," Hayden said. "Sure."

"All right," his father said, already stepping into the study again.

Hayden looked back once at the gun cabinet and then walked into the kitchen. It was like having someone's eyes on your back, and he tried not to think about it. He filled a salad bowl with ice cubes and took a tumbler down from one of the cabinets.

He stopped in the doorway of the study. The worn smells of paper and cigarettes hung at the door like a curtain, as if all the dead people and places in the books lining these walls had solidified into a single ghost whose presence now filled the room. Bookshelves rose from the floor to the ceiling and beside them books were stacked in tall piles on the floor. In the corner a small table held the typewriter his father used for letters and two wide leather armchairs sat in the middle of the room footed with ottomans, another small table between them. Weak-bulbed lamps rose in every open space and gave the room the rich, sewn-together light of an old library. Hayden's father sat in one of the armchairs looking out the dark window on the far wall, his finger still marking his place in a book, as though he only half expected Hayden to come. The dog lay stretched out between the bookshelves and the ottomans, his breath rising in slow, labored heaves that caressed his golden coat with a dull reflection of the lamps.

When Hayden stepped into the room, both his father and the dog looked up. He stepped over Sam and put the bowl of ice on the table between the chairs. The dog sniffed once and lay his head back down on the floor, closing his white eyes again.

"Perfect," his father said, finishing the last of the whiskey in his glass.

Hayden's father picked up a bottle from the floor beside his chair and dropped a small handful of ice into each of their glasses. Hayden thought he looked handsome as he poured the whiskey, his face trained on the liquor climbing the sides of the glasses and his skin golden and flushed with whatever he had already drunk, the metal streaks in his hair polished by the lamplight. But it was really this tiny room, with all his books, where he always seemed more complete, that set the feeling. The book now lay open on his lap, facedown on the page he had been reading, the spine rising slightly off his leg. Looking at him now, Hayden thought that he could almost remember what he had been like before his mother died, but as soon as he thought it he knew it wasn't true.

"Cheers," his father said as they touched their glasses. Hayden wasn't used to sipping whiskey like this, and it burned his mouth more than just drinking it from the bottle. The song changed and then another began. He felt the whiskey stretching out in his belly and his chest and growing warm inside him.

"Listen," his father said after a minute. "I just wanted to tell you that I was sorry about the other day. Before the service, what I said. I know you could've maybe used more from me than that." He shook his head a little. "I mean, who gives a fuck if you've read *Antigone*?

"Maybe I'm not much of a father. Maybe I drink too much and

smoke too much and work too little. I know all that." Hayden lifted his glass and his father held up his hand.

"Wait, don't say anything," he said. "That's not important, either way. What I'm trying to say is, I don't always know what to do. And I feel like I'm probably wrong a lot, and I want to apologize if that came out wrong. Reading all these old books." He smiled a little, raising his hand and letting it flutter toward the wall. "I think maybe that's about all I'm good for."

He stared at the wall, the books, his fingers gently running back and forth over the chair's leather arm. "It doesn't seem like much, I guess, does it?" he said. "And it probably isn't winning me any parenting awards. But I try, you know? This, it's just what I have. It's what I have to give. But I didn't want you to think I was being unfeeling."

He reached over and held on to Hayden's arm for a second. "I love you, though. You know that, don't you?"

Hayden nodded. "Of course," he said. "Of course, I know that."

His father nodded again. "Without your mother," he said. He lit a cigarette and breathed out the smoke. "Shit, I don't know." He spoke slowly and took another sip of the whiskey. His eyes seemed heavy to Hayden, the lids slipping down just a touch behind his glasses. "She was so good with everything, it seems now. She always had this knack, especially with you, of knowing somehow not only exactly what was needed but just how to get there, you know? I think that's why I gave you those letters, in the end. I thought maybe they could stand in, or something. I thought they might be able to do what I couldn't figure out. Me," he said. "I probably would have kept them forever, like an asshole. You'd've had another reason to hate me when I die." He smiled, looking at Hayden over the glass as he took a sip of his drink. Hayden smiled.

"But, funerals," his father said. "I'm not that good with them, you know. With death, I guess. I suppose I used to be different, but—"

"I know," Hayden said. It seemed like it wasn't what he meant to say, or wasn't enough somehow for how he felt, for how close he suddenly felt to his father.

His father nodded. "I know you do," he said. He finished his whiskey and filled his glass again and topped up Hayden's. Hayden took a sip of the fresh whiskey and it was strong again, without the water from the melting ice, but it was different, too. He was surprised at how much the taste could change in only the time it took to drink one glass; now it was all smoke and wood and not just the thin burning of alcohol.

His father nodded and closed his eyes, leaning his head back against the chair. There was something about his face, the slack lines running from closed eye to temple, the soft flush of his lips, something about the way he held the burning cigarette up in front of him, which made Hayden think that, tonight at least, his father wasn't drinking for that fast escape it sometimes gives, but for the slow warmth that it always promised. Hayden knew his father had been thinking about all of this long before he walked in tonight, of apologizing, of death, even of Hayden's mother, and with what he had to say said, you could almost watch him turn back to it, whatever separate world his memories had quilted, a close, private nostalgia, which always hides death inside of it anyway, and is probably, if we are honest with ourselves, just the mask that death wears in its more tender moments.

"I was at the church," Hayden said. "Today. I went by there."

His father nodded slowly, but didn't say anything. The smoke from his cigarette coiled around his fingers and then dissolved.

"You been thinking about that boy a lot?" he said finally, pulling himself only with difficulty from wherever he had been.

"That," Hayden said. "And all of it. The funeral. The letters. I don't know."

His father's cigarette had died between his fingers and he reached out and dropped the butt in the ashtray.

"You haven't been there in a while, have you?"

"No," Hayden said. "Not since her funeral."

"What'd you think? Being back?"

"It was beautiful," Hayden said. "In a way."

"That's the point, don't you think?" his father said. "There's a reason they call the whole religion 'The Church.'"

"But it was weird, too. It wasn't the same. Not as I remember."

"No," his father said. "It never is."

"But what's the point, then?" Hayden said. "I mean, if it's not the same. What's the point of remembering it at all?"

"Whatever made you think remembering had anything to do with what's real?" his father said. "The point is not that it's not the same. It's that it's different. There's more to it, like dreaming. You know?"

"No, I'm not sure I do," Hayden said. He took a sip of his drink and it was much softer now. "I'd just rather not remember, I guess."

"Maybe," his father said. "Maybe you would." He cleared his drink. "But that's not an option."

Hayden nodded at the book on his father's lap.

"What you reading?" he asked.

"Oh." His father looked down at the book. He turned it over and let the pages flip through his fingers as though he needed to see the ink, the words, to remember. "It's a new book on Shiloh that just came out," he said.

"Shiloh?"

His father laid the book down on the floor between the chairs, and his fingertips ran almost sadly over the cover as he let it go. "You know Shiloh," he said. "One of the big early battles in the Civil War? In Tennessee?"

Hayden shook his head.

"It was one of those first really bad ones. Nearly twenty thousand dead, I think, at the end of it."

"Is it good, the book?" Hayden asked. "What do you think?"

Hayden's father looked down again at the book on the floor and then reached for the whiskey. "What do I think?" he said, almost as if he were asking himself. He poured more whiskey into his glass and held up the bottle for Hayden, who shook his head. "Maybe I think we're animals," he said. "Maybe that's what I think. It was all so gruesome, Hayden. Maybe I think we're just animals moving through the world the way we've been built to do."

Hayden took another sip of the whiskey and looked at his glass as he swallowed it. Where the liquid touched the ice, it grew thick and swirled like oil. "But it was right, though, wasn't it?" he said. He looked up at his father. The lines in the older man's face caught the lamplight as though they were nets in an ocean of it. "The killing there?" he said. "Wasn't it right to fight for that?"

"Maybe," his father said, nodding. "Maybe it was. But what does that change? That's the irony of history. Lies fought in the name of half-truths, and it's the best fight. That's what Churchill said about World War Two. And what, Hayden, did we fight Shiloh for, exactly, anyway? Or, all that war? For what did a whole generation die and a whole country burn? So that fat redneck assholes can run around this valley with their muskets, re-creating every Southern victory that burned up the South? What, a hundred and fifty years later? All so a bunch of eighteen-year-olds can drive around in trucks with Confederate flags hanging out the back windows, while black babies are still dying almost three to one to white? Was it so we could have the privilege of just incarcerating black men instead of slaving them and nobody can say a word about it 'cause polite people don't say nigger anymore in mixed company? Fucking wonderful."

"Doesn't it still mean something, though?" Hayden said. "Even if all that's true, it was still right, though, wasn't it?" The whiskey was cold against his hand.

"No," his father said. "Don't get me wrong." He knocked another cigarette out of the pack on the table and lit it, his words coming synaesthetic, like small bundles of smoke. "It still means something. It just doesn't mean everything. Not like they want you to believe it does."

"I don't know," Hayden said.

"This whole country is like that, Hayden," his father said. "Either it's some kind of promise that just hasn't been kept yet, or a lie that was never meant to be. But maybe it's something else, too. Maybe everything here is kind of like this, like a dream house. The architect makes these almost perfect plans, everything is right, and then he spends his life building it. We won't even talk about what it's being built on, what kind of ghosts. But, still, he's building it, and he's using rotten wood and rusted nails the whole way through. Eventually, it begins to crumble, right, and when it does everyone keeps saying, this can't be falling." He held his hands palm up in front of him. "It can't be falling apart. The dream was so perfect. And you know they're right, too. So what do you do with that? It was right." He nodded. "Yeah, maybe it was right. But being right isn't like being rich, Hayden. You don't get to pass it on."

He stared out at the blunt, colored spines lining the wall in front of him. The old tape popped behind the music. "So we're animals," he said. He took a sip of his drink and then waved his glass at the books. "But then you have all of this, too." A long lock of his hair fell out from behind his ear and hung over his face. "Animals," he said. "But, maybe, sometimes, beautiful ones."

He smiled at Hayden. "You know what I mean?"

"Do you think about it a lot?" Hayden said. "The death, I mean?" His father looked at him again. Sometimes, with his father, if you said the wrong thing he would just stop, shut down, and move away in his mind. Hayden nodded toward the book on the floor. "Like in those old battles? All the people that died, but all the ones that didn't, too? What they had left," he said. "After?"

His father nodded. "Sometimes," he said. "Sometimes, I do. But there are lots of kinds of dying. What are you asking me?"

"I don't know," Hayden said. "I don't know what I'm asking, really. Just about death, period. All of it. What you said the other day, about me being too young when Mom died, not to know what happened but to understand it. I don't know. Maybe I was."

Hayden looked at his glass and it was almost done.

His father reached over and dropped a handful of new ice into his glass. It cracked as it touched the warmed liquid still left. He reached down between them and brought the bottle up. It was a little more than half gone and Hayden wondered how much they had drunk and how much his father had had before he came. He felt not drunk yet, but light, dizzy.

"The Celts were once all through Europe," his father said as he filled the glasses. A new cigarette hung from his lips, the long, blue threads of smoke making and unmaking sweet, bluish flowers around his head. "Did you know that?" He took the cigarette from his mouth and ashed the first, white ashes.

"No," Hayden said. "I've never heard that." Sam scratched at the floor with his paws, running, Hayden supposed, in his dreams.

"It's true," his father said. "There are sites of Celtic settlements as far east as Hungary and Romania. They think that the Celts held most of Europe for twelve, thirteen hundred years. But there's this great story, Hayden. I don't know if it's exactly true or not. Hell, I can't even remember now where I read it. I know Livy wrote about it, but it was a poet that wrote what I'm thinking of. Roman, definitely, but I can't remember for the life of me now who it was. Catullus? Shit, I don't know. Anyway, it's a great story. After those far eastern settlements, about how these Celts attacked Rome once."

He took a sip of his whiskey and held it in his mouth for a long time before swallowing. He was pulling himself into wherever this story was, falling back into whatever time it had lived in.

"The story goes," he said finally. "That there was this band of Celts, probably the ones who would become Irish, knowing them. You know, maybe at most a few hundred warriors. And they were sweeping over northern Italy for some reason, destroying everything they came across. The Romans, though, they decided not to bother about it. That was part of ruling an empire, you see, knowing what to leave alone. And Rome never really controlled the Celts. They were there, eventually they got there, but they never held them, not really. But they wanted to, so they figured this thing, it would sort itself out."

As he had spoken, his bangs had fallen down over his glasses and he swept them up. Hayden realized he was matching the cadence of his voice to the slow, warped blues that spilled out of the tape player, and he wondered if he was conscious of it. He had always thought that his father had been born in the wrong time. He should have been a bard, or one of those Indian storytellers that just sit around and tell about the world. It was something that Hayden envied. He felt that he could hardly talk most of the time, could never

get the words to match what he thought, but every time his father
began to speak, even if it was just to tell about a bar that used to be
on such and such a block, it sounded like he were retelling the story
of how the world had begun. He had that special thing, a quality of
voice, maybe, that kept you there, right with him, and Hayden waited
for him to keep going.

"Sooner or later," he eventually said, his eyes lit with the grinding, slow, frenetic energy of the story, moving, in a way, with it. "It
became clear to Rome that this was getting out of hand, that it was
going to have to be dealt with somehow. I don't remember what
it was about, or even know that anyone ever knew, you see. But, I
mean, these people were moving down the peninsula. They were
actually headed for Rome, Hayden. That's what everyone started to
realize. These few hundred goddamned, lunatic Celts were going to
attack Rome, for Christ's sake.

"And they were terrible adversaries, you see, and Rome knew
that because they used them as mercenaries. They fought naked,
Hayden, paint streaked over their bodies like they were demons
come straight from hell for you. They were brilliant in that way—
the same as Rome actually, but just done differently. You see, both
understood that the enemy can be defeated before the first strike.
If they are scared. If they are scared enough, you've already won.
That was the way the Celts fought. And even out-manned, even
out-trained, they won because of it. You see, Hayden, they had no
fear. None at all."

His father held up his glass and his cigarette and swept his
hands slowly through the air in front of him and his fingers and the

glass became the Celts moving across Italy and the smoke of the cigarette the smoke rising behind them, the smoke of the scorched earth.

"So, they moved toward Rome," his father said, watching his hands. "And this, remember, is the greatest military force the world had ever seen up to this point. And Rome knew now, they knew what was happening. So when the Celts camped just north of the city, the emperor sent out an envoy to talk and make peace. The Romans, you understand, Hayden, they respected the valor of these warriors. They understood courage."

He leaned in his chair toward Hayden so that his hands were between them, the smoke rising into the bowl of the lampshade and becoming a solid thing there, an atmosphere. "But even more than that, Hayden," he said. "They wanted these people as subjects of Rome. Rome wasn't stupid, and subjects fight for their empire, you see. The envoy, it brought out gold and furs, cups and jewels and all kinds of things as gifts.

"Well, the Celts took them in, these officials, and they gave feasts every night and they danced and got them women and threw festivals for days in their honor. But they wouldn't take any of the offerings. They refused them all. And finally, see, after a week or so, the Romans were just furious. Of course, they weren't used to not being minded in their empire. I mean, they felt like they were being generous to these insane people by not just killing them all outright. So they got fed up.

"One of the Romans finally went to the leader of the Celts, a druid, probably. He said, 'Listen, you can't attack Rome. You'll all be killed. You have no chance of success. So what can this bring you?' The Celts, though, they listened to what he had to say. But when he finished, they just said—and this is great, Hayden, truly great—they said, 'What can you do? You cannot kill us. Already, we walk in both worlds. There is nothing you can do.'"

Hayden looked at his father. He was looking out, blindly. He ran the fingertips of one hand over his jaw and shook his head softly. Again, he repeated it, "Already, we walk in both worlds."

"Well," he said. "You can imagine what the Romans thought of this kind of attitude. They got on their horses and they rode back to Rome. No one understood it. They all said, these people are crazy. There's nothing to be done with them. None of the officials understood it, none of the historians. Only the poets understood it. It was powerful, you see, stunning. It was more powerful than any show of might could have been. They were a sacred people, Hayden. Saints in their way, I suppose. I guess it's why they went in for the Roman church eventually, to walk in both worlds still. The soul in that religion is something that no one can take, that no one can force you to give up or give in. It's in the other world. The last stand of the truly defeated. You know?"

"What happened?" Hayden asked. "What happened after?"

His father finished his whiskey. "They rode on Rome," he said, slowly, as if every word were a thing to be cherished, cupped in your hands and savored. "Every one of them was killed, to the man. Their women made slaves and whores. Their animals sacrificed to Roman Gods. Their children were slaves, and then became Roman."

"Jesus," Hayden said.

"Yeah," his father said. "But there's something beautiful about that, isn't there? Walking in both worlds."

Hayden didn't think he had ever realized this about his father before, where the distance led him, where he was, or where he was trying to be, when he wasn't ever there. Hayden looked down into his drink. His father shook his head.

"It's not always easy, though," he said, pushing his hair back off his forehead again as he leaned over for the bottle of whiskey between them. Hayden held up his glass and his father filled it and neither of them looked at the other, as though there were a privacy in the moment but it wasn't a shared one.

The tape snapped off and the silence seemed to cover them like a blanket. Hayden hadn't realized how much the music had filled the room. He put his drink down and stood up. As he walked to the tapes, he pulled a cigarette from his pocket. He felt freed slightly, with his back turned, and tears came into his eyes though he kept them from falling. "What do you want to hear?" he asked without turning around. From his pocket he pulled out a book of matches and lit the cigarette.

"Something soft," his father said behind him. "Something good for whiskey."

Hayden squatted down and looked at the tapes stacked beside the old player and let out a long breath of smoke. Most of the tapes were old and their plastic cases had become cloudy over the years. Hayden pulled out an Emmylou Harris tape. There was a story that his mother and father had once taken him to a bar in D.C. to see her play when they couldn't find a babysitter. He had no memory of it, of course, but it made her one of his favorites, anyway. He pushed the tape into the player and smoked his cigarette as the empty static on the beginning of the tape started and then the first song came on.

"Not this," his father said behind him.

Hayden opened his eyes. "Why not?" he said. "I like it."

"Hayden, goddamn it," his father said. "Just not this, all right. It's too damn soft."

"Fine," Hayden said. "What then?"

Hayden could hear his father push himself up in the chair to look.

"Put on that John Prine tape there," he said. Hayden started to take one out. "No," his father said. "The other one, to the left."

Hayden took it out of the stack and put it on. He heard his father strike a match and blow out the first, whispered breath of a new cigarette. "Angel from Montgomery" began to play and Hayden looked back at his father. Right then, it seemed like the saddest song he could think of. His father had his eyes closed, his head rocking up and down softly. "Thank you, Hayden," he said. He had pushed his glasses up and they rested high on his forehead and his drink sat on his thigh and the cigarette burned slowly down in his fingers. The blue smoke looked like incense, tracing his body. Hayden thought about the church, about the crucifix and how the sinewy cords of Christ's body, the shadows carving each muscle that kept him up on the cross, had reminded him of Evelyn in the truck the other night. The expression on his face, the tightly closed eyes and open mouth, it seemed almost sexual, like he was coming, his face turned away from the pleasure, and Hayden wondered if it wrong to think that, or if that was in fact the point. That it was so foul, so strong, all of this, that even he had turned away then.

"That's all right," his father said behind him. "Sure, now, that sounds all right."

10.

The distant trees seemed dressed in the bright and gleaming costumes of a slow and marching autumnal parade. Through the wide front window of the sheriff's office, Dan could see almost the whole valley, the roofs of town and its neighborhoods trickling away into the long, flat slope of farmland, peopled now only by cattle and stilled, lunchtime tractors. Each building and house rising out of those great rows of low, threshed crops grew more improbable, more picture-postcard, as the eye moved farther into the valley, wiping all specificity away, until the land was swallowed again by the woods sheathing the river winding somewhere at the bottom of all of this. And then the other side, the opposing hills, their mirror, looking so much simpler, reduced finally to pure aesthetic by the distance. The sun hovered above it all and turned the rain gutters and car bumpers into blades against the softened, midday colors of everything else. Though he had already seen it, it was only hesitantly that Dan allowed his eyes to settle on Robert's Mercedes pulling into the parking lot.

Whoever made this world, he thought, they certainly didn't make it easy.

The acid in his stomach churned up again and a vague feeling of nausea reverberated through the network of his bones until even his fingers tingled. Excited, he had called Robert the night before when one of his deputies had matched the fingerprints they found on those beer cans in the clearing to a girl in Grant's class. It had been sort of genius, actually; he had run them against somebody's class project on forensic evidence that he had helped with from the year before. Calling Robert was unprofessional, and Dan had known it, but it was the first time he had anything at all to offer his friend and he couldn't help himself. Though, after having spent the last two hours with the girl and her father, he wished he hadn't; had thought, in fact, that maybe if he were given, right now, the choice to take back any single action of his life, this one might be it. Snowy static rang in his ears and he closed his eyes. The girl's father stood beside him and the way his fingers squeezed Dan's elbow let him know the man was speaking. Dan opened his eyes.

"I'm sorry," he said. "What was that?"

"You know young girls," Mr. Warren said. "This death, I think it's been hard on her the last few days. All that carrying on in there, I know it must seem a bit strange. But like she said, she saw that boy earlier, before he was killed. That's quite something for a young girl. I don't think she's righted it in her head, is all. You understand."

Dan wondered if she ever would right it. He looked back at Evelyn, standing behind her father. She had pulled the sleeves of her sweater into tight balls around her fists and her eyes were still, shining, and teary. But there was something else, too. Something other than the protective curl of her body into itself, the fear that trembled her lips, there was a hardness in the set of her mouth, in the clean, flat way her green eyes regarded him, even behind the tears. For perhaps the hundredth time in the last few hours, Dan's gaze ran over the skin of her throat she had tried to cover with her dark hair, searching out the four yellowing bruises, which, if he let himself, he could guess the age of, probably to the quarter hour. She was pretty and he tried not to think about it, any of it. Sometimes in this job, all you wish for is to be a more stupid man.

"Yes, of course," Dan said, nodding his head. "We can all understand that. This kind of death's hard on all of us. Especially the young."

Evelyn's father smiled. He seemed relieved. "Yes," he said. "Exactly. Well, Sheriff, if there's anything more we can do for you—" He had the voice of a salesman, Dan thought. He reached his hand out and Dan took it.

Dan thought about how protection was a kind of instinct in a parent. This man probably didn't even know what it was he was protecting her from, or maybe that he was protecting her at all, but he did it nonetheless. The thought made him remember Robert outside, and he looked again at the big, German car pulling in, all its chrome like so much heat lightning against the cold daylight. Another stab of pain cut into his belly.

"All right," Dan said. "I will do."

He watched Robert stumble out of the car. He looked as though he hadn't slept in days and when he shaved that morning, he had missed several spots of dark, day-old stubble, which gave the impression of some unseen mobile hanging over his head, small bits of its shadow pressed here and there against his face. Under his eyes, a purplish-yellow swelling stood out against the gray skin and made him look like a drunk three days into a binge. The impression was corroborated, too, by the heaviness of his limbs on his body, the swinging way he moved, as though only with the help of gravity could he orchestrate himself.

Mr. Warren opened the door and a wash of cold air swept into the room. Evelyn began to follow her father out, and Dan, without realizing he was going to, reached out and put a hand on her shoulder. When she looked up at him, he was almost surprised as their eyes met.

"I'm sorry," he said. "For all of this. You know, for everything."

She nodded and then walked quickly out of the station. Whatever it was that he had actually just said to her, even he didn't know what he meant, a feeling that he shouldn't have tickled in his belly beside the ulcer. Dan reached into his pocket and fingered the rough, worn rabbit's foot that his son had given him years before and that he had carried ever since, and the feeling of it, the rough boned end, the leathery places where he had worn the fur off, made him feel a little better.

Through the window he watched the girl walk out into the parking lot, her hair catching long streaks of light when she pushed it back behind her ears with the balled ends of her sweater. Robert stared at him as he trudged up the walk and the two almost ran into each other, the girl and he. They stood, looking at one another, for a long second, and then Robert took a step back and looked down at his feet, mumbling something that Dan couldn't make out as she stepped past him. She looked back once, Robert still standing there with his head down. Dan's stomach pitched. He looked over to the pot of coffee that sat in the waiting room. Never since the doctor had forbidden it, along with the cigarettes, had he wanted a cup so badly.

He turned back to the secretary. "Shelly," he said. "I'm going to head out for lunch. I shouldn't be long."

"All right, Dan," she said. She smiled at him and turned back to whatever she was writing on her desk. In the doorway of the lobby, Edgar, who had found the girl and been with him when they talked to her, watched Robert through the glass. The sparse red beard he wore gave his pale, freckled skin a fierce and also vulnerable look, and Dan nodded to him once before turning away, unwilling right now to even engage his expression and what it might mean.

Pushing the door open with his shoulder, he slipped his other arm through the sleeve of his heavy coat. It was cold and bright and the concrete sidewalks had the matte gray shine of dirty snow.

Robert looked up and Dan had the impression that he had forgotten where he was. "Dan," he said.

"Robert, you're just in time to come have lunch with me. I'm glad you came by," he lied. They shook hands weakly.

"Right," Robert said. "Is it lunch already?"

"Sure," Dan said. "How's Buck's sound?"

"Okay."

"Good." Dan tried to smile.

He turned to go but Robert stood where he was. Dan fingered the rabbit's foot in his pocket, his other hand palming Robert's elbow. At the touch, Robert looked up with that expression people have when they've been caught not listening to the conversation, suddenly realizing they're supposed to respond without any idea of the question. It took him a second, but he nodded and they turned together toward Main Street.

It was just noon and the sun stood directly above them and laid, like a separate and opposite frost, only the thinnest sheet of warmth over the cold air. There wasn't a shadow on anything. It wasn't something that Dan normally noticed, shadows, or the lack of them, but the effect seemed eerie today for some reason. It made him feel like he was dreaming, only knowing it, and in his pocket he worked the small ridges of his fingerprint over the ragged bones.

"How's Deb?" he said.

Robert looked up into the clear sky above the simple, blockish skyline of Main Street. "Oh," he said. "Not so good, I guess."

"And the little one, too?"

"I don't know, really," Robert said. "She doesn't say much anymore. But to be fair, I don't feel like I've been present much, either. You know, in my head. So—I'm trying, though. I mean, I think we're all trying."

Dan rested his hand on his friend's shoulder as they came up to Buck's. "It'll get better," he said.

Robert nodded. "Sure," he said. "It has to, right?"

Dan opened the door and stepped into the warm bar. On his right the dining room spread out through an open archway, all its tables covered in the checked oilcloths that made Dan think of his childhood. He smiled because they were designed to do it and he could never remember without also being aware that the memory was manipulated. The place was run entirely by Buck's son, who was about ten years younger than he and Robert, while Buck himself sat at the bar from open to close, drinking.

Buck turned his massive body slowly around on his barstool and looked them over.

"You have a warrant?" he said.

Behind the bar, his son smiled and flushed.

"Buck," he said. "I'm not a cop at lunch, I'm just another armed citizen of this great state of ours."

Buck smiled and took a sip of the whiskey and Sprite in front of him, crushing a piece of ice between his dentures. His face was grizzled in a way that let you know he had probably been beaten badly when he was young. "Good for you," he said, smiling. He gave Dan a little wink and reached out his gnarled, almost brutal hand and they shook.

Nights, Buck ran a small card room upstairs and Dan sometimes played in the poker games. The greeting was kind of a ritual, just a way to say they liked each other.

"We sit over here, Joey?" Dan said, nodding to the far table in the bar, which was the smoking section.

"Anywhere's fine," Buck's son said. He waved his arm over the empty tables.

He walked to the last table and took his coat off and swung it over the back of the chair. Sitting down, his body shifted quickly and pain sliced through his belly again and he closed his eyes and waited for it to pass. When he looked back, Buck had Robert by the arm, talking softly into his ear as Robert nodded. Dan liked this about small towns—they were small towns, always, no matter what happened. Everybody knew everything and somehow that bred empathy, not the self-help bullshit but the real thing, the thing that happens only when you watch someone's life too close for comfort. Even if Buck didn't particularly like Robert, which he probably didn't, considering what Robert did for a living, he still cared.

Robert nodded one last time and then came over to the table and sat down. They didn't say anything. Dan fingered an unlit cigarette lovingly. Robert seemed to be thinking about something else and Dan wondered what Buck had said to him. The waitress came up to the table and she and Dan said hello and then she let her eyes come to rest on Robert, who didn't look up at her. For a second, Dan thought she might start crying. When she looked at him again, he ordered the roast beef lunch special and a sweet tea, which was as close to coffee as he could get.

He couldn't stop thinking about the girl, about how pretty she was and the low moaning sound that came just before the tears, the yellow bruises, and how complicated and ugly this had all just become.

He let the cigarette sit in the ashtray still unlit and took the rabbit's foot from his pocket and put it beside him on the table.

"Oh. Nothing for me, thanks," Robert said after the waitress had asked him twice.

"Robert," Dan said. "Get the lunch. It's good and you look like you need to eat something. My treat."

"Oh," the waitress said. "No. Buck's picking up y'all's lunch." She patted Robert on the shoulder, smiling. "I'd take the opportunity, honey. It might never come again in our lifetime."

Robert smiled. "Okay," he said. "The lunch sounds good." He turned and lifted a hand up. Buck, at the end of the bar, raised his drink, watching the waitress's ass as she walked back into the kitchen to drop the order.

After the girl left, Robert began to roll the saltshaker around in his hand, back and forth.

"You know," he said. "I've been thinking a lot about my father and my grandfather. Since all this started. About the farms and that. Do you ever miss it? You ever think that we all made a mistake not staying with them?"

Dan and Robert had known each other as kids. They had both grown up on farms around this town, and Dan had gone out to Vietnam half a year later than Robert. After, he joined the sheriff's office while Robert went to law school. Dan had always guessed that it was the war that had separated them a little when they got back, but it could have been a thousand other things, too. In the end, it was just life, just life that got in the way.

"Hell, I don't know, Robert," Dan said. "Sometimes. Sometimes I guess I miss it. But it's that time I miss, not the life. You remember how they were. I mean, you must still see it all the time, the heartbreak that comes with trying for that life now. What's even to farm anymore? There's no place for it, anymore, that life. Not in the valley, anyway. A single farmer, in this America. You're dying as much as you're living the whole time."

Robert nodded. When he had come back from the war he had had a plan to consolidate all the farms in his family to compete with the bigger corporations, diversify crops to beat the price fixing and the subsidies, but his father had made Robert promise to sell the farm when his mother died. "Sometimes, Bobby," he had said one morning when they were hunting, his faraway eyes pretending to search the woods for game. "Sometimes, you just have to give up. Sometimes it just comes to that."

"I know," Robert said, shaking his head. "I know. It's just that I feel like maybe we lost something. Or I did, anyway. Like there was something they had, that even I had then. Some kind of clarity, an understanding of what they were, or something. And I don't have it anymore. I feel like I'm swimming, you know. I can't even name what it was exactly, but I can feel that it's gone, that I've lost it."

"It's the whole world that lost that," Dan said. "Not just us."

"You think so?"

Dan nodded. "Yeah," he said, "I do."

The waitress brought their plates and despite the pain in his belly, Dan realized how hungry he was. He looked down at the green beans and potatoes, the fatty, heavy slices of roast beef, and the thick, dark gravy smoking over it all, and he was glad, guiltily, to have something other than Robert to look at. Robert looked down at his plate, too, and slowly he cut off a piece of the meat and put it in his mouth, letting it sit there for a long time before he finally began to chew.

Before Dan took a bite, though, he drank half of the sweet tea in a single sip. The cool liquid rushed through his middle and calmed the acid roiling in his stomach enough for him to start. They sat silently, for a while, as he ate. Robert pushed a bite of food into his mouth every so often but mostly just dragged the tines of his fork over the plate. He seemed to be watching something behind Dan, though there was nothing there but the wall.

Eventually, he let his fork rest against the side of his plate. "We never talked much about the war after we came back, did we?" he said.

Dan shook his head. "No, not really," he said. "A few times, I guess."

Robert nodded. "I never thought about it much," he said. "I know there're lots of guys who could never stop thinking about it, but it was never like that for me."

"You're lucky," Dan said. "Me, too, I guess. Though right when I got back, I used to have these dreams. Nothing specific, just about the place. I hardly ever have them anymore."

"Sure," Robert said. "But here's the thing, I've been thinking about it a lot lately. You know, since the other night. It's been a long time since I've seen anything like that."

Dan ran a piece of bread over the gravy on his plate and as he chewed it, his insides shifted and he was glad it was the last bite. Robert had begun to play with the saltshaker again, spinning it slowly in his fingers.

"What I've been thinking about is this," Robert said. "Well, you know how you said it'll get easier. That's what I keep wondering. This thing, here. Seeing Grant. It's different from all the things I saw in Vietnam. Seeing him out in the clearing, seeing him opened up like that. And now, every time I close my eyes, I see it again. I can't put it out of my mind like I did all that stuff. It's like it's haunting me. And I keep wondering, Is it ever going to go away?"

"From what I've seen?" Dan said. "Is that what you're asking me?"

Robert nodded without looking up from the saltshaker in his hand.

"Honestly?" Dan asked. He looked down at the cigarette and the rabbit's foot lying beside one another.

"Please," Robert said.

"No. Not in my experience. No, it never goes away. But that doesn't mean it doesn't get easier."

Robert nodded and closed his eyes. It was the saddest expression that Dan had ever seen, even more so than that first night. Softer, less violent, but still, sadder. There are worse things, though, he reminded himself. Aren't there? Worse things even than this.

"I was never super-religious," Dan said. "But after I came back, I used to think a lot about original sin." He wanted to say something that would help, and he couldn't think of anything. Nothing from his experience, nothing out of all the years that he had been watching other people deal with their losses, provided him the slightest idea of what might give Robert what he needed, and it felt cliché, thin in a way, to fall back on religion now. But isn't that what it was, in the end, the only thing left when there are no other explanations?

"Just the concept," he went on, trying to articulate something he never had before, something he hadn't even thought about for years. "That maybe it's just a part of being a person. All the pain that will come in the course of a life. Some of us have more of it and some less, but everyone's got it. Everyone carries the evil. No matter what you do, there's all this pain in the world, all this ugliness, and you have a share. And I thought maybe that's what they meant about original sin. That we have it inside of us, that the bad things are part of us, too, just because we are. Nothing else, no special thing we did. But just because we are, we have to carry it, too. It seemed like that might explain something at the time."

"I don't know," Robert said. "I don't understand that." He shook his head. "It seems to me that if there's any such thing as that, then man's not the one who sinned. God is. God made the original sin." He looked up. His eyes had filled with a shining, porcelain wetness. "That's what they never tell you in Sunday school."

They looked at each other for a while. Behind Robert, Dan could see the cars skimming past the bright windows and their picture-frame curtains. Finally, he had to look away. He studied the cigarette in the ashtray, waiting. And he looked at the gray rabbit's foot.

Neither said anything as the waitress came and cleared the table.

"That girl," Robert said when she had left the table. "Outside the station. That was her, wasn't it? The one from the fingerprint?"

Dan looked up. This is what he had been afraid of since the first second he had seen Robert's car. His stomach turned over the heavy food and his eyes fluttered with the pain before he was able to control them. Robert was staring at him. He wondered if this question was why Robert had seemed so quiet, so distant and thoughtful this whole time they had been together.

"Yes," he said. The word almost caught in his throat. He did not want to have to talk about this, did not want to face it before he had thought what to do.

"I've never seen her before," Robert said. He nodded. "But I knew, anyway. Isn't that funny? She looked at me like I had done something to her. Like she hated me. She looked at me like she was scared of me, Dan. She was there, wasn't she?"

Dan didn't say anything.

"Her lip," Robert said. "It was busted."

"Yes," Dan said.

Robert's fingers closed around the saltshaker. His voice was trembling and so was Dan's, though he was trying to steady it.

"And the scratches all down his throat and chest," Robert said. The tears were red and glassy in his eyes. "And him being naked, there. Those bruises all on his shoulders."

Dan held his palm across his mouth and looked at his friend. "Yes," he said.

"My God," Robert said. The tears crowded onto his lashes. Dan didn't want to look. Yes, there were worse things than what Robert had already known.

"You know," Robert said, shaking his head. "This whole time I've been scared that he was there with a man. Can you believe that? That's why I didn't want to push you. I was scared of that. This whole time I was scared to find out he was gay. Isn't that the stupidest thing you've ever heard?" He looked up at Dan and two tears dropped over his cheeks. He didn't even bother to wipe them. Dan reached across the table and put his hand on Robert's arm.

"Oh my God," Robert said. "That little girl."

Dan wrapped his hand around the rabbit's foot. He knew, suddenly, that he stood in one of those moments in which you define your life. He had always thought that if he had the brains to recognize that kind of moment as it was happening then the choice would seem as obvious as it always did in retrospect. But it didn't. He let the rabbit's foot roll over his fingers and then he pushed it into his pocket. The fans above whirred softly in the quiet, and he could feel the slight movement of the air against his neck. He picked up the cigarette.

"Robert," he said. "You know, we could not find whoever did this."

Robert waved his hand weakly in front of him. "Oh, Dan," he said. "I know that."

"No, Robert," Dan said. He stared at this man in front of him, his friend. "We could not find whoever did this."

Robert looked at him and Dan could tell he understood. Tears thickened the comprehension in his eyes and he leaned forward over the table as though he didn't have the strength anymore to hold himself up.

"But how?" he said. "How can you love a boy like that?"

The Children of God

Behind him, the boy shifted, the hushed cadence of his breath quickening. Walker turned away from the window and looked to where he lay asleep still in the bed. On the table just beside his face, a deflated condom lay in a tiny heap, the thin, caked patches of brown and white stretching like scales across the dry collapse of latex. The mussed sheets twisted around the boy's shoulders and thighs like a rope, the mute daylight painting the pale arcs of his features an ashy gold. He looked so young now, no more than nineteen, Walker guessed. Sprawled over the bed like this, he gave the impression of some classical statue, his body a simple, pure geometry, both taut and relinquished, a brand-new Daniel in the teeth of the lion.

Walker didn't want to wake him up, couldn't bring himself to begin those awkward morning moments just yet, but just wanted him to be there, still and simple and beautiful. This was getting harder, the quick and staid good-byes, the stiff kisses, and the eyes that were so fast in the night, but now, in the day, would be flat, a stranger's eyes.

He turned back to the window, to the comfort of the city smoking outside. He had been thinking about the same things he always thought about in this kind of mood, this kind of morning, when the emptiness is like a rush through your belly and the day is so overcast it doesn't help anything at all, which is to say, trying not to think about anything.

Below, people moved in and out of shop doors, running their Saturday errands, and Walker watched them spinning around the buildings like discarded leaves spiraling through a river's stones. He didn't hear the boy get up and wasn't aware of him again at all until he spoke. When he did, it was only the sound of his voice, not what he said, that Walker heard. The cigarette he was holding had burned out in his fingers and he dropped the butt on the windowsill before turning around. The boy stood shirtless, clutching his socks and his shirt in one hand while buttoning up his jeans with the other. Awake, his features animate, articulated, he was prettier than Walker remembered. His light hair was scattered over his face in the wreckage of sleep, his flat chest and belly tattooed with impressions of the ruffled sheet. His lips were swollen and cracked from their sex and he smiled nervously as Walker looked at him.

"You're leaving," Walker said. He didn't know if this was a question or a statement, but it didn't really matter.

The boy nodded. He hooked his hand over his shoulder, his thin bicep and forearm laying a limp, hollow chevron over his chest. "Yeah," he said. "I've got to, you know, get back."

"Sure," Walker said. They stood looking at one another, both shirtless and in the jeans they had worn out, and Walker could smell all the complicated layers of sex still on their bodies and in the bed they stood beside. The smells culminated in the air directly between them, creating, Walker thought, a fecund but invisible third party, a sort of ghost of the night before. "You want a cup of coffee or something before you go?" he said. He had started some when he first woke up and thought it was probably ready by now.

"Maybe a quick one," the boy said.

Walker walked to the kitchen and filled two cups from the pot. A delicate and breathy steam rose from the mugs. When he turned around again the boy was fully dressed, balancing himself on one leg and then the other as he pulled his shoes on.

"Milk or sugar?" Walker asked.

"Both."

"This feels so domestic," he said when Walker gave him the cup. They both smiled, as if it were a joke that didn't need an explanation.

They drank quickly, their eyes lingering on one another over the porcelain. Walker worked to keep his body hard and he liked watching the boy's eyes drift over it, matching up what he saw now with what he remembered from the night.

"You going out tonight?"

"Maybe," Walker said, though he knew he was, knew that Desmond and he had plans.

The boy finished his coffee quickly and then leaned over the counter where a pad of paper and a pen sat beside the phone. "Well, if you do," he said as he wrote. "Or, if you want to, sometime, later, call me, okay?"

"Sure," Walker said. He thought, though, that he probably

wouldn't and he wondered when he had come to be like this. Was there an actual point, a line somewhere in his life that he crossed over without knowing it? He remembered being this same boy only a few years before, but he couldn't remember becoming this man. He leaned over the boy's shoulder and looked at the name he had written. *Bobby*. Walker smiled as he tried to imagine him in the uniform of a suburban little league.

At the door Bobby stopped and turned around. He raised one hand to Walker's chest and the fingers were soft and cold and wormy against his skin. They ran their tongues over one another's lips, and Walker felt like he was remembering something, some already distant encounter.

"It was hot," Bobby said. "Last night."

"Yeah." Walker nodded. "Okay."

"Okay."

Walker opened the door and Bobby kept his eyes on him and then turned and walked down the stairs and Walker closed the door. He felt as though he were just now coming out of sleep, as though he were suspended in his life, almost cushioned by the days that had come before this one and the ones that would come after. He lit another cigarette as he walked to the bathroom. Reaching behind the curtain, steam began to fill the tiny room almost immediately.

Just off West Fourth, Walker found himself on one of those small streets that seem to lose themselves as they go. He loved this neighborhood; cobbled sidewalks—didn't that say it all? These old, winding streets could be anywhere in the world, and the only things that placed you in time and space were the voices of people you passed, the brief flashes of neon pressing their faces, like children, through the otherwise dark windows of bars and restaurants. The closeness of these buildings, the low, huddling awnings and roofs were so much more human than the rest of the city, probably not worth the half of his salary he paid to live here, but still.

As he walked, he thought of New York, of how it had changed for him since he had first come here and how it had changed him, also. Although he didn't like to, he thought of Virginia, of those tight hills, the safe and secluded ignorance and violence and love of his parents' world. He hadn't been home since the Thanksgiving of his first year in college, when he had tried to explain it all to his father, how it had always been like this for him, how it was never going to change. His father had stood up slowly. Walker heard the screen door slam shut and then press open again and then come to rest, finally, quieter the second time. His mother had cried, not because she was hurt or surprised by what he had said—she had always known, he guessed, had felt the lack of desire in him as all women do on some level—but because she knew that she would lose him, or maybe both of them, now. And though she still loved him, and he knew it, it was only in quick phone calls and letters now, lipstick kissed over her good-bye.

When his father returned later that night, he stood in the doorway of Walker's room, silently waiting there. He forced Walker to turn and look at him, which was an almost unimaginable cruelty. They had the same wide build, he and his father, and he was framed by a thin line of yellow that stretched weakly into Walker's room from the hallway behind him, the angles of his shoulder and neck, the wide length of his arm weighted by a large book, all edged in that brackish light. Even after Walker had turned toward him, he stood there for a long time, staring at his son as though it was only there that he was finally deciding what he would say.

His father pulled a chair into the middle of the room and sat down. He hadn't taken off his boots and Walker stared down at them. In that moment he memorized the dirt and the lines of shadow that crossed and recrossed them where the leather buckled, the creases and scars cut into them like lines across a palm. When his father finally spoke, the sound surprised him.

"Walker," he said. He opened the book and the gilt cross on its cover sparked under the lamp. Walker had to make himself look up, but he did.

"Walker," his father said again. "You shall not lie with a male as with a female. It is an abomination." Although he didn't, Walker thought his father might cry.

His father looked up at him as though this might have changed something, and his eyes were pleading for Walker to take this last chance to make everything right. Tears slipped over Walker's face and he hated them and hated himself for crying them. He held his jaw so tightly he was afraid his teeth would break apart in his mouth. "You will never, ever, be happy, Walker," his father said. "Because this, it's not love." He stood up and walked to the door, but he stopped there, holding on to the door frame. He looked back and his wet eyes caught the lamplight, so blue, they were the softest part of the man, and Walker thought for a second that he might say something else, something different, hoped so hard that he never forgave himself for it, and then his father reached into his pocket and let drop a small fold of bills onto the table beside him.

"Be gone in the morning," he said, turning away. Walker could hear the boots clapping against the floor as he walked away from the room, and the sound was so clear in his memory he could still hear it now, twelve years later, wandering through the West Village.

He had never seen the valley again, and he hated to remember all this. These are physical things, he had come to understand, memories. All that we feel, pain and hatred and love and happiness, they aren't some existential experiment of the mind, but they played themselves out in the body mainly, and the thoughts came after, a justification of what the body already knew.

Walker lit a cigarette and looked around him. He had become lost in himself as he walked. The rush of cars along the streets and the hushed voices of people crashed against the buildings like an ocean sound. The silhouettes of city birds, black against the hidden light of the sun, circled above like scavengers. There was a bar on the corner that he liked and he headed toward it.

The light inside the bar was low and comfortable. Groups of young people sat huddled around their small tables fingering Bloody Marys and glasses of beer, while the dirge of a rock band leaked from the jukebox in the corner. Walker recognized the bartender and nodded. His hair stood in shining, razorlike spikes, and the delicate whispers of his ribs, the small muscles of his shoulders, pressed against his t-shirt. He watched Walker as he came up to the bar and he worked the glasses he was cleaning like they were flesh.

Walker ordered a drink and he made it without a word. Walker paid and drank the whiskey in a single, quick and burning sip. He ordered another one and the boy smiled. "It's on me," he said as he turned the bottle up above the glass.

"Thanks," Walker said. He dropped the money on the bar and picked up the drink and walked to a small table in the corner, the bartender's eyes still on him as he sat down.

Across the bar a woman sat at one of the tables reading a book that Walker had edited. She had that savage beauty that he saw in some women, strong and unforgiving, as though, in another time, they would have been something more holy than what this world allowed, something fertile and earthen, he imagined their skin like stone, but ended up now just like everyone else, only a little bit stronger. He watched her as she read. She was reading quickly, and it gave him a weird pride to think that she liked it, the book. It was one of the best parts of his job, these artifacts you helped create, that were fixed, solid, but floating, too, continually moving through the world like quiet, hidden pieces of yourself.

He pulled his phone out of his pocket and scrolled through his numbers before getting to Desmond. After that time with his parents, he had come back to New York ferocious. He thought that the city, the buildings in place of the hills he had just left, the confusion, might save him. And, for a time, it kind of had. For a short time, he had been awed by the freedom here, the quick love and the glistening bodies in the clubs, the smoky darkness, which were so much like those dark adolescent dreams he had cherished, held close as a locket to himself, that he had nearly felt saved. He had thrown himself into it, offering himself, it seemed now, like some kind of sacrifice.

That was when he had met Desmond, who had been a grad student where Walker went to school. Desmond taught him, really, how to exist in this new world. When Walker thought of that time now, he realized how quaking and gormless he must have seemed, despite how brazen he felt. Desmond was the most beautiful thing he had ever seen, and though they had never been lovers, Walker had grabbed hold of him then and in some ways it wasn't his father's face or his mother's that Walker saw when he thought of growing up, it was Desmond's.

It wasn't that Walker had been ignorant, exactly, but just that the world had been an abstract thing for him. Before coming to New York, he had never known an openly gay man. The one sexual experience he had had—the quick touching, the pounding heart, the thing he had wanted forever suddenly there, real, and then all too real, in his mouth, without knowing how but being thankful anyway, being thankful even for the gagging and the hot feeling of the tears sliding down—it had been a silent thing, a thing you knew not to talk about even as it happened, much less not to fall into it as you might have wanted to fall. And, really, the shame and the fear were the only things that made it real after, the only things that separated it from the dreams, and when they fell away, finally, it had been no different from a dream at all.

But Desmond's life had been so different from Walker's. He had grown up in a city and been out since he was little more than a child himself. God, Walker thought, he couldn't believe how stunning he had been then. Of course, he still could be called beautiful, but it was different now. Walker took another sip of the whiskey and walked to the doorway of the bar, pressing the call button on his phone and lighting a cigarette as it rang.

"Hello?" Desmond said.

"Hey, it's me."

"Walker?"

"Uh-huh," Walker said.

"Hey, baby," Desmond said. "What's up?"

Outside, it had started raining, and Walker watched the people on the sidewalks begin to scatter, coats and papers held above their heads as they ducked into doorways and under awnings, long strands of wet hair clinging, already, to their faces.

"How was it today?" he said.

"What?"

"Desmond, goddamn it," Walker said. "The doctor's."

"I think he's a fag," Desmond said. Walker could tell that he was looking at something else. He had that distant, automatic tone in his voice as though he were trying to decide which CD to put on next. "He definitely likes playing with my balls. No joke."

Walker smiled despite himself. "What did he say?"

"Nothing good, I can assure you. He did, however, insist on my phone number."

"Blood work come back yet?"

"Walker, please," Desmond said. "Are you still coming over before dinner?"

"Yeah," Walker said. "I'll be over in an hour or two."

"I can barely contain myself," Desmond said. "Then again, I think my pants are too tight."

Walker laughed and coughed out the smoke he had just inhaled.

"You sound good," Desmond said. "Maybe you should go to the doctor. He's cute."

"Okay," Walker said. "I'll see you soon."

"Bye-bye."

Walker hung up and went back into the bar. He dropped the phone down next to his drink and looked at the woman on the other side of the room again. She smiled to herself and pushed her hair unconsciously behind her ear. It was a girlish thing his mother did, and he suddenly missed her here, in this city she'd never seen. She used to sing to him when he was a child and for some reason the song came back to him, perfectly clear, as though she were singing it in his ear.

Jesus loves you, oh yes he does.
Jesus loves you, oh yes he does.
And you'll know it because the Bible tells you so.

Walker turned out of his apartment and headed across town toward Desmond's. It had grown cool and he buttoned his jean jacket up to his throat. The sun had just fallen and Walker felt the lengthening shadows and the alcohol like a reassurance in his body. He felt nervous, but better in the night than he had all day. The last of the dusk crept over the clouds and gave them shape, finally, above the city.

Walker pressed the buzzer to Desmond's apartment and stood waiting until the small speaker spit out its grinding sound and the lock dropped. The walls of the stairwell were tiled to look vaguely Middle Eastern, but whole patches of tile were missing, exposing the raw concrete behind them. The door to Desmond's apartment was open and Walker went in and shut it behind him. The walls were a startling white; with paintings and pictures hung at random heights and intervals, the furniture laid out at strange angles to make several spaces out of the tiny front room, the apartment was small but decorated to seem bigger than it was. The beat of a decades-old house song pushed through the walls between this room and Desmond's bedroom.

"Walker?" Desmond yelled over the music.

"Yeah."

"Make yourself a drink, honey."

In the corner of the room stood a small table covered with bottles and glasses. Walker poured a small shot of whiskey and drank it and then put ice in the glass and refilled it. Desmond walked into the room in his underwear, which was thin and white, nearly translucent in the fluorescent lights. A single, new lesion stretched from under the waistband and rose up the line of his hip like one of those tribal tattoos. Walker watched his body move and thought about how much it had changed in the last years. Now it was gaunt and corded, white as alabaster, like a gothic figure study. He remembered the opulence of Desmond's old body, not thick, but fleshed, flushed as though the blood inside could barely be contained. He met Desmond's eyes and then looked away, taking a sip of his drink, the heat flashing dull inside him.

"It's that bad?" Desmond said.

"What?" Walker said.

Desmond smiled and leaned forward and kissed him. He reached down and picked up a half-drunk cocktail from the table. The small, melting ice cubes looked like tiny, almost invisible coins thrown into a wish pool. Desmond stepped back and took a sip of the drink and looked Walker over. As he leaned his shoulders back, his ribs rose against the skin like a hand reaching right through him.

"You look good," he said. "I hate you. Why do you always look so good? And I know you didn't spend more time than it took to put those clothes on, either." He shook his head softly. "In a t-shirt and jeans, too. Shit."

"Maybe if you spent less time you'd look better," Walker said. He smiled.

"Fuck you, bitch."

"C'mon," Walker said. "You look good to me." He arched his eyebrows and smiled.

"You wish, honey."

They both smiled and Desmond lowered his eyes. When he looked up again they were milky with something that Walker couldn't place exactly, sadness, or gratitude, maybe. He had that gift of the drag queens, where everything is so far down, so covered over, that it could always be something else. Walker held his drink in front of him and ran his finger over the edge of the glass, watching Desmond nod, slowly, almost to himself, before he walked back into the bedroom.

Walker thought about the night, so many years ago now, when he had found out that Desmond was sick. They had been watching a movie and smoking a joint in Desmond's apartment. He had noticed it in the months before, Desmond's body becoming stingy with its flesh, the pills he had started sneaking. But Desmond hadn't said anything to him. It took the specific courage of being stoned in the dark room, almost anonymous, for Walker to say anything at all. He remembered how he had run his hands up and down his legs as though pushing himself from the outside.

"Desmond," he had said. "Can I ask you something?"

So silly, he thought now. So scared, like a kid who asks a question he doesn't really want the answer to.

Desmond had looked over, the whites of his eyes flickering in the small light of the television. "Walker," he said. "You know I'm a movie nazi."

"I know," Walker said.

"All right," Desmond said. "What?"

Walker looked at him. "Do you know what I'm going to ask?"

"If I knew what you were going to ask, wouldn't I just answer you so we could watch the movie?"

"I guess," Walker said. "Yeah." He realized he was still holding on to his legs, that his hands had grown tight on his thighs.

"Okay," Desmond said. "I'm sorry." He reached for the remote control on the couch between them and the screen froze. Walker felt disconcerted in the still light of the paused movie frame, he remembered, as if time had suddenly stopped around them. "Shoot," Desmond said.

Walker nodded. "You're thin," he finally said.

Desmond looked down at the remote control in his hand and carefully put it down. "That's not a question, Walker," he said.

"I know."

Desmond looked up and smiled. It was that smile gay men sometimes use in an ironic pantomime of feminine coyness, and Walker found it distasteful when Desmond used it with him. He didn't like the big beating eyes, the false retreat of posture. "Well," Desmond said. "I'm glad you finally noticed."

"Desi," Walker said. "Are you—Baby, are you sick?"

Desmond didn't say anything at first. He looked down at his hands lying empty across his lap, the long, parsimonious fingers barely flexing in the air, like a pianist dreaming. The light from the television carved deep shadows between his cheekbone and his jaw, along his neck.

"That's how rumors are started, Walker," Desmond said finally, without looking up. The words came out like so many breaths. It was something meant to be defiant, pointed, but there was no force to it and the words trickled out of him, pleading. Walker could almost feel his heart breaking. He reached out and tried to touch Desmond's leg, but he moved it and Walker's hand fell to the couch. Desmond looked up at him, and his eyes were wet and fierce-looking.

"What kind of thing is that to ask?" he said. "What kind of thing?"

"How much do you know?" Walker said.

Desmond looked down again, and the movie snapped to motion on the screen.

"Watch the movie, baby," he said. "It's a sad one."

Walker didn't say anything more then, but just watched the tears sliding down Desmond's cheek, colored by the television, almost ethereal, he remembered thinking, almost separate and bearable in the darkness.

Now, Desmond walked back into the room, and Walker turned from the window to look at him. He was wearing tight black pants and a pressed black dress shirt with oversized cuffs and collar. The shirt was open at the top and showed just the beginnings of his sharp, marble collarbone. Facing the mirror, he pressed black eyeliner across his eyes, and when he turned back it was as though he had become something different, not the tragic, skeletal figure he had been naked, not Walker's friend, but some small god, borne of and wholly of and holy within the night, and Walker thought, looking at him, yes, time will stop for this man.

"There," Walker said. "Beautiful. And in no time."

"If only. You know how long it took me to get my hair this way?"

He took a half-smoked joint from the ashtray on the table and lit it. The smoke rose around him like an aura, and he leaned his head back, his neck a delicate topography, and exhaled a white column of smoke. He handed the joint to Walker. The smoke burned down Walker's throat and into his lungs, and he watched as an ember fell off its tip and died in the air. He handed the joint back and walked to the bar. Even from just the one hit, his head was light. He filled up his glass. It was the whiskey that his father named him after and he thought of his father and then he didn't.

"We have to meet Tomás and Daniel pretty soon," Desmond said. "But I'm feeling reckless and I want to do a line before we go. You want one?"

"No," Walker said.

"Okay. Just wait a second then."

Walker sat on the couch and lit a cigarette while Desmond kneeled on the floor and pulled a vial out of his pocket.

"Should you be doing this?"

"Walker," Desmond said. "Shut up."

Desmond spilled out a tiny pile of the white powder and pushed it into a makeshift line on the table. He pulled a straw from a small box at his knees. His hand was white as the powder as he leaned down into it. He took the line in a breath that made Walker think of someone drowning and then leaned his head back. His eyes closed, shuddering, and the black makeup made them look deep, sunken.

"Fuck," he said.

"You ready?" Walker said.

"Yeah."

They stood up and Desmond pulled a black jacket around himself and flipped the high collar up. Outside the air was cooler still and they lit cigarettes and paced each other as they walked.

"It didn't go well with that boy?" Desmond said.

"Which?"

"The one last night."

"It was all right," Walker said. "Why do you say?"

"You haven't said anything," Desmond said. "He was hot." He looked over at Walker.

"Whatever," Walker said. "I guess."

"What?"

'It just seemed kind of stupid. Pointless."

"What?"

"The whole thing," Walker said. "I'm tired of just getting off. I'm tired. The nights, the sex, it doesn't mean anything anymore, does it? And that's all it ever is."

"That's all it ever is," Desmond said. The streets were still wet from the rain, and as they walked past the bars, neon reflected in the puddles like something hanging just below the surface of the world.

"No," Walker said. "There is fucking something more than that."

"There's not, baby," Desmond said. "Sorry."

"There has to be," Walker said. He said it quickly, and it sounded desperate even to him. And Desmond watched him as they walked.

"What are you doing to yourself?" Desmond said.

"I don't know."

"There's not," Desmond said. "There's nothing more. You know that. Damn, Walker, you know this shit. Look at the world you're in, baby. When you're young and pretty everyone wants you. And you take it, all of it—the nights, the sex, because that's all you're going to get. And if you know it then you've got a chance. Because boys don't love, baby, not really. It only lasts until the next one. The night only lasts until the sun comes up again. You want all this shit, all this reality and romance; you want to get married, and live in some nice middle-aged dyke brownstone in Brooklyn. Me, I'm just hoping for a little more nighttime. You know what I mean?"

He looked over at Walker and, yes, Walker knew what he meant. It was an impossible thing to argue against, dying. Walker could hear the coke pushing through Desmond's voice, though it didn't change anything he was saying. They had had this conversation before. "Don't say that," he said.

"And then you old, honey," Desmond said, a quick flourish of drag. "And either you're totally destroyed or you've survived, but either way you're not young anymore. And you're definitely not pretty. And you end up at the bars, like one of those ghosts, just wanting what used to seem like it wasn't enough. But now it's plenty, baby. More than enough. Now it's the fucking stars. And then you die, because when you were young and pretty, when you were a baby, some fucking asshole gave you the plague. And now your body can't even beat a cold."

"Desmond—"

"And it's better that you're alone then," Desmond said. "There're less tears for you to cry."

"I don't want that," Walker said. "Any of it."

"Oh, but you do, baby. You're fucking right you do," Desmond said. "Because that's life."

"There's something else, too," Walker said. "The Thing. Whatever it is, that fucking thing that pulls you out of the rest of this shit, that saves your ass from all this world in the end."

"Look around you, Walker," Desmond said. "It doesn't exist.

It's a myth. And how we got dragged into it, I'll never understand. For straight people, there's the suburbs, marriage, the propagation of the species. But we don't even get that. All we get is the truth of what people can really do, the hot, hard truth." He made a motion in the air like he was slowly stroking a cock. "And let me tell you what, baby. There ain't a thing in this world that saves you in the end."

"I don't want that truth," Walker said. "It's not for me, thank you."

"Who does, baby?" Desmond said. He laughed. "Whoever wants any truth?"

Suddenly, they were standing outside the restaurant. They stood there looking at each other and then they dropped their cigarettes onto the pavement. The embers shot over the gray cement like so many stars and Desmond reached out and touched Walker's arm.

"Walker," he said. "For real, though. I'm getting out of all this—" He lifted his hands and looked around, as if there were no words for the place he would be leaving. "You need to be ready for that."

Walker looked away. "You always say that."

"I know," Desmond said as he opened the door. "Baby, I know it."

It was one of those restaurants that open and become important for a year and then close. The shattered sound of so many conversations made a wall around everyone and behind that was the slow, grinding beat the DJ spit out from a platform in the corner. Beautiful people laughed and talked with food still on their forks, looking at one another through the alleys set up for the waiters.

Desmond and Daniel and Tomás all talked and laughed, but for some reason Walker couldn't concentrate on any of it. All he could do was think about Desmond, how they had found his cocktail years ago and then for some reason it had just stopped working, his body suddenly decaying again as though this were twenty years ago. How the doctor told him all he could do was wait for something new. And Walker thought of his father, too, bathing in his stupid innocence, his religion, arcane and miserable, and where was his God now, anyway, when everything in the world was suddenly bowing down to death? Where had his God been when all these beautiful men were dying? Don't tell me about the wages of sin. Where the fuck is redemption?

He wondered what it was that he wanted from his father now, why he was thinking of him so much, but he knew that most of all, he just wanted his father not to be right.

Desmond wouldn't talk about the doctor during the night, as if they stood on some holy ground. Walker drank. It was maybe the one thing, he thought, almost laughing, he had learned from his father. After dinner, they decided to go to a few new clubs on the Lower East Side. The darkness outside the restaurant was swollen with the false, orange dusk of the city lights reflecting on the low clouds, and it was stronger even than the real dusk had been.

They went to one club and then to another, but they were the same place. You could smoke in both, illegally, and it was the only thing Walker liked about them. The darkness inside was a thick curtain hung over everything, broken only by the canyons of colored lights that twirled and spun across the dance floor. Cold-looking girls in beautiful clothes sat along the walls or danced with slow, still steps, smoking and looking bored, touching their hair and slowly sipping cocktails, while the boys twisted their bodies in and out of the lights, slick and gleaming with sweat. Most of them were high on something, and they seemed to touch each other without any discrimination, to lick each other as though they were just tasting the salt, as if it were all about something as basic as that, as simple as remembering.

Daniel leaned over and told Walker that the DJ was from London and was in New York to spin someplace big but had agreed to do a couple of nights here while he was in town. Tomás and Daniel went out on the dance floor, and he and Desmond walked to the bar and ordered drinks. They watched the people dancing, their arms thrown up in what looked like desperate praise or prayer and reminded Walker of the revivals and churches where he had grown up, and they all seemed to be saying, this, there is this, only this, only now. Hallelujah.

Walker turned toward the bar. And there were the other men, the ones who didn't dance but just circled the young with their eyes like predators, hungry, their tongues slick and gaudy over their lips. Desmond leaned into his ear, saying, "Okay. Show me your something more." Walker could feel his breath against his neck, in his ear, and he turned to face him.

"What about Tomás and Daniel?"

"Oh, please," Desmond laughed. "They'll take one of these boys home tonight."

Walker looked at Desmond without thinking, just letting his eyes take him in, the black makeup and his dark, almost black eyes below it, the smile that was so sardonic and scared, the clear, pulsing acorn of muscle in his jaw, and the hard set of his black, manicured eyebrows, like scars cut into the smoothness of his skin. It seemed to Walker that Desmond had become like that hero, who, returned from war, cherished, cheered, is lost in his own country, sleepless for what he's done in her name. He thought, too, about what Desmond had asked and he thought that maybe he had an answer, but that it was unwanted, maybe even unsayable, and he swallowed it down anyway with his drink and then he ordered another one.

In front of them a boy pushed up through the crowd at the bar. Walker recognized him as an old lover of Desmond's, from years and years ago. His eyes were big and blank, and Walker thought he had probably taken pills. He stood before Desmond with his feet set wide apart.

"Hey," Desmond said. He pulled his lower lip in between his teeth. "You look great."

The boy slapped him, his hand almost too fast for Walker to see, but the sound was like a whip cracking against the air. Desmond's head snapped down and his jaw fell into his shoulder and while it sat like that, for the half second that he was still, he looked shy, almost embarrassed. When he looked straight on again, his eyes were wide and his mouth was open, but only for a second.

"I didn't know you liked it rough," he said. A blossom of red had opened over the flesh of his cheek.

"You're so fucking trite," the boy said.

People had begun to turn around, to watch them, and Desmond's eyes flashed back and forth across the faces. The boy leaned into the space between Walker and Desmond. When he spoke, his words were a whisper.

"I'm fucked," he said. His voice trembled, and Walker couldn't tell if it was from the drugs or what he was saying. "And I know it was you that did it to me. I know it, Desi."

He reached up slowly and touched Desmond's lips with his fingers. "You remember? When we were in love, right? You remember that time?" Walker looked at Desmond and tried to find his eyes, just to let him know that he wasn't alone, but Desmond was staring at the ground. "I didn't know," he whispered. His face, where the boy had hit him, was flushed and red and the color was moving, stretching farther over his skin as though you could watch the blood pumping through him. The boy pushed slowly off Desmond's chest and took a step back.

"This faggot is sick," he screamed. He shook his head and wiped the tears that Walker hadn't noticed in the dark out of his eyelashes. "This faggot's so sick," he said, softer. His voice was small and held the perfect trill of one person's terror, and someplace else it might have been the kind of thing that struck you, that stuck with you, that you remembered later again and again, and every time, from that moment on, your heart would break a little just remembering, but here, amidst these people and their chaos, it was lost, swallowed. The boy wiped his eyes again before turning into the crowd, disappearing.

Desmond covered his face and ran out of the club. Walker tried to go after him, but the bartender reached over the bar and grabbed his shoulder. When Walker turned, he was holding the check, and he paid quickly, throwing several crumpled bills from his pocket down on the bar. Before he had a chance to get out, he saw the people who had been watching the scene turn around and push into the darkness of the club, leaving him standing totally alone at the bar. He knew that it wasn't some kind of politeness or even fear that turned them like that, but the sense of being tainted, of wanting to be taken in again by the darkness and to believe again, however briefly, that they were protected, and that those who had just been touched by another world, a world beyond this night, were alone, far from them, and alone.

Outside, the air was cool and somehow huge, as though Walker could feel it moving, not just the breeze but the whole night, streaming blindly over the world. Desmond wavered in the middle of the street like a drunk. He had lit a cigarette and he raised it absently in front of him as though he were speaking and then he let it down again. Walker ran to where he was and pulled him onto the sidewalk. He tried to hug him, but Desmond turned out of his arms, heading down the smaller street beside them.

"That faggot," he said. He was crying. "That tired, fucking bitch. How could he do that to me?" He collapsed onto the steps of a small apartment building beside them. The black makeup ran down his face in burnt, charred-looking streams. He put his face in his hands and Walker stood and watched him sob, watched his shoulders shaking. All around him the stone and cement of the building and stairs glittered wet in the streetlights.

Finally, he looked up. "Walker," he said. He wiped at the tears and the makeup stretched over his face and made him like some fierce, defeated warrior.

"Don't," Walker said. "Don't say anything."

"Walker," he said again. "I'm dead."

Walker didn't say anything. Tears welled in his eyes and bled down and everything grew soft behind them, shimmering, radiant.

Desmond stared at him. "You want to know what the doctor said? He said I'm dead, already dead. He said that when it comes, it'll come from nowhere. And it's coming, baby. I can feel the sea changing."

"No," Walker said. He shook his head and sank down to his knees in front of Desmond. The cold, wet sidewalk soaked through his jeans. He took hold of Desmond's legs in front of him and pulled himself up his body until he was pressed against it, gripping his shoulders and then his back and his neck.

"Together," he said. "We could do it together."

"Don't do that," Desmond said.

"People do it," Walker said. "Everyone gets that. People get to do that at least."

"Not us," Desmond said.

"I'll take care of you." He could feel the heat of his own breath between them, curling up Desmond's neck and touching his own face again, hot and breathy and boozy. "Right now. Right now we're alive."

"No," Desmond said.

Walker reached his hand around Desmond's head and pulled it toward him until he could feel the curling and hard bones of their skulls pressing into one another. He breathed in and let the air out slowly. "I love you," he said. "Desmond, I'm in love with you."

"You can't say that to me," Desmond told him. He tried to push Walker away, but he held on, pulling them closer still, and they stood up connected like that. "Please don't ever say that to me," Desmond said.

"I'll be with you," Walker said. His lips formed the words over Desmond's cheek, the rough bristle of his beard pulling Walker's lip down as he spoke.

"I'm leaving," Desmond said. "Here, you, everything. I've got to. I'm too scared for this."

"No, you're not," Walker said. He moved his hands to the side of Desmond's face so that they were looking at one another.

"I can't do this, Walker. Please don't ask me. I can't watch you watch me die. I can't see that."

"I don't care," Walker said. "I don't care if you die. I want what I can get. All of it. I don't care about sickness. I don't care about pain or doctors, any of it." Desmond shook his head and Walker could feel the ridges of his brow and the cuts of his cheekbones rocking against his palms. "You wanted me to show you something more? This is it. Right here, right now. This is the thing that saves us."

Walker brought his face into Desmond's and the first thing he could feel was the wetness of their tears, cool and thick with the makeup, and then Desmond's lips, soft, shaking against his. Their tongues met gently, knowingly, as if they were old lovers. It seemed to Walker later that all the world was there between them in that second, the hope and faith that's always sacrificed and almost never survived. It seemed that time did stop, in that second time stopped for them. When they broke the kiss, their faces still touching, they were both shaking. Desmond nodded. "Yes," he said. "This is it."

He pushed his hands into Walker's chest as hard as he could and Walker stepped back. The heel of his boot hit one of the stairs and in the flashing feeling he knew he was drunk. He fell hard onto the stoop. The rain soaked in cold lines across his back where the stairs dug into him. He looked up at Desmond, who stood just beneath the streetlight, his skin and hair and tears shining, his dark tears shining. He covered his mouth and then turned and ran down the street. Walker tried to get up quickly but his foot slipped out on the wet pavement and he fell back down. He only heard Desmond get into a cab.

Sitting in that doorway, Walker pulled his knees into his chest. He could still see Desmond in his mind as he had been standing there, and he knew that he would always see him just like that, and when he forgave him, as he would, standing beside his coffin several months later, he was forgiving this same, beautiful man. Because it wasn't the wasted, washed skeleton that Walker had prepared for that lay there, but this man, here, because it hadn't come that way, his death, not the long fight of sickness, but a final gift, the quick release of his life dripping, dripping into the water of a bathtub in his mother's house, an image that Walker thought could even have been lovely, so purely his, the rouge against his skin, the aesthetic chosen always, the aesthetic the last, the final sentiment. And Walker forgiving him again later and again later, as he would again and always, because maybe if you tried hard enough you could forgive anything, even the unforgivable.

And he closed his eyes, soaking wet and freezing on the stairs, rocking with his own sobs as he pulled his knees tighter and tighter. And this far east, he could almost smell the ocean closing in on him. Fetid and unthinking, it suckled at the pilings of this city beneath him.

Eden

II. Was something as small and discrete as a body—eyes, ears, tongue, gut—Robert wondered, a thing that itself could be haunted?

Against the window the air seemed sharper, more precise, the cold contracting every line into a crystal tension that showed the exact distance the outside bled in. Despite this, this cold, Robert was sweating; single, warm drops falling across the tender skin of his ribs, cooling even as they were caught in the fabric of his shirt.

Above his own half-reflected face, the moon carved a high, delicate crescent into the dusk. Its whitish sheen clung to the mist that had come in with the evening, glimmering tinsel-like over the long, shallow arcs of wetted telephone wires. Along the sidewalks, the large trees that stood hulking between the streetlights became strangely colorless above the milky sheets of pink and green, pearlish light spilled over the fog-beaded bodies of parked cars.

All this, though, like the half-lit room in the window, seemed to be just superimposed over what Robert was really seeing, a

memory that had suddenly filled his mind earlier in the day and had
stayed with him ever since, repeating over and over and becoming
strangely and inexplicably connected to that girl, her frightened,
hateful expression, the eyes themselves shockingly pretty, so that
along with the memory, the feeling of her staring at him turned
over again in his stomach each time, spilling gooseflesh down
his arms.

He was running. A child still, he was running through tall rows
of corn on their farm. Above him, the flat, blue sky made a low ceiling and in the distance the long rows closed in on themselves, opening always just before him until they seemed infinite. The wide leaves
of the corn reaching out and slapping, caressing his shoulders, and
his arms pumping and his legs pushing up and down against the soft
earth, the turned earth, and the wide, curling husks fingering his hair
as he ran. He was playing or had been sent to get his father, he
couldn't remember which, or if there was anyone else with him. What
he remembered now was just running for the sake of it, because he
was young, because he had a body that not only knew it could but
had to. His memory of the feeling was lovely, this imperative physical
force, this driving motion to nowhere, through nothing, totally free
in the way that only those who don't know the concept are, but that
only made it worse somehow; so obviously nostalgic, the memory felt
contrived and specious, the needy push to move at the heart of it desperate, even frightening.

Deb opened the door to the study behind him and he had to
stop himself from jumping at the sound. He had turned the arm-
chair to face the window and had to twist around now to see her in

the doorway. She had been cooking since he came home and he knew she would be telling him the food was ready, but he had trouble making out the mumble of her words.

He was surprised to find himself thinking, even now, how lovely she still was, the dim light just edging each of her features; even behind the sad restlessness and the new wrinkles cut down into her cheekbones, the cracked, ashen lips, he loved her. Maybe, in the end, he told himself, there will be nothing so surprising as love, as what it can be, what it can live through.

When she stopped talking, he realized he hadn't heard anything she said. "Okay," was all he was able to get out before she closed the door again.

He stood up and his body was heavy, aching. He was filled with a physical hollowness that felt something, though not exactly, like anxiety, a strange, quiet, and terrifying feeling that his body was not only his own anymore, but held in equal share, suddenly, with so many memories and impressions, a random connecting tissue of thoughts and images that he, of his own accord, would have cut, but couldn't.

Running. When he closed his eyes, the top-heavy stalks of corn, still green in their husks, bent and blinked above him, tiny threads of silk reaching down for his face. He could almost feel the scratches the way only a child does, pleasantly, tickling pain stroking his cheeks. Robert shook his head and forced his eyes to open again, to focus on what was here. The town stumbling out the window down toward the river, tiered, parceled, like some kind of agricultural experiment. *New revolutionary techniques in the growing of America,* he imagined one of those governmental pamphlets from his grandfather's era saying. He finished the drink he had been nursing since coming home and turned away from the window.

Under the lamp on his desk, the white rose from Grant's funeral had sat now for days, each petal curling back until the outermost had fallen into a close scatter over the wood. He didn't know what to do with it. In fact, he had almost, or at least tried to, forget that it was there. It's flesh glowed beneath the lamp's glass shade, brownish and thin, the veins running through it like empty flourishes, slightly whiter than the rest. Suddenly, he remembered how the other flowers had lay against the coffin, limp and sagging as a snake pile cleared from a new field and thrown in a heap somewhere by its edge, each headless, doused and waiting to be lit. It made him shudder. No matter what else, he thought, that was my son. My poor son.

The strong overhead lights turned on in the parlor and the dining room made the rooms look flat and bright as photographs. The sun was hidden behind the ribboned husks, but the brightness, he could feel it pressing all around him, forcing the shade down into the rows with him, cool air licking his straining shoulders and neck, touching him everywhere in fact, the light stretching only between the long stalks and there darkening the earth. Each piece of furniture sent several long shadows skittering across the floor. Rachael was already at the table and behind her, the crystal reached through its glass case to splash tiny pools of rainbow against the wall. She had pulled several strands of hair taut over her eyes and she watched him through their dark lattice. She turned away and he realized he had been staring at her without meaning to. The thick, heavy leaves; the tall stalks like arms reaching up.

He felt hunched, his body exhausted, and he tried to pull his spine straight. He could almost see that girl's face in front of him; her pale skin and dark hair weren't so different from Rachael's. The thought embarrassed him and he didn't want to think of all the reasons why and he was glad that Rachael wasn't looking at him anymore.

Love is not an act of will.

No, he thought, love cannot be just will, because will can fail. Maybe will always fails. And love cannot be will.

As he walked around the table, he rested his hand on Rachael's shoulder. So tiny, it brought him back to the night he had done the same thing as she walked down the stairs to her mother. He was trying to find, he knew, some form of continuity between the moments, between this day and that, between that and every other day he had lived. He wondered if the running memory was the same thing, an attempt at continuity, as if everything he had ever experienced, or would, could be all held each in the other, a whole life encrypted in every second. He had never liked the thought of predestination, ironically un-American he thought, and this, this impression of time, comforting as it was, left the same uneasiness, the same vague feeling of rebellion in him that that idea always had.

A large roast sat on a platter in the middle of the table, and all around it lay white bowls of roasted vegetables and sliced tomatoes. The table reminded Robert of a garden, of the pools of color, the care that goes into making something beautiful. He looked for Deb but she was tucked behind the wall of the kitchen. The food was still steaming and where she had sliced the meat, you could watch the rare center bleeding onto the porcelain. He felt nauseous, empty, and he realized that the only thing he had eaten today was the few bites of food with Dan. Everything felt still, reduced to only this, this table, this second, as if a life could be broken, continuity itself made moot, transcended by something so simple as a table laid out and a little girl in a chair, as food prepared and waiting to be eaten.

Walking into the dining room, Deb filled the three water glasses carefully from a pear-shaped pitcher, which had already begun to sweat in her hand, wetting the tablecloth in a ring when she put it down. Robert picked up one of the bowls. Hungry tongues of steam stretched out over its lip and sucked at his fingers. He served himself and then handed the bowl to Rachael. When everything had been passed around, he cut into the pink meat on his plate.

"Aren't we going to say grace?" Rachael said.

Beneath his feet, in the thin furrow, the soft dirt gave, a tiny alley of dirt, and on either side, it rose, this damp earth, to meet the stalks, the yellow-green stalks that were straight and moved only with his body, only as he ran.

Robert looked up from his plate. "No," he said. He shook his head. "No, the food is hot."

Deb looked down at the table. Rachael nodded. "Oh," she said. She stared at him and he felt the morning, the girl, Dan, the whole of it rushing up and he tried to silence it. He looked at her and told himself that she was just his little girl, his child. But she didn't look, suddenly, even a bit like a child, but like someone who had already seen through it all. Someone pushed to it, pushed by this, he thought, maybe even by him. He had to be more, that's what he decided. More than this emptiness, this receptacle for life's heaped horrors. He had to fight, to take what there was left beyond that, and bring it back to them. Absently, Rachael ran her fork back and forth over a small red potato. "It's his favorite dinner," she said. Robert looked at her. "This," Rachael said, her hand gesturing over the table. "It was his favorite, right?"

Deb looked up at her and Robert thought her eyes were unfairly fierce, as though the girl were telling their secrets in public. "Stop it," she hissed. But Rachael was right. It was Grant's favorite dinner. There was a part of him that didn't like the thought, that grew queasy at the idea of such an invocation. But there was another part that was less just than that, less willing to measure the world out so equally, and that was even now holding the boy's hand, kneeling facedown in the wild grass of a clearing. He closed his eyes. The small muscles all through his body, stretching, pulling, stronger than the air; running.

"I guess we'll enjoy it, then," he said, each word forced shaking from inside him.

Nobody said anything more. The silver scratched against the plates, and behind that only the whirring of the heat. Robert watched the tears gathering in Rachael's eyes. Her dark lashes were strung together, made solid, by the wetness growing inside them, the light from the chandelier above like an adornment painted onto them. Eventually, Deb stood up to clear the half-eaten plates.

"Why do we have to be like this?" Rachael said finally. The

thickening of her lashes had grown too heavy and the tears now began to fall.

Robert looked at her. "What do you mean?" he said. Even in his own ears, his voice held the specific, petty tenor of somebody else's fear, distant-sounding, as if he were only half listening to himself.

"Like this," she said. She lifted her hand off the table and it hung there in the air as though she didn't know what to point to. "Does loving someone have to mean this? That you aren't even alive anymore. It's not fair to love someone so much that you can't live."

In the kitchen, Deb dropped a plate into the sink and Robert heard the pieces of porcelain skidding across the metal.

"Love shouldn't be able to kill you," Rachael said, turning toward the kitchen. "Should it?" She had begun to scream. Robert was surprised how quickly the emotion came into her voice, how loud it was. He almost didn't hear the words. They didn't matter anyway; he could feel what she was saying, see it spelled out in the blind, inky reaching of her eyes. Her neck and face flushed in patchy, blood-pinked dollops.

"You all walk around like without him none of us have any reason to live," she yelled. "It shouldn't be like this. It's not fair. Is this what life is?" Robert could hear Deb crying in the kitchen, her fingernails making a small scratching against the wall between them. It seemed, as he watched Rachael, that they were both miles away from him. It wasn't her saying any of this, but some middle voice, some invisible presence, that knew so much more than she did. She stared at him, her eyes accusing him of something he couldn't even understand. She was so pretty, that's what he kept thinking. "I don't want to love him," she screamed. "I don't want to love him anymore."

What Robert could feel was the perfect fulcrum of his elbow as it sprung out. The sound clapped through the air and her head turned and carried her chair onto its back legs and then over. Before he knew what was happening, he had followed her to the floor. The corner of the table clipped his hip like a hammer to the bone and turned his body, canting him on its fulcrum. Through his own tears, he couldn't see anything. He fell on top of her. He was running, again, the blood filling each vein, warming, now hot. His arms rose and fell blindly against her body, but he couldn't feel the impact of his hands against her. All he could feel was their heat, this profound, living heat radiating between them. This was inconceivable; he was not doing this. She was screaming and he finally began to hear again through the rushing sound in his ears.

"I'm glad he's dead," she was screaming. Her face and arms were flushed red from his incompetent beating. His hand froze in the air. His breathing was so hard, so labored, he wondered for a second if he was having a heart attack. Reaching out, he grabbed hold of the table to steady himself. Rachael's arms were held up above her face against his flailing. He looked at her. He had never hit one of his children before, and he felt exactly as weak, as bullying now as he had always feared he might. In a sense, it was the feeling, not the act, that shamed him.

"I'm glad he died when he did." She was bawling, barely able to get her breath in between the words. She pushed herself up quickly from the floor and he was left kneeling there by himself, trying to breathe. "I'm glad he died when he was still young," she sobbed. "I'm glad he died before he had to know what this was like, before he had to see you. Both of you."

Her tiny fists shook beside her face as she screamed at him. He could see the veins throbbing against the skin of her throat. Robert felt so tender all of a sudden, whatever blind anger had come up in him falling away as suddenly and blindly as it had come. Her eyes were swollen and red-rimmed, long strings of her black hair stuck in the tears on her face. Thick ropes of spit stretched between her trembling lips. Inside he began to tremble, too, aware now that he was lost totally as to what was happening in his life.

"I'm sorry," he said. His voice was weak and shaky between his sucking breaths. "Darling, I'm so sorry. I don't know—" As she turned, running away, he reached out. His hand hung in the air as though she were still there. Her footsteps made an erratic rhythm up the stairs and then the door to her room slammed. Slowly, his fingers curled down and he let his hand come to rest on the floor. He pushed himself up. The sting in his hands had begun to vibrate over his skin, pins and needles cool, as though they were falling asleep.

Robert turned slowly toward the kitchen, where Deb stood. She was watching him. Her jaw trembled half-open, tears glossing her lips and falling into her open mouth. She leaned on one hand against the kitchen counter and with the other held herself by the throat.

"Deb," Robert said.

"I know."

He walked into the kitchen and she turned half away from him. Reflected in the little window, he could see them both as he pressed his chest against her, watched her eyes fall shut. He wrapped his arms around her middle and he was surprised that she let him touch her after that.

"I'm so sorry," he said.

She shook her head. "They have no idea how long time can be," she said. "They want everything." In the sink the shards of porcelain shone like pieces of bones thrown over the ground.

"Love," he said.

"Not yet. Please." She turned inside his arms and faced him. "I can't be here yet. Not for this," she said. "Please, don't make me."

Robert nodded. He had thought that if he gave her time, she would come back, and he still hoped so, but also he was beginning to understand how someone doesn't come back. This was too much, though, even to think about. He felt as though he were sinking, like those pieces of the earth he had read about, whole countries sinking an inch or two every year, a millionth of that every second.

She lowered her face. "Not yet," she said again. He ran his fingertips over the soft skin at her temple, tracing the edges of her hair.

At the door, he slowly pushed his arms into the sleeves of his jacket. Outside, the night closed around him, the fog swallowing everything whole, without discretion. He made his way down the porch steps and at the bottom he closed his eyes, trying to imagine himself disappearing in the white.

Besides Buck's, the only other bar anywhere near town was out on 211. It was just a little redneck roadhouse, the kind of place he had hated all his life. He was almost positive that he wouldn't see anyone he knew there. He would be a coward to go someplace like that right now, when he was leaving what he was leaving. He walked to his car anyway.

The newly dark air was viscous, thick with the mist, and he could feel it as it moved over him and then away, slipping into itself again. He closed his eyes. And for the first time since it had come, he couldn't recapture the memory. Running, he thought, you were running.

12. The mixed scents of urine and bleach crowded the small room. From the stained faucet, a slow leak tapped its hollow finger against the cracked porcelain. Hayden had already thrown up once and he tried not to dwell on it, the smell, that dizzy, unnerving rhythm. He turned the faucet on. The bare fluorescent light dressed the water in a dull gleam as it gurgled into the drain. He cupped his hands, splashing the water onto his face and then filling his mouth. The pipe's rust tasted sweet against the vomit still on his tongue. He gagged again and the water spilled out.

He wondered why it had taken Evelyn so long to tell him, why she waited until they were sitting in this bar. But then again, maybe he'd known as soon as he'd seen her. Not everything, obviously, not the details, but the fact, spelled out in the scattershot tapping of her foot against the floorboard, the tremble in her voice as she asked him to take her somewhere away from town. And he hadn't asked, had he? He tried to imagine her in the sheriff's office, but he didn't want to, didn't want to imagine that.

He stared at himself in the mirror, this almost stranger with water dripping off his chin and nose, his wet skin glowing, here yellow, here pink, where the fluorescents touched it. Heaving in the stall, Hayden had started to sweat, and his shirt was already beginning to stick to the skin across his back. The two long bulbs hung from the ceiling, squeezing the white fixtures until they shone with the bluish glare of teeth. Through the walls he could hear the music from the bar. The muted sound became small and sharp against the filthy tile.

Another man opened the door behind him and they looked at each other in the mirror before he nodded and stepped past Hayden into the stall. Outside, his back pressed against the wall, Hayden could still smell the acrid urine through the door. The song on the jukebox changed and the wailing sound of a guitar opened in the dark. The dance floor in front of him began to fill, people rushing to catch it before the song ended. Beside it, he could just make out the dark, blank shapes of bodies leaning into one another in a small side room packed with tables. Evelyn was sitting in a booth on the far side of the dance floor, but the lights and bodies between them seemed too frantic, the music too loud for him to make his way through them.

He could hardly see anything and he closed his eyes, waiting for them to adjust after the bright bathroom. For some reason, he remembered the bar as it had been when they walked in. With the doors open, the strip mall's neon and streetlights, the last of the evening still palpable this high on the hill, all mixed together and submerged the almost empty, already dark bar in a kind of muddied, colored light. There were the middle-aged women pulling wet labels from their beers with long, colored fingernails, the wiry old men squinting beneath their tall, careful baseball caps, their pressed blue jeans and cowboy shirts. They were spotlit, all of them, their resigned, upturned faces bathed in this vulgar, reddish baptism as they stared at the two entering. It must have been glaring. But they stared anyway. They didn't even raise a hand to cover their eyes.

Hayden pushed himself off the wall and into the bodies of the dancers. Long, smoking shafts of light spun over them and where one touched a face, the rapturous, closed-eyed visage was frozen in an unlikely purple or red grimace, which stayed suspended, briefly, above the blur of twisting arms and legs.

Evelyn sat at their small table, her legs crossed and tucked underneath her on the bench, smoking one of his cigarettes and nervously tearing at the skin beside her thumbnail. He watched as she ran her hand through her hair and took a quick sip of the beer in front of her. She looked up only as he stepped beside the table. She was wearing mascara and it made her eyes deep, quiet in a way that seemed misplaced in the bed of her expression. She started to say something, but Hayden couldn't hear it over the music, and she stopped, waiting for him to sit down.

When he had, she reached over the table for his hand. Words had been carved into the wood, one over the other until eventually they had become meaningless, just a texture below your fingers. For what seemed a long time, they just looked at each other. He didn't know what to say. Behind her, the bar was packed with people trying to get the bartender's attention.

"Are you crying?" she said.

"No," he said. "My face—it's just water."

"Are you mad?" she asked.

"At what?"

"I don't know," she said. "Just please don't be mad at me."

"Of course not," he said. "But can we leave? This place is just a little too much right now."

"Of course," she said.

Pushing the door open, Hayden turned. Nobody was looking. It was too busy for anyone to notice they were leaving, but still, he wished somebody would. Sitting along the bar, he tried to find those men and women from before, but if they were there, they had been eclipsed by the bodies of the young couples pressed between the stools, by the false solidity the colored lights provided the dark.

Outside, the early mist had settled into fog, the air growing dense as the night got colder. Fall claimed the dark with the smell of harvest scraps burning somewhere nearby. Evelyn balled her hands in the ends of her sleeves and folded her arms tightly against her belly. Walking to the truck, Hayden could see his breath, his wet hair freezing against his head. Dim rainbows stretched over the oily puddles spotting the parking lot. The overhead lamps hung their curtains against the fog, sheer but solid.

In the truck, Evelyn reached out and stopped his hand before he turned the ignition. "Hayden," she said. "I don't care anymore. I just want you to know that. I don't care anymore who knows what happened. If that's what you want. Okay?"

Hayden looked at her. He nodded and turned the engine over.

Heavy raindrops churned the air as they began to fall, exploding one after another against the windshield of the truck and leaving wide, clear pockmarks over the glass. He drove fast, past the strip malls and gas stations near the bar, past the long empty farms. In the few fields where the tall rolls of hay had not yet been taken in, they stood now in long, slovenly rows, the tight coils grown bloated and disheveled in the weather, like packs of slow-moving elephants.

For a while, neither of them said anything. But before Evelyn finally did, he heard her pull in her breath. "It might be okay, though, right?" she said. She looked over quickly and then turned toward the window. "All of this, it could just be nothing. Couldn't it?"

"Yeah," he said. "Of course."

"Right," she said. She smiled but didn't look at him.

He skirted the edge of town and then crossed the river. If he hadn't known better, he would have thought the water was still. Only a clear ribbon of air between it and the fog, which was held above the banks, belied the sure, invisible current.

At the gate to the hill, Hayden got out of the truck. Walking through the headlights, he could almost feel the fog clinging to his body, the air moving visibly over his hands as he swung the metal gate open. It was all beautiful and disconcerting, too, in a way, this moment, this literal erasure of the world you knew, replaced only by a jacklighted, solid picture of white, as though his shadow swam through nothing so pedestrian as water and air but through the void itself, whatever lay before the world had been. And he was glad to be here, away from that frantic bar, the confusion of bodies moving all around them, where, at least right now, this, whatever it was, hung above them, patient, willing to take possession of them again.

As he opened the door, he looked at Evelyn, who touched his hand as he put the truck into gear and pulled just inside the fence. The grass brushed against the door, whispering. Everything around them was solid, the split rail fence just an idea running beside them. He turned off the headlights and they were cradled again by the dark. Against the roof, the spare drops of rain did not break the silence but gave it form, flesh. He turned his legs out from under the steering wheel and Evelyn lay back against him.

"Is it all right?" she said as she pulled his hand over her shoulder. "I mean, if we don't—" She turned to look up at him. "I'm not sure I could handle it right now. You know?"

"Of course," he said. "No. Me, either."

She lifted his hand to her mouth and he could feel her entire spine curling against him as she kissed it.

"I can hear your heart beating," she said. "Like this, against you."

"Evelyn," he said, after a while. "We could leave, you know. We could do that. We could leave—" He looked around. "All of this," he said.

She turned again and looked at him for a long time. "No," she said. "No, we couldn't, really. Could we?"

Hayden thought about it, turning to stare out the empty windshield. "No." He shook his head. "I guess not. Not really."

She laid her head back against his chest.

"You know, when I was a little girl, I used to think that angels lived in the fog," she said. "My mother and I, we would sit at the window and point out where we saw the air moving because that was where the angels would be walking through it. You know those little whirlpools that happen when the fog is really heavy?" Hayden nodded, though he didn't know if she could tell or not. "My mother told me'" she went on, "that angels were supposed to be terrifying to see. She said maybe that's why they came in the fog. But I never believed her. I was sure I'd almost seen one a hundred times, and I knew they were beautiful, no matter what she said.

"In the mornings, we'd go out and try to find their footprints where we had seen them. But they were never there. I used to tell myself they were just too light to make footprints, just too beautiful for us to see."

Their breath had begun to fog the windows on the inside of the truck, and Evelyn pushed off her shoes, drawing stick figure angels on the glass with her toes.

"We don't have to leave," she said after a minute. She lifted their clasped hands above her and pushed them slowly through the air. "We'll never leave. We'll live here, on your hill that no one owns. We'll trespass here for the rest of our lives. We could do that, couldn't we?" After their hands fell back to her stomach, she still held on to his wrist, tracing the lines of his palm with the fingertips of her other hand.

"Sure," Hayden said. He smiled. "We could do that."

"The fog will never lift," she said. "And no one will ever see us. We'll disappear in it. We'll eat flowers, and they'll taste like anything we want them to. There'll be a house made out of the grass where we'll live. Over there," she pointed up the hill to the west. "The house will be right over there. We'll use these plants to catch rain. They're just little silver bowls, anyway, and whenever we want, we'll just turn one up and drink." She leaned forward and unrolled the window. When she brought her hand back inside she put it to his mouth and her fingers were wet.

"We'll drink only rainwater," she said. "We'll wear the fog. We'll only ever wear the fog. And, we'll never think about any of this again. The only thing we'll ever see is this hill.

"Can't you imagine it?" she said. She was crying, he thought, but he didn't want to look down and see it.

He wanted to believe that the rest of the world could suddenly fall away, could be generous enough to unleash them, to leave them here, protected behind these gates. He remembered that feeling outside the truck, and he imagined them again, the first two souls in a brand-new, totally clean, and, at least for this second, unformed world, and if it would let him then he would run headlong into it. Backward through time they would carry each other until neither remembered that time moved only one way.

Yes, he could imagine it.

"We're safe here," she said. "Hayden, we'll be the angels."

She wiped her eyes and pulled his arm tighter around her.

"It's beautiful, isn't it?" she said. "The fog."

"Yes," he said. "It is."

The rain had grown harder, its sound tapping, tapping on the metal roof. You could see it through the fog, the sky just beginning to expose itself. The stars were brilliant, condensed by the freezing air above into precise wounds within the dark. In the lowest part of the valley, the round heads of silos began to rise out of the mist like animals standing.

"It's beautiful," he said.

She nodded against his chest.

The Children of God

His whole childhood, he was beginning to realize, had been buffered, protected from this, by the valley he had come from, and Jesse felt lost now in this surreal heat, unbalanced in his first summer in the Deep South.

Outside, the air buckled above the sidewalks and the street in its knee-high waves, like water rising. Jesse stood by the window and pressed his cigarette into the ashtray. The dog lay panting on the tile floor by the small vent that breathed cool air into the laundry room. The landlord had called it central air, but it was just the one vent and by the time it reached Jesse the air was tepid and wet.

The house was a small square, one story with chicken wire running in a rectangle around it. Outside this fence sat an empty half-block. There were meant to be other houses but the landlord had run out of money and only the one was ever built. Inside, the house was split in half. On the left was a single, long room carved into three sections by different types of flooring. The living room had wood, the kitchen linoleum, and in the small laundry room were laid heavy tiles that stayed cool throughout the long summer days. On the right of the house were two small rooms with a bed and a desk, respectively, in the back a bathroom.

The landlord had painted the outside purple, thinking, he once told Jesse, that the color would bring white people into the neighborhood, though Jesse was the only one who had come to see it. His lot used to be empty but for a lean-to shack where his house now stood and which had acted, Jesse found out, as a makeshift crack house. Sometimes, evenings, Jesse would still open the shades to see a thin man or woman standing at the edge of his yard, looking into the lit house and nervously fingering their pockets.

Jesse buttoned the light, blue dress shirt up to the collar and tucked the tails into his slacks. On the chair back beside him hung the blazer he had bought for his college graduation. He ran his hand over the shoulders, brushing off the lint that freckled the dark fabric. He couldn't stand the thought of a tie in the heat and he told himself that no one expected it anyway.

The clock in the face of the stove flipped to 9:30 and Jesse walked quietly into the bedroom. Meagan lay in his bed, sleeping. She had pulled the sheet up to the back of her head unconsciously when he got up, and it now lay taut over the left half of her naked body. Jesse watched her breathe slowly into his pillow. Her dark hair was scattered over her face and her heavy lips were slack and her eyes fluttered in the light coming through the window above her. Her skin was stark and white and Jesse wondered how she kept the color in the sun-drenched summer months. She lay on her stomach and the arcs of her ribs pushed out on the skin, defining themselves, before falling back. Beneath her, her small breast pooled against the mattress. In the bowl-like small of her back, the sun turned the tiny hairs golden. Her right leg stretched out where Jesse had lain and where the thin tangle of hair opened, the skin was pink and delicate.

Jesse thought about not leaving, about lying down again and closing his eyes and letting the Sunday drift away. He remembered when they had come to his house the night before, her body angled at the jutting point of bone bared above her low jeans as she smiled and waited for him to kiss her. From one of the cabinets in the kitchen he took a small glass and put it on the counter and filled it carefully from the gallon bottle of whiskey that stood next to the sink. Without lifting his head from the tiles, the dog's eyes followed the blue blazer as Jesse swung it over his shoulders and righted the collar of his shirt beneath it. The dog was huge sprawled like this, and the following eyes made him look like a bull who, already fallen, still dreams of the cape. Jesse took a deep breath through his nose to settle himself before drinking the whiskey. Then he closed his eyes while the taste moved across his tongue and the nervous heat spread through his belly.

The air was hot and so thick you could feel it against your skin, weighing on your clothes. Jesse pulled the door shut softly against his hand so that it didn't make a noise. Through the front window he could see Meagan where she lay on the bed, totally still, exactly as he had left her.

His house stood at the very end of the small neighborhood and the lot was surrounded on three sides by borders of tall woods. To his right and behind the house, a thin curtain of trees stood between the neighborhood and the train tracks. Since Jesse had moved in, heavy summer kudzu had grown up the bodies of the trees and swallowed them whole, leaving only a dense, lush curtain of green. To his left, a narrow swath of land had been given over to forest and held within it the single, long sewage pipe that connected the housing projects in the neighborhood. From the tree branches, lavender wisteria blossoms toppled over one another in long arms like melted candle wax. In the evenings Jesse could watch prostitutes slip in and out of the purple fringe; stiff, nervous men behind them. The light smell of honeysuckle came from everywhere.

Across the street, Will sat in the recliner on his front porch. A collection of his relatives stood around the house in their Sunday clothes waiting for church. The heavy women crowded in the shade beneath the porch roof, fanning themselves with paper plates, while on the steps below them their brothers and husbands stood drinking beer, their suits catching the sun in oily streaks of color. Small children ran through the five or six car skeletons scattered over the yard and disappeared altogether as the women yelled for them not to muss their clothes. On the walkway near the street, the young men stood in a circle passing a joint and the smoke crowded around their heads. Everyone watched Jesse with slow, careful eyes as he walked toward them.

Tony, one of Will's sons, reached out for the joint that had been cuffed as Jesse walked up. Will raised his hand from the porch in a silent hello.

"Goining for church?" Tony asked. His face was round and

OUR BURDEN'S LIGHT

clean-shaven and a long, wet-looking, nearly black scar ran down his cheek. He held out his hand and Jesse shook it and the others stared at them both blankly. "Uh-huh," Jesse said.

He watched the children as they ran through the yard, the small suits and stiff, pastel dresses ill-fitting to the simple grace of their bodies. Tony held the joint out to him and it took Jesse a moment to realize that he had spoken. "You right," he said again. Smoke threaded out of the joint's gray-red tip and the wet, open back end. "Get you some of that Spirit, son."

"No," Jesse said. "Thanks, though."

He turned up the street and he could hear them laughing as the hard soles of his dress shoes clapped against the pavement. Most everyone in the neighborhood thought Jesse was a police officer because he was the only white person there and because of the dog. When he walked out from the house the youngest kids would run out of their front doors and sing made-up songs and scream at him from the safety of the project lawns. The older kids, the ones on the corners, disappeared like shadows behind the low buildings, and from where they stood out of sight the mock sounds of sirens would rise up and echo out in front of him as he walked.

The neighborhood had once been a pecan plantation and Jesse walked in and out of the dense shade of the huge trees that still edged the sidewalk. Dogs, staked and chained in the front yards, no longer barked when he went by but just pulled against the length of their heavy tethers, following him with their noses. The ancient grandmothers and tiny, shrunken men watched him from their porches, lifting their gnarled hands into the air as he passed.

Jesse took a cigarette from his pocket and lit it. The whiskey had begun to lighten his head as he walked and small drops of sweat ran over the skin beneath his jacket and shirt. The main street leading into town was quiet as Jesse crossed it. Already he could see the small spire of the Catholic church rising through the treetops on the other side of the road. The blue-green copper roof shone dull and uneven in the sun as though it were wet.

Everywhere in the South, older Catholic churches seem to hide themselves in the trees and houses where they sit, as though built to protect the identity of their believers. This one was the same and it reminded him of home. Small statues stood in the yard of the church and the wide, white and pink flowers of a magnolia tree hung above their heads, delicate as parasols over the effeminate stone faces. Jesse followed several young families up the stairs to the open doors and a little girl turned back and stared at him as he came. Her thin white dress caught on her stockings as she turned, clinging to her knees and only falling loose again when, after a strange, almost romantic second, she ran into the church.

It was dark inside and cool, and the cool air settled against Jesse's skin and dried the sweat. Two old men in pastel blazers stood just inside the door and watched Jesse wet his fingers in the stone bowl and trace the shape of a cross over his forehead in a habit he didn't know he had. The walls were rough stone, and polished, shining stones were laid over the aisle and carried the hushed sounds of footsteps into the air. Dimmed lights hung from the tall ceiling and shone upward onto faded, flaking portraits of angels.

Jesse sat down in one of the pews in the back of the church and let his eyes close.

The church, the hard curl of the wooden pew, the shade and candles and the young, easy families, it all seemed more familiar, more his own, than he had thought it would. He had never thought of church as a powerful part of his childhood, though his mother told him that she was going to mass several times a week now. The doors scraped against the floor behind him and the band of light that had stretched over the aisle to the altar drew thin and then disappeared altogether.

The organist began to play in the front of the church and Jesse turned around in his pew to watch the procession. The white cotton robes of the priest and altar boys whispered against the stone floor. Two of the altar boys held tall, white candles and the flames leaned toward them in the air. When they had passed, Jesse let his head fall back against the pew. The whiskey and the perspective of the tall, arcing ceiling mixed in a pleasant, dreamy vertigo.

The mass was as far away as a dream, too. He did everything from the instinct reactions of memory, the whole hour like a dance he had learned as a child and now slipped into again; the confusing, almost bodily nostalgia of ritual eclipsing everything else. You see, time does not exist in a church for a childhood Catholic, it is held outside the vestibule, with the light. A dream in your mother tongue.

He kneeled. The notes of the organ rose through the air and overtook one another in the corners of the building. At the offering of peace Jesse looked around, but there was no one near. When he walked to the altar to take communion, all he saw were the tired and loosened face of the priest, the taut and shining crucifixion hanging above it. He tried to remind himself what he was supposed to believe as he tongued the dry wafer in his mouth, that this was flesh, that in it was some sort of salvation. And then it was over. The priest shuffled by quickly. The whole thing felt too quick, really, as though he wasn't ready to leave yet, wasn't ready to give up the dark and the sudden, unexpected comfort of knowing all this without thinking.

Jesse stood up and walked through the big doors into the day, which was garish and stunning after the twilight inside. His legs felt stiff from the wooden pew, and the whiskey, gone now, had left him flat and slow. Outside the church, Jesse looked around for the little girl but couldn't see her anywhere and he lit a cigarette.

While he had been in church, the world had woken. People streamed in and out of shops and smoked, sitting in lazy poses at the outside tables of restaurants and coffee shops. This town was unlike any other place he had been. A university town, it wasn't like the small place he grew up or the city he went to school in but somehow separate from either. The town was a kind of oasis in the South and in the summer you could feel it; the religion of youth, pulsing out of the speakers of every bar, and the people in the cars and on the street were all young and in the right kind of moment that can seem precious.

Jesse walked quickly down Washington St. and turned up Lumpkin. Low, abandoned storefronts peppered the vintage clothing stores and bars and record shops and then fell away as the down-town took hold. He was headed for a restaurant called The Last Resort and when he got to it, he stopped and finished his cigarette, looking at the old hot rods parked in the lot. Every Sunday until five they had a half-off deal for people in the service industry, called the bartender's brunch, and though it was still early the bar was already almost half full when he opened the door.

The air-conditioning was strong and cold and the long, pol-ished, zinc-covered bar stretched out shining and cold beneath the smoke and the lights. The people sitting on their stools looked up from their cigarettes and eggs, their Bloody Marys and Greyhounds, and most of them nodded a silent hello. Tattooed arms lay on the bar like colorful flags draped over a coffin. It was one of the things Jesse liked about the town and which made it so different, as if by coming here you joined a different America, set apart by a gray economy and the opulent color of skin.

Jesse shook hands with the bartender, Eli, who had been his first friend when he moved to town six months before. He walked to the end of the bar and took the far corner seat. Two seats down from him sat Biker James, a fixture whose family had something to do with the founding of the university. James's eyes fluttered as he tried to focus and Jesse figured he hadn't been to bed yet. "Faggot fancy," he said, looking at Jesse's blazer. Jesse thought he meant to say more, or at least something more eloquent, but couldn't get it out.

"Church," Jesse said.

Biker James nodded and turned back to his half-eaten food. His long beard caught on his forearm and gave his face a windswept, dis-appointed look. In the South, religion is a vaguely irreproachable thing.

Jesse looked down the bar at who was there. Many of them probably already knew about his father, he thought. This was that kind of town. There were one or two he almost remembered seeing that night, a week before, when he had come back from what would probably be the last visit. He had bought a bottle and crossed three states fast enough to almost outrun the vision of his father in the hospital bed; the loose skin and tiny skull that had somehow be-come his face, the tubes that he gagged on like a drunk. Later that night Jesse had crashed his car in the kudzu forest behind his house and then walked into town with a freshly broken nose and another bottle of Jack Daniel's.

"What you drinking?" Eli said from behind the bar. Jesse hadn't seen him walk up.

"Irish coffee," he said. "Please."

Eli nodded. Jesse watched him pour a glass three-quarters full of whiskey and then top it off with coffee. "You say you were in church?" Eli asked as he slid the cup over the bar.

Jesse nodded and Eli let his face become soft, sad-looking, in an expression that Jesse thought was probably supposed to mean that he understood, that he was sorry for what Jesse was going through. But who could understand this strange nakedness, the specific shivering that rolls over you when you are asked, finally, to be something, a man, and you realize you don't even know what the word means? What do you say when your life comes to get you and you aren't ready? Even once it's happened, Jesse wondered, how do you understand that?

Jesse finished the coffee before Eli came back with a menu. The heat of it scorched his throat as it went down, hotter still when the whiskey hit his belly, stretching long, tawny fingers up like vomit to the back of his tongue. Jesse held up the empty glass. "Another one of these," he said.

Some time later, Jesse looked up as Jules, a girl he worked with, pushed through the door. Her husband, a thin, waifish man named Michael, huddled just behind her. Jesse was on his fifth Irish coffee and the cup warmed his fingers as he held on to it. The whiskey had put a pleasant mist into his head and the coffee beat out a steady, manic rhythm on his knees under the bar. A plate of food that he had ordered sat in front of him, untouched, and he looked down at the curdled eggs and hash browns, wondering why he didn't wave Jules over. When he looked again, she had seen him and her eyes grew big as she pulled Michael toward him through the crowd that had grown in the bar.

Jules always looked like a 1950s housewife, and today she wore an apron over her dress and fake pearls in her ears and around her neck. Her blonde hair was tied into a tight bun on the back of her skull and her smile was taut and delirious. She asked Biker James to move over a seat and he obliged with a half-audible grunt and then put his head down on the bar. Earlier, Jesse had watched him crush a pill in a dollar bill and snort small mounds of it off his butter knife.

"My," Jules said. "Aren't we the dapper dandy this morning." She laughed to herself and slowly pushed James's plate from in front of Michael.

"I came from mass," Jesse said.

Jules raised her eyebrows into two startling arcs. "Well, you are a complicated cad," she said. "And I hope you've confessed to everything. The Lord above, my savior and yours, knows that you have yet to answer a single of my letters." Even the mention of the words Lord and savior made her giggle. Michael lit a cigarette and handed it to her without a word. In all the time Jesse had known them, he could barely remember hearing Michael speak. Jules took the cigarette and pushed the filter into a small ebony holder that she sometimes used and which always indicated a certain volatility of mood. Michael lit one for himself and it hung trembling between his thin fingers over the ashtray.

"I know," Jesse said.

At least once a week, Jules wrote him a letter, despite the fact that they had three shifts a week together on the bar. He had never written her back.

"I will," he said. "Answer. Sometime, you know, soon."

"I should hope so," Jules said.

Jesse pushed his plate over to her and Michael. "If y'all are hungry," he said. "I'm not going to touch it." Michael took a quick pull off his cigarette and Jules contorted her face at the sight of the food. "No. No, thank you," she said, pushing the plate back into the exact spot that it had been. "Michael and I," she said. She looked poignantly at Jesse and nodded her head. "We're on a strict mental health break."

This, Jesse knew, was euphemistic for an all-out drug binge, the base of which, he guessed looking at them, was probably speed, but could also include, he knew, any known psychotropic. "Ahh," he said.

Eli had come over and was talking to Michael, who stared up at him blankly but curiously, nodding his head like an agreeable foreigner. Jules leaned over. "We'll have two Brandy Alexanders, dearest Eli," she said. "But no egg, please. And whatever for Jesse."

She waved a hand queenlike toward Jesse's empty glass and then became hysterical, laughing and covering her mouth. Michael leaned his head against hers and they began to whisper to one another. Eli looked at Jesse. He thought that Michael and Jules were too strange too tolerate and clearly wondered why he was friends with them. Jesse had never told him about the letters. He didn't know why.

"Another coffee?" Eli asked.

"No. A shot and a beer."

Eli set a huge glass of whiskey in front of him and popped a beer off his church key. "You done with that?" he said, pointing at the plate of food.

"Yeah," Jesse said. "Guess I'm not really hungry."

"Right on."

Eli disappeared with the plate and Jesse drank half the whiskey in the glass and when he breathed out again his breath was steam. Jules and Michael seemed to have forgotten about him and he was grateful for it. The sound of the bar was an assault, but it was a wall, too. He leaned into the bar and let his eyes close, his hands wrapped around the cool glass bottle. The bar had filled up and he could feel the heat of the bodies pressing against his back. The people behind him were talking about politics, and he tried not to listen because it can break your heart just to think about this country. He finished the whiskey and Eli filled it up again without saying anything. When Jesse finally pushed his chair back from the bar he didn't know how many he had had. Eli dropped the bill onto the bar and Jesse looked down at it. "I took off the food," he said, but even still it was far too small and Jesse paid it and left thirty more.

As he took a step back from the bar, Jesse almost fell over the chair. He reached out for the bar and a shiver of pain slipped from his nose down his spine. Somebody from the crowd put a hand on his shoulder to steady him. Jules turned around and caught him by the sleeve of his jacket.

"You're leaving?" she asked.

Jesse nodded and she reached her hand up to his face and touched his cheek. "Be careful," he said.

"I can see, my tragic little prince," she said, nodding. "I can see."

"Hold on," she said. She pulled her purse into her lap and reached into it. She leaned into him and kissed his cheek and almost subtly pushed something into his hand. Jesse opened his palm and tried to focus on the small paper envelope.

"You know I don't do drugs," he said. "And besides, I hate speed."

She gave him a strange, wistful look that either came from the drugs or some kind of complicated emotion. "Not speed, my dear boy," she said. "Cocaine."

Michael ashed his cigarette. "In case the whiskey fails you," he said. He smiled. His voice was soft, almost pretty.

"Thanks," Jesse said. He slipped the envelope into his coat pocket.

Jesse nodded to a few people as he walked by them, but didn't stop. He wasn't ready, he thought, for all the sad, knowing eyes glaring down on him, the weighty patience that comes only when people think they understand why you're stumbling drunk in the middle of the day. He didn't want to give anyone the chance for sympathy, it felt so shallow. It's the solipsism of grief, he understood, though, that may be its ugliest part.

Outside, the heat had become grotesque, every object bright and misshapen in the still, boiling air as if the world were bubbling up under its skin. The sun was blinding and invisible in the white sky, and he stopped just outside the door and leaned back against the wall. The glare and the alcohol and his healing nose together made his eyes tear and he closed them. There was a second, a visceral, stabbing entry into him almost, if memory can be said to be something so physical, so external as that, if it can be said to cut, to stab, where he had the terrifying feeling of being turned over in the ocean, the cold and spinning salt swelling over him. He had only ever felt this once, caught in a breaking tide, submerged, his body limp as the waves formed and reformed it, breathless, the world revealed briefly for what it is, so different than you thought, its typical sounds reduced to a simple roaring, or unheard altogether. He thought he was going to pass out and he opened his eyes again and tried to shake the feeling out of his head.

He felt more drunk for its only being early evening, and he stared closely at the broken sidewalks and bricks as he walked home. At the driveway, Jesse turned stiffly back to look at Will's house. There were only a few men on the porch now and Jesse didn't know what he was looking for. Will raised his beer when he saw him. Something seemed different. It was the children, they were gone.

His house was cooler than the air outside and Jesse took off his jacket and threw it on the couch. His shirt was soaked through from the walk home. He looked quickly through the house for Meagan, but she had gone.

Taped to the whiskey bottle on the counter was a note.

Helped myself to a drink and let the dog out for you. Did he eat the note you left me?—Meagan

The dog, slow from the heat outside, licked his hand once as Jesse let him in and then collapsed over the vent in the laundry room. He went back to the note and peeled it off the bottle. Beneath the paper, Meagan had taped a photo she had taken with his Polaroid camera. In it, she was naked, lying back over the unmade bed, the camera held above her. On the thin white strip below the picture was written,

PS I missed you this morning.

Jesse stumbled into the bedroom and, holding the picture up in front of him, he began to unbuckle his pants. He lay back on the bed. He thought of Meagan the night before. He closed his eyes and went harder and he couldn't come and he thought of Jules and then of the little girl at the church door. He started to cry and then lost consciousness, his half hard cock still held in his hand.

When he woke the house was pitch dark all around him and through the open windows only the barest light bled. A gunshot exploded somewhere in the neighborhood. He stood up and then tripped over his pants, which were tangled around his ankles. The impact of the floor ricocheted in the swollen bones of his face and he threw up onto the cool wood. He coughed and spit the last of it out and then walked into the living room, naked from the waist down. From the pocket of his jacket he took out the packet Jules had given him. On the table lay the rosary he had meant to take to church that morning and forgotten and beside it he spilled the white powder and began to shape it into clumsy lines.

Four more gunshots rang out, closer this time, as if someone were walking through the streets crying out what was becoming obvious on the horizon.

The night had passed without his knowing, this was dawn.

Eden

13. The rain had passed, but not before dispersing the fog, leaving only discrete, hovering tongues now to wander and collect in the dark corner-pinned congress of the river. And it's only now, only after the fog, that its vacancy, its vacuity even occurs to you, the empty world grown suddenly dense without it.

Outside the truck, the cold seemed to shiver, to descend, cascading, through the air, and, held beneath it, every solid thing became clearer than it was, sharper, as if each molecule had taken shape only now, only in this cuspal moment between seasons, the total ascension of the fall. The dark sucked from the cabin's lit windows long banners of yellow silk, and even turned away from the house, Hayden could see them, their ragged, dissipate ends aflutter in the dark periphery. The stars, above it all, spit out their million-miles-distant light in perfect, flickering clarity.

In front of him lay the late garden they had planted after taking up the early summer vegetables, the vines and leaves reaching already toward that place where the sun would come in the morning. But for now, only dim, curving fingers of the house lights rested over the taut skins of the tomatoes. He was surprised that his father hadn't taken them in while he'd been gone. It would frost tonight, he could feel it, and depending on how badly it did, the tomatoes, the most delicate of those late crops, would freeze, shrinking inside their skins, ruined.

Hayden turned back to the house. Inside, the warmth felt like ice on his skin until his cheeks began to flush. The two lamps on either side of the couch were lit and, through their thick canvas shades, bathed the open room in a shadow-heavy, bone-colored light. His father sat slumped in the corner of the couch, asleep, a book spread facedown over his belly. His glasses hung crooked off the bridge of his nose, one of the temples loose against his cheek where he had knocked it, sleeping, from his ear. A long fringe of his hair fell down and curled over his cheek. Hayden wondered why he was out here rather than in the study, and it occurred to him that his father had been waiting up for him.

Sam, lying at his father's feet, lifted his head when Hayden walked in, his pale eyes moving lazily back and forth, and now his tail slapped a slow, two-beat rhythm against the floorboards before he let his jaw come to rest again on his paws. Hayden slipped his boots off quietly. The room felt so perfect, so quiet, that he was scared of disturbing it with his presence. Against the far wall, the pipe of the woodstove hissed and around it, the air wavered slightly, softening in the heat. A fire burned, too, in the wide, stone fireplace, its shaking light like a silent, private music that only the long, swaying shadows heard. The fire lit the dog's coat, bathing his wrinkled forehead in still more exaggerated mournfulness.

Something, Hayden didn't know exactly what, didn't know what intermingling of senses, of images and thoughts and smells and memories that didn't seem present but of course were, made it all seem so terribly fraught, the coming winter and the burning wood smell, the flames like tiny tabby kittens reaching up and highlighting the silver-gray stones in flickering red and orange winks, and above them his mother's photograph, darkened on the mantle by all this light below; and he himself, a part of it of course, even just looking, and his crumpled, exhausted father, crooked glasses solid with firelight, long, delicate fingers still balancing an empty drink against his thigh.

Hayden wanted to let everything here remain exactly as it was, to sneak quietly to his own room as though he had never been here at all, never muddied this picture with his pounding, deliberate heartbeat, the uneven breath he could hear in his ears. Gunshots, the wind sound through tall grass and the wingbeats of birds.

But he couldn't sneak away. His father was working this week, refurbishing the carpentry in an old farmhouse, and was starting early every day straight through the next week. Hayden knew he would be upset to wake up on the couch, stiff and alone, dawn coming through the windows. He had to wake him up. Still, he waited a second more before stepping farther into the room.

Gently, he lifted the book off his father's stomach. The thick cotton shirt his father wore hung open, unbuttoned at the collar. Under the lamp on the table, a clear bottle stood with the last glowing, amber inch of whiskey still in it, and beside it lay an ash-tray, crowded with short, bent cigarette ends.

Hayden leaned over his father and began to shake his arm. Only then, leaning down like this, did he see the table where they ate tucked in its alcove in the corner. Over a cheap plastic tablecloth, the shotgun lay broken apart. Spread around the barrel and the stock were the long wire brush and oil bottle and chamois cloth they used to clean the guns. Two plastic shells stood on the table, the metal base of one colored in the rainbow oscillations of burnt copper and below that the black stains of spent powder. Along the barrel of the gun, long, oily lines of fire and lamplight stretched like an accent to the dull, plastic sheen of the tablecloth. From the wet blue-black metal, the sudden smell of oil that came only as he saw the thing, Hayden could tell that his father had cleaned it.

A cold, stunning stillness wrapped itself around him. It wasn't fear, not exactly, but something much deeper, far more compli-cated, more wordless than that. It was as if the world had, for one second, contracted to nothing, to a single square inch in which everything that was, that had ever been, was enclosed within a tightening knot around his heart, burned and then blown away like ash. It was almost religious, this feeling, rapturous and impersonal. It lasted only a second, though, before Hayden could feel the snowy rush of blood again through his veins and his heartbeat came back to him, not violently, but almost gently, beating drum-like in the bent junctures of his arms and legs.

"No," his father said beneath him. He waved his free arm in front of his face. "Don't."

Hayden looked down. His father's eyes were still closed. "Dad," he said. "You're sleeping."

His father opened his eyes, and Hayden watched them focus, the pupils opening and then closing inside their blue rings. "Oh," he said, thickly. "Hayden. I was dreaming." He reached across his body and followed the line of his glasses, righting the temple over his ear again.

"I know," Hayden said. "You were talking in your sleep."

"Hmm," he said. He began to straighten himself and the rocks glass fell from his leg onto the couch, the last drops of whiskey rolling like tiny beads over the fabric until they were absorbed. They both watched and then his father put the glass onto the table. "When did you get home?" he asked, rubbing his eyes under his glasses.

"Just now," Hayden said.

His father nodded. He stumbled as he tried to push himself off the couch. By the lethargy of his arms as he threw them out, by the stiff, open-palmed grab he made for the couch back, Hayden could tell he was drunk. He caught his father by the elbow as he pivoted around and finally steadied himself against the cushions. The way their bodies had turned, they were both staring at the shotgun on the table. Behind them, the fire popped and hissed, tossed their shaking shadows against the wall above the table.

His father looked up at Hayden and crawled his hands up the couch until he was almost standing. "I was doing laundry," he said. "I took some of the clothes from your closet in, too. The shells, they were in your jeans pocket. I thought it'd be nice. If I threw some of your things in."

Hayden was still holding on to his father's arm and he let his hand drop. He could hear the question, but he didn't say anything. He just nodded.

"This wasn't—?" his father said. "I mean, there's no way you were—?"

He was searching for the words to a question he was afraid of or thought too ridiculous to voice. He was hoping Hayden would answer it without his having to ask, to name it, his eyes skimming back and forth across Hayden's face.

"Hayden, what was it? What season is this?" he finally asked. His breath was rank and his eyes were liquid behind his glasses from whiskey and from sleep and he blinked too quickly, as though he were still trying to focus. It was strange that he would even think it, but maybe it wasn't, too, and maybe, in fact, he wasn't even thinking it and it was just what Hayden heard. It didn't matter, though. Hayden had always thought that when this moment came, finally, he would say it, would be thankful in the end to let himself be lowered slowly down into whatever came.

"No," Hayden said. "It was a rabbit." He looked at their shadows flickering in the warm light. "I lost it, though," he said.

Hayden could feel his father still looking at him. And though he hadn't said it, maybe that was what it came to in a way. He remembered sitting at the river with Evelyn, those little boys, and how at the time he had thought that maybe they were ruining something, holding that rabbit up, taking it from the burrow, but now, in his memory, it seemed different, perfect; and so maybe what he had just said was true, truer than any simple account of actual events could be; whatever that was, whatever that boy had held up, he had lost it.

Shaking his head, his father waved a hand in front of him. "Well," he said. "I've cleaned it, the gun. So."

"Thanks," Hayden said. "I guess I should have."

They stood there, not saying anything more. The dog's breath heaved with all the commotion of them moving around. "It's cold out," Hayden said finally. "It'll probably frost tonight. Should we take up those tomatoes?"

Hayden's father looked at him again. "No," he said. He tried to touch Hayden's arm but pushed into him instead, misjudging the distance, and they ended up nearly embracing until his father grew steady again. "No, they'll survive. We'll do it tomorrow, huh? When I get back."

"Okay," Hayden said. He stepped aside as his father began to walk past him.

"I was having a dream," he said, shuffling toward the hallway. "I can't remember exactly, but I have the feeling your mother was in it." He straightened his back and grew taller as he pushed the hunch of the couch out of his spine. He looked around the room as though he were forgetting something before continuing toward his bedroom. Hayden didn't say anything but just followed him. He had never been one of those children who resented their parent's drinking. Rather, he had always sort of cherished it, because when his father was drinking it seemed that the reticence of his devotions were all stripped and he became a kind of sorcerer, conjuring for Hayden memories and stories that they may as well have shared by now. It was only in these, too, that his mother seemed to come back to them, not the one he remembered best, sick and tiny and careful with him, but the one that lived just barely behind her, just out of sight, taken by the hand of his father's remembrance and brought forward, where he could finally see her again. And if now was going to be one of those times, then Hayden didn't want to say anything to stop it.

His father sat down heavily on his bed and Hayden watched, leaning in the doorway, as he slowly pulled each of his socks off. He sat in the shadow of Hayden's body, the hall light drawing his outline over the bed and the wall above. His father took each of his feet and bent the long, yellowed toes back and forth. He shook his head.

"It's strange, though," he went on. He stood up and unbuttoned his shirt and laid it on the chair beside the bed. Hayden thought that his eyes were closed, as though he was trying not to cover the feeling of the dream with too many other sensations. He unfastened his pants and stepped out of them, walking to the side of the bed and pulling down the blankets and the sheets. Taking off his glasses, he folded them and laid them carefully down on the bedside table.

"When I dream about her I'm always asking her not to go," he said when he was finally in the bed. "Did I ever tell you that? Isn't it funny? Seven years, and I'm still just trying to get her not to go. Jesus," he said. "Seven years."

"Just," Hayden said.

"That's right," his father said. "Just." He rocked his head back and forth on the pillow until it cradled his skull.

"I've been dreaming about her, too," Hayden said.

"It's those letters," his father said. "All of it."

"I guess."

"You read them yet?" he asked. His voice was heavy and slow, already sleepy again.

"Yeah," Hayden said.

His father lifted up his head and looked at Hayden. "Pretty tough. Huh?"

"Pretty tough."

His father let out a long breath. Hayden watched the sheets and blankets rise with his stomach.

"Dad," he said. His father was already nearly asleep again but Hayden didn't want to be left alone, not yet.

"Yes?" his father said without looking up.

"Tell me something."

"What?"

"Tell me a story," Hayden said.

"Hayden, c'mon," his father said. "Let me sleep." And then, after another second, "You'll spread out the fire for me?"

Hayden nodded. "Sure," he said.

"Okay."

Hayden stood in the doorway long after he knew that his father wasn't going to say anything more, his breath grown slow, steady, then deepening into the drunk whistle that meant he was gone.

Sam was still lying in front of the fire when he turned away from his father's door. Along the logs, the flames were receding into the shifting, grayish embers that would burn through the night. The dog's eyelids barely shuddered open as Hayden walked past him into the kitchen. From the cupboard he took down a wide wicker basket and a knife from one of the drawers. Reaching for the basket, he thought he could still smell Evelyn's shampoo on his fingers and he closed his eyes and tried to breathe it in.

He thought about when he had driven her home earlier that night. Leaving the hill, they sped into a solid wall of fog the whole way and only behind them could he see it falter, the air spinning in the mirrors, streamers of white twisting off the back of his truck.

When they got to her house, he turned off the car. The streetlights and lit windows of houses cut through the thinning gray. The rain had filled the silence. Beneath the sound, Hayden could hear her breathing.

"Hayden," she said. "Can I ask you something?"

"Of course."

"How long were you there?" she said. "I mean, before. How long had you been there before you came out?"

He knew exactly what she meant. Behind her parents' house, he noticed the empty bones of a child's swing set in one of her neighbor's yards. It stood out from the fog, rusted and leaning, the triangle frames empty of their swings and slides. It had the bygone look of an artifact, the children obviously grown.

He stared at it. "I was there for a while," he said. "I was there for too long."

She had looked at him for a long time and then, brows cinched together, she turned his face toward her and kissed him, her hand still on his cheek as she opened the door behind her.

He wasn't able to place her expression as they had looked at each other. He couldn't figure out if she was trying to forgive him for being there without stopping it, or if she was sad that he had seen it, or if it was something else altogether. Thinking now, he still couldn't.

"I'm so sorry," was all he had said as she left.

Now, the cold outside was enormous on his bare arms. The wicker basket tapped against his thigh as he made his way down the steps. The night seemed whole, an unbroken skin, until the house lights began to carve out the shapes around him. Squatting down at the very edge of the garden, Hayden started to take up the tomatoes, the knife slicing through the stems easily and coming to rest against his thumb as he had been taught. He lay his hand down to steady himself and his fingertips sank into the wet, cold dirt.

The whole night was running through his mind, though already he knew there was no peace to be made with everything that had happened. It was too much. But there had been a single moment, hadn't there, when it had felt as if at least one small corner of heaven had actually existed, had been set aside for them, but only as long as the sympathies of time had lasted, only as long as the angels had conspired for them. And it felt now as though even that had a price, had been unforgivable in its own way. The secret prize of grace is only that you will always have to wonder if it wasn't real, that you'll be left to suspect that all paradise is stolen, all innocence lost and then contrived, that in fact there are no angels to conspire, and that time has no sympathy. Most terrifying, though, was that it might not be the promise of anything greater at all, but that the touch, the dream you're holding on to, the single stolen, precious, and fleeting moment was itself the whole fulfillment, and you didn't know it, and now it was gone. And none of this mattered, anyway. Because sooner or later, he would have to turn away from the garden and walk back into the house that was waiting behind him. As much as he might want to, he couldn't stand here forever.

He cut above the bunches and lay them slowly, softly into the basket. They were so ripe, the green vines that held them were pulled taut by the weight. You could almost see the flesh pushing against the skin that held it, as though each were a single, perfect heart, cresting with the inrush of blood, stilled, somehow, just before it beat.

14.

"Hon?" a woman's voice said.

He heard her when she said it, but it was only the touch, finally, the fluttering weight of her fingers against his shoulder, that brought Robert back to himself, vertiginous, as if he had risen slightly and now had only to fall backward into his own body, found suddenly, still in this place, in these clothes, this life. She was leaning close enough to him to be heard over the music and he could feel her warm breath against his ear, surprised that even now, even right now, the sensation could register as it did, an animal flicker through his groin.

He didn't want to open his eyes again, didn't want to take his face from his hands and make the scene that a crying man makes, not here, not in front of this girl. But he understood immediately that he was going to have to. From the tone of her voice, he could tell that she had watched him lean into his hands and thought now that he had passed out against the table, which, shortly, would lead to a scene of its own. Through the web of his fingers, he could see the table, and around it, the darkness of the bar, the glass of vodka, his fourth or fifth, half drunk, what ice remained floating around the lip of the glass, the legs and hands and voices of people just discernible around other tables. He looked at each of these things without moving, naming them silently in his head as if this list would find him, of its own accord, somewhere inside it. Trying to wipe the tears from under his eyes without her noticing, he could feel himself blushing, the skin growing hot beneath his fingers. What would it take, he wondered, what do you have to face to finally break free of these petty cornerstones like embarrassment, so many paper-thin despots inside us, each jostling for the chance to lay its cattle prod against our neck.

The waitress leaned over the table and this close, their bodies together made a kind of human lean-to, sheltering them both from the weight of the colored lights, the trembling, false illumination that reached out through the dark bar and actually lit only the smoke that hovered in giant swirling galaxies beneath the vents. She was maybe twenty-three, he thought, a limp, chestnut ponytail just too young for her face hanging over one shoulder, and the summer's tan fading quickly, leaving her skin an in-between, leftover shade of gold. Small discs of white spilled over one side of her body as the disco ball started to spin again.

Her arm's cant pulled the front of her blouse open beneath her throat, exposing the smallish breasts hanging into the ivory lace cups of her bra. Just above the slack, heavier flesh, the uppermost of her ribs showed through the skin as they sometimes do on too-skinny women. From beneath her skirt, her thighs leaned slightly toward the table, her custard-colored legs bent, so that the dim lights directly overhead reflected in two dull, satiny, salt-white streaks fading and then disappearing just above the bulbs of her knees. He had the vague feeling that there was something remarkable in the image of her, that he had caught her in the split-second of some spontaneous, banal miracle of time and flesh, neither young nor past youth but complete, wrapped somewhere in that unbearable moment when innocence and age can still face one another. Suddenly, almost desperately, he wanted to touch her, this girl with her cracked, worn lipstick and high-school ponytail, the overly pretty, compensating bra and the small breasts that had never seen milk, wanted to run his hands over her newly shaved legs, to pull her into him and taste her, collapsing her against his body.

Her smell grew stronger as he turned to face her. Robert realized that he had actually smelled her before she spoke, smelled her even as she first stepped toward him, something feminine, the honeyed smoke smell of a woman in a bar, clearer now, cleaner as she leaned farther into him and the soap smell of her skin asserted itself underneath all the rest. He imagined kissing her, the surprised flutter of her lips over his.

And he almost did, almost reached out and touched her without thinking, but there was something in the way her hand lay on his shoulder that stopped him immediately, shamed him even before the urge was articulated; the light, careful tension of a woman touching a man because she has to, her fingers a fulcrum ready to push away, an instinctual defense against the damages that men inflict, the gross, stumbling reduction of their desires, of hands, the coarse instruments of that desire, which itself is a two-headed thing, a fire-breathing, sweet-nothing argument between violence and love, because men are simple and old, and that is what they were made to be, the poetic, brutal machines of protection.

Anyway, it was gone as it occurred, the desire, the moment of their bodies colluding toward something, lovers in a way, already, because when she saw him fully, when he managed finally to raise his face, he saw himself in her expression—and, yes, it is awful to see how you've fallen, to see yourself reflected in the eyes of something good—and it changed, the feeling, evaporated, as she took a small, unconscious step back. And besides, he didn't really want to touch her, because even at the best, even in the impossible fruition of consent, it would be only mimicry, only a soft, maybe merciful pretending, but still without feeling, without love, an empty sating, which is certainly the cruelest kind of protection. She must have seen all of this, whatever it amounted to, play across his face, because he watched her expression collapse, her eyes filling with the heavy rubble of his emotions, that instant, instinctual sympathy that of all the world only almost-pretty women could ever muster believably. And from desire to shame to tenderness he had moved in the nauseating quickness of a second.

"Are you okay?" she said. She was unprepared for whatever strange intimacy they had shared just looking at one another and he could hear it in her voice, an uncertain wavering not unlike that of a child who has stumbled upon her parents. "Can I get you anything? Another drink, or something?" She blinked, her gaze rising upward and her hand pressing against her chest, searching, he thought, for what words could possibly be appropriate for an inherently wordless moment.

He should have been prepared for it, he knew, having noticed, a few minutes earlier, the late local news replace the football game on the television above the bar. It shouldn't have caught him as off-guard as it did, but it had.

He had been watching silent footage of several of these storms that had risen all around the world in the last months, thinking how they seemed, coming so close to one another, merciless. How maybe if there's no mercy then that means there's nothing else, either; no God at all, just weather, just the perfect indifference of weather. And he sounded even to himself like a kook, like one of those desperate end-timers who boil every random thing in the world down to a personal revelation. But wouldn't it be nice, wouldn't that at least be an explanation, and wouldn't the world then, ugly and cruel as it might be, make so much more sense? Justice being just another word for cruelty and it coming to everyone alike in the end. In weather there is no such thing as innocence, just like Dan said, and if there is no such thing as innocence then there is no such thing as guilt, and no need of mercy and no gift of grace that can be given or withheld.

And it was just then that he had looked up and noticed Grant's picture on the television screen, hanging there as it had every day since he was found in the woods. And he should have been more prepared for it, but it wasn't even that, the picture, a handsome black-and-white school portrait, it was the certainty that rushed through him as he saw it, the certainty that he had been trying to argue against since he had watched them leave the bar, or actually even before that, since he had left Dan earlier.

Robert felt even more embarrassed now as the waitress stood looking at him, waiting for him to say something that would release her, he knew, that would let her again rise to the comfortable surfaces that strangers inhabit. But instead his silence forced her to watch him crying in these silly, flickering lights that suddenly made his life seem like some flimsy and cheap county carnival. He wanted to say something, to explain, or at least to let his voice provide some gravity to this, to him, to prove that he understood it was inappropriate, that he was in fact a man and not this sad, quivering beast, or at least that he could summon the voice of one, even just to say yes, another drink, anything. But he couldn't find it. He lifted his hand up toward the television as though that in itself would be an explanation.

"That's my son," he finally said. "That was my son, there."

The waitress followed his hand away. Her other hand fell off his shoulder and he wished it hadn't, because now he could feel its absence and that seemed worse than anything. But how had he come to this, he wondered, nearly ready to beg this poor stranger girl just to keep touching him.

"Oh my God," she said through her fingers. She looked at him again, closely, and then shook her head. "Oh my God," she said again. Robert didn't say anything. In his skull, the sound of his breathing, the light, liquid rattle in his nose, the hissing collapse of his tightened throat on every breath, eclipsed even the music. "Honey," she said finally. She looked up at the ceiling, and, as if it was all she could find to give in the end, said, "those drinks are on us, okay?"

Robert shook his head. "No," he managed. "No, I couldn't do that." It was time for him to leave. He should be at home; he needed to go home, where he had something, where he could be covered, joined and found again inside of this, this terrible thing, because it was theirs, wasn't it, theirs to fight through, like Grant had been theirs.

"It's already done," she said. "I'm serious. Okay?"

He nodded. "Thank you," he said.

Robert stood up as she turned and disappeared through the tables. Blood rushed to his head and the droning pump of his heart whispered into his ears like somebody making promises. Only now, after so many hours, did he really feel the confusion and hum of the bar around him, the bodies dancing, flash-frozen by the lights, and everything spinning, the lights, the people, the heavy spirals of smoke like a palsied, paisley ether above their heads. Dizzy, he tried to take a step away from the table and stumbled against the leg of the chair, almost falling. The people at the tables beside his looked over and then turned away quickly, before decorum would demand someone try to help him.

Robert steadied himself against the table and waited for the static in his head to fade. When it had, he took a twenty-dollar bill and slid it under his glass and then pulled his coat on and made his way through the tables and around the dance floor. He didn't know who had come into the bar first, but he hadn't seem them either way, hadn't seen the girl, in fact, until just before they left the bar.

At first, he had been the only person in the back room, the dance floor an empty, waiting space in front of him. At the tables just beside the bar, the old widowers had been finishing their dinners and watching the evening football game.

But as the music changed, pouring louder and faster from the jukebox, the bar had filled up, the dimming lights throwing bluish sheets over the tables. Eventually he found himself forgetting about the football game and Rachael and watching only the couples dancing, these stunning, terribly young bodies clutching on to one another. It was lovely in its way, everyone so young, he had wondered if Grant had ever come here, thrilling silently at the thought that he might be somewhere where his son had come before. Nostalgia, which is what the pleasure of the thought amounted to, is always somehow pure, he thought, miraculously unmarred by whatever we might know about the truth, which is why we love it, why we cling to it so desperately. Like these young people, these children, we are dancers together, we and our private, cherished lies.

It was the Clyde boy he had seen first, Owen's boy, making his way through the dance floor to the bathroom. Hayden was his name, Robert remembered. Owen had brought him to the funeral. The boys had played together when they were little, before the mother died, and he remembered wondering if they had still known each other well, he and Grant. He probably wouldn't have noticed him at all if he hadn't been thinking about Grant. It was the split-second that the boy could have been Grant that caught Robert's attention. Though, as he looked more carefully, they weren't built all that much alike. They both had wide, clean shoulders, but Hayden was taller, longer in the torso than Grant. Mostly, what they shared was that fierce, unconscious kinetic grace that comes at their age, the body a tool that has outgrown the mind, precise despite the blunt fingers of the child still wielding it.

He almost called Hayden over to him as he came out of the bathroom, but something stopped him, something in the way the boy looked as he stood outside the door. Robert was almost sure Hayden looked directly at him, but then he stepped away, pushing through the dance floor toward the booths by the bar. That was when Robert saw her, his eyes following Hayden through the crowd. At first he thought he must be wrong, that in the same way he had confused Hayden and Grant, he was now projecting her face onto somebody else. But he wasn't wrong. And there was something else, too. The way their bodies leaned into one another, such a strange mix of intimacy and discomfort, became like a flashing in the dark room once you began to look, the fear between them visible as sparks when they touched each other.

Watching them, he had just known. It was that simple. He couldn't trace how exactly, but he saw it all, not just some small piece of it, but the whole appearing as if it had always been there, as if it had been worked out beforehand. Each piece of it connected intractably to the others, where the Clyde place was out in the woods, and the way—of all the faces, his now suddenly remembered—Hayden had looked at the service, the girl's eyes staring at him outside the station earlier and the way she was touching him now, his face, his hand, and he was crying now. Wasn't he? He could almost hear what she must have brought him here to say, *they know,* the horror. Each part cascading invisibly down to the next until it all pooled at the bottom, where Robert lay, covered now in the thick water of their secret, whole and shimmering cold and true. And he was sure of all of it, all that he had told himself might not be true, he knew suddenly, was.

As he watched them leave together, his mind was totally silent. It wasn't until he saw the picture on the television that he said it to himself. That boy killed my son; he watched him on top of that little girl; and he spilled him out into the grass for it. These like three objects rotating around one another, triangular and perfect as some horrible, intrinsic geometry. Not weather, but something much, much worse than that. Clarity.

He almost expected them to be outside waiting for him, though of course they weren't. The last, slowing drops of rain fell invisibly through the dissipating fog and splashed against the windshield of his car as if from nowhere. Home, he thought, I need to get home. The electricity wires, sagging beside the road, paced the car with their slack, gentle waves, rising and falling, barely visible above the fields and then turning away altogether. A semi truck passed him, tires hissing against the wet pavement. Spitting a dirty mist onto the glass, its red lights bent away into the distance.

On either side, as he left behind the strip malls around the bar, fields stretched out glistening beneath the fog. Standing along the fences, the dense, anvil-headed cattle stood like an audience to his passing, their noses rapt and bleating out the wet, shining black glare of his headlights. Robert noticed the horses standing deep in a pasture on his right. Even partial, even within the fog, they were stunning. Or perhaps more so because of it. Maybe it was only in that bare shroud that their now vague arabesques, the pure, muscled curvature of their bodies, seemed like a perfection of the blunt and sloping world around them, as though they were the earth's gift to itself, so that even if it could never, due to sheer magnitude, achieve the insular grace they had, it could at least possess it.

Up into town, the fog began to thin. In his mirrors, Robert could see where the river crawled through the woods, could follow it by the heavier wisps of white still rising above it as though it were some pilgrim road and they the streamers of a colorless procession. What would his father have done, or his grandfather, if they had known all this? But this is not that world and he was not them. The shapes of familiar houses and buildings stood along the sides of the road as if to prove it, strange and partial in the mist, as though the town had burned and was left now only half standing, hidden in the heavy smoke of what remained, the few yellow window lights as irrevocable and frightening as the last embers.

He pulled into his driveway and there was his house, leaning out to him. The dormant, brown vines threading through the porch slats and rusted chains of the old swing receded into the white air and then out again as though they were stitched through its fabric. This is how you do it, he told himself. You love them, you love them and you tell yourself that means everything. You tell yourself and tell yourself until you start to believe it.

He realized for the first time, as he stepped out of the car, how cold the night was. The soft warp of the wooden porch steps had grown yet more exaggerated, as it always did in wet weather, silencing his footsteps, turning him weightless and giving him the impression again, for the second time in the last weeks, like an eerie déjà vu, of being a ghost walking up these steps. Inside, the dark house was so warm it felt painful against his skin. He let his coat slide off his shoulders to the ground. The blood pushed through his fingers and hands in a thick, hot pulsing, as though he were thawing, his body gulping down its own blood. He stopped at the top of the stairs. Standing in front of Rachael's door, he pressed his palm and head against it, as if so paltry a gesture could stand in for anything, as if he had been left the privilege of believing in gestures.

Deb had left the bedroom door cracked and he opened it just enough to slip inside. It was black almost, the room, and he was grateful for it, the sudden blindness as he entered. His body ached beneath the cold liquored numb. The moonlight laid its pale hands against the windows, but through some specific tenderness of light did not come through the curtains, did not seem to touch anything inside.

Beneath the blankets the bed was shockingly warm. Deb was turned toward the window, her body a thick, basic shape in that heat, the nucleus of it, the heart, pumping blindly, bleeding into him unknowing, umbilical, as if she were the dumb, blind center and origin of life. He closed his eyes.

"You're home," Deb said without turning over.

"You're awake."

"I was waiting," she said. She turned over to look at him. Her arms were crossed over her breasts, her hands tucked underneath her chin.

"It's so cold outside," he said. "Come here." He reached for her and pulled himself against her.

"Jesus, Robert," she said. She laughed a little. "You smell like you've been swimming in it."

"Deb," he said. He found her mouth only clumsily in the dark, his teeth gnashing against her lips. "Come here."

"Come on," she said, pushing him away. "You're drunk."

"This isn't about drunk," he said. "Rachael was right, Deb. I want to live, now. We need to try to live again." He put his hand on her leg and began to pull her nightgown up.

"Robert," she said. She held his wrist where it was. "You know it's just not this easy. You don't just get to fuck it away."

Robert turned his hand out of hers. "I need you, now," he said. "You don't know all that I know."

She put her hand against his chest. "I don't want to know," she said. She shook her head. "I don't want to know any of it."

"You don't have to," he said. He was crying. He pulled her nightgown up and pressed the heel of his palm against the slick satin pouch of her crotch inside the panties, the soft flesh of her inner thighs hanging over the back of his hand. "I don't need you to know, I just need you to love me."

"What's the difference?" she said.

"Deb," he said. "You can't imagine." He rolled her onto her back. His eyes were growing accustomed to the dark and he could see her now.

"Stop" she said. "Robert, come on. You're hurting me." Her hands tried to push against his chest and he could see every little bone in her wrist. "Not yet," she said. "Please, and not like this. Not all drunk and meaningful. It can't hold up."

"Just love me," he said. He was on top of her now. "You just have to love me now."

"What are you doing?" she said as he pushed her arms off her chest. Her face was contorted with the effort she was making to turn out from under him. "Just not yet," she said. She was wriggling beneath him. "All right, Robert?"

"Deb, goddamn you," he said. He grabbed her jaw and stilled her face. "Just open your fucking legs."

She went suddenly still beneath him, and slowly, her legs opened. "My God," she said. Her eyes began to fill beneath him, shining steadily, her ribs just barely shuddering beneath his. He put his hand down between them and pulled the cotton nightgown up to her waist.

"Robert," she said. Her voice was soft, barely audible.

"Love me," he said. His face was pressed into her neck, but he only half felt the wetness of his tears against her skin, only half felt, in fact, any of this. He took her underwear down, the crotch like a handle, and pulled them until they ripped, pulled them again until they came off of her. As they did she let out a breathy grunt, her body lifted and dropped limp again on the bed. Beneath his knuckles, the wiry curls of her pubic hair dusted his fingers. "Love me, goddamn it," he said into her throat, shaking his head. "Deb, love me even for this."

He held her legs apart with his thighs as he pulled his own underwear down. "You have to," he cried.

"Robert. I need to get up now," she said, her voice calm as he opened her with his fingers. "Robert," she cried. The skin of her thighs pulled against his hips.

"Goddamn you for this," he said. He held his eyes so tight that colors swam through the darkness.

And then there were the dry, ripping insides. He opened his eyes only as he pushed into her. Her collarbone sucked into tight, small cups and her eyes rolled back, flickering, flickering beneath him. There were no more words, only the squelched clap of their loose bellies against each other. Her throat gurgled as he pushed further and then further inside her until there was nowhere more to go and he was seizing, hot, rancid against her, and her panties still torn in his hands, balled tight in his fingers, and those children walking out, holding on to each other as they left, and her green eyes, and the fish-bellied insides in gray-bleached grass, and lights, and lights, and from the back of her throat a scream, a guttural, unbearable moan, and her flickering, flickering white eyes, and her lips pulled back to bare the screaming, and teeth, teeth shining and broken and shining in the moon. He recognized the sound she made now from when he had told her about Grant and it was the same and maybe it was the sound of death.

He curled up, gasping, and fell off of her, stepping off the bed and tumbling onto the floor, his arms wrapped around his knees and crying, crying, "Goddamn you for this." And he lay on the floor, covering himself, the wetness of his come and her insides growing cold in the hair under his hands. He shook his head against the floor, the silver light of the window above him sinking down as though through water. He pressed his hands down, palm to bone, covering himself.

"Mama?"

Robert looked up from where he lay. Rachael stood in the empty, open doorway. She looked back and forth between them, and Deb did not pull down her nightgown, did not cover herself at all but lay on the bed in the dark, blue and still, her legs spread open and the dimpled flesh of her thighs shaking and catching the light in tiny, silver mouthfuls, the dark in between them darker somehow still, darker than the dark. The lit blue lines of her tears crossed and recrossed her temples and wet the hair against her face.

She didn't look at Rachael but her eyes were open, staring up at the ceiling. Quietly, almost with no sound, her voice hoarse and crying, she said, "It's over. Go to bed now."

The Children of God

He is an American, this boy, this man, or was, sitting at a makeshift desk pressed against the window of this rented room, or always will be, shirtless and alone now, the smoke of his cigarette pressing its feeble hands against the glass, a backpack and a bathroom down the hall all he has. The rainy season has just begun here, and each day, long before twilight, the storms turn the flat, cobbled gutters into fast canals for the gray water of the city. The mountains disappear into the dark. Some of the people like him that he's met like to call themselves travelers, but he doesn't feel like that, too much agency in that word. Wanderer might be more like it. Or foreigner, an exile who has somehow cast himself out, and like all of them, the slightly sniveling dreamers and ex-soldiers he meets in the bars, he is lost everywhere.

Why does he sit here still, then, just watching this drowning city happen around him? There is a kind of muddied innocence in it, he thinks, a belief that if he waits long enough some sort of explanation will come, that he deserves it, an assurance that life is not as halfhearted as it seems. It is a strange thought, even as he thinks it, one in which the entitlement of adulthood mixes imperfectly with the last vestige of a child's trust in the world, a brackish moment in time where he finds himself holding on to something he no longer believes in. And in fact maybe there is no innocence at all, because he already knows, but he wants there to be, even if it's a lie, and perhaps that's the innocence.

The windows across from his grow thick in the rain as though they were newly covered in Vaseline or doused with oil. In the sky dull sheets of roiled nickel lie one on top of the other, and above the ancient cathedrals forked tongues of lightning reach out and lick the man-sized crosses, while beneath their roofs, all gilt and gold tiles, the peasant women will be pulling their brightly colored shawls tighter against their shoulders, their muttered evening prayers skittering between the stone walls in the suddenly dense air. Even the falling of water in this place, the hard ricochet of rain against stone, sounds foreign. It is a kind of static, the rain, stunning, and so whole it is somehow both the silence and the sound of it that he cannot get used to.

The siesta is over, but he can see the old, whitish men, *los viejos,* still standing under the eaves of the square and sitting in the small, covered second-floor terraces, drinking their coffees and smoking tiny cigars. Their eyes watch the water slowly filling the squat palm trees' fronds and they watch as the leaves bend, bend until they empty in great, sudden washes of rain onto the white stone and the thirsty grass of the square, and each time it happens the old men nod their heads and blow long, appraising streams of smoke into the air. And also the Indian men, standing in the arched doorways of the churches, waiting for their women to come out and waiting for what money the women have managed during the day from their begging and the selling of fruits and sunglasses and the ornate or simple rosaries their daughters carve from wood, they watch, their lined, ancient faces profoundly silent, silent and still as the mountains they come from, that form them like rock, and they seem not to notice the rain, nor the dark that has come too early, nor anything else.

The Indian children are held in slings on the backs of their mothers and grandmothers inside the church, or, if they are old enough, and boys, they run between the feet of the praying women and their fathers outside, throwing their small arms out from the steps and catching raindrops on their fingers, smiling the toothless, children's smiles that will soon be saved for occasions more special than rain. The two sets of men, the Indians and the *viejos,* they do not look at each other, but they have lived long enough amongst each other that they do it naturally, without malice. They all wear small, felt fedoras and hide mouthy flashes of gold behind their lips, and these things seem, after so many weeks of watching them, the only things they share. These, and the rain.

A man walks slowly out into the square, terribly thin, black, the first the boy has seen here, while all around him men and women and children in school uniforms run, sodden books and newspapers held over their heads. He must be from the coast, where the boy's heard that the people are darker and more beautiful, the mixed remnants of sailors and slaves shaping their features. What he notices first about the man is his hair, the loose, thick curls, because they seem not to get wet at all, though his face shines with rainwater and his thin, pastel shirt has grown transparent and clings now to the dark fingers of his ribs. He is smiling, his wide, almost Asian eyes turned to slick, opaque shards above his flat cheekbones, his walk so slow he seems to see a different world than the rest.

An immense clap of thunder shakes the entire square and rattles the loose panes of glass in the boy's window. The single, bare lightbulb, which hangs loose from a socket in the tin ceiling of his room, flickers, threatening to go out again. Along the streets off the square, the lowered grates covering the windows of siesta-closed shops rattle in their bearings, and the small children, still standing along the sidewalks where they had watched the storm come, jump into the doorways behind their mothers' legs at the sound, which is sharp, louder than a gun. Birds, the large, wide-winged pigeons and the white, speckled doves, lift suddenly from the open eaves of buildings at the sound and hover for a delicate, frantic second of beating wings before settling again into the darkness waiting beneath the roofs.

The thieves and hustlers of the square lean against the dark door frames of cafés and *hostelerías* below. Their dark faces seem mute and dull and anonymous behind the sheets of rain that fall from the ramshackle gutters, but their eyes are bright and alive and moving, and they follow, close and hungry, the white faces of foreigners who push quickly across the square. They mark them, he knows, and wait to see them again later in the bars and on the streets. They use everything from sex to knives to drugs to quick tongues and even quicker fingers, and there is an indifference here that is total, cruel, and their fatalism, their poverty, is written in the bright eyes and the way they stay on you. These men are dangerous, dangerous in a way he's never seen before, and he knows it and he lives here knowing that he can never escape their eyes, never be anonymous, and he wonders if it could be as simple as that, why they come, him, all of them, if they are willing in the end to risk their lives just to be seen.

The wind shifts and a sheet of rain covers his window until everything outside it has disappeared into a wash of colors and shapes, a palette of simple forms, and everything outside could be nothing more than the movement of water over glass. He cannot see the men in the doorways or their wolfish eyes and for a second they could be a dream, only a dream. But when the wind changes again and the rain falls straight down again, he can see them and they are not a dream, none of this is a dream, and though they are dangerous, there is something compelling in them, too, something brutal and pure, as though they had escaped time's second-guessing, free, but only to act. This is too simple, too tempting a condescension, and he knows it, and even if it's true it means nothing, and he tries to remember their faces, because he is young but he is not young enough anymore to believe that purity makes them better. The black man is gone from the square now, and the boy feels as though something has been lost here, and though he could not say what it was, he knows it has nothing to do with a black man in a soaking shirt.

Above the houses in the distance, clothes hang on lines stretched over the red tile roofs. Nobody bothers to take them up in the rain because they will be dry by the evening regardless. The shirts and pants pitch back and forth in the wind and they look like the ragged and worn, wind-weathered prayer flags he has seen strung up in the mountains in Asia, except there are no prayers written on these. He wonders why he lingers so long in these places around mountains and hills, wonders if he has really moved across this massive globe chasing the tiny valley he came from, which doesn't exist, not anymore, because he already knows he will never return, and that makes it little more than a dream that he has and wakes from and has again.

It is difficult to believe that this storm, this darkness and white-green lightning color, which is not a color at all but just a sheer, vicious and brief brightness, belong to the same sky, the same country that bleaches these buildings to the color of bones. It is difficult to believe that this same sky, just an hour before, was so brilliant and bare that it seemed only a scorched, white, empty space above the world. And mostly, he thinks, it is difficult to believe that this is the same world he was born into, the same one in which was built the precious and tiny house of his memories.

He has gone out of the city before to watch one of these storms come over the mountains and was stunned in a way by the violence and the quickness, but also by the sheer grandeur of it. To see it sweep the long fields of wild grasses and cane, devour the ridges, pouring through the ragged passes of sheer rock, to see it without the protection of walls, the perspective of buildings, felt like watching a volcano erupt, what it must be like to know, irrevocably, as it came, that it could not be stopped, that everything would change, that people would die in this, that you would die, but also, first, to be awed, to be simply taken by the vision.

There is another moment like that in these storms and it is right now and it is the reason he watches, because the storm is terrible but also, occasionally, so lovely that you cease to breathe in front of it, so immense that you are left somehow stripped bare each time, shaken. It begins to break, the storm, as the sun starts to fall into the mountains. The clouds, as they tear from one another, still carry the heavy load of their unspent rain, and the water becomes a prism for the daylight and the falling sun. Colors rush across the sky as though you could see the shadows of Hermes coming for you, as though through some trick of the light time itself had been frozen midstride, the ineffable mechanism of the world laid bare, finally and for only one second, to be witnessed. And then it is gone.

And then there is the shaking hum of bus wheels over a dirt road as he leaves the mountains, high enough still that solid, white clouds hang beneath them, as though death, which is what they amount to, were pleading to be reconsidered, to be seen as gentler, more loving, than it is. And there is the hoveled port city where he changes buses, where they videotape his face and a huge mulatto searches every part of him with his heavy palms, spitting out a slurred, Creole slang the boy doesn't understand, and laughing; and there are the miles of tenements, and then the walled and whitewashed compounds, razor wire wrapped in dense and dangerous helixes over everything, and beyond even them the corrugated tin roofs held on by the weight of rocks, until they are leaving the slums of the port behind and the morning finally exhales its hot breath all around them, as though it has been carved, a solid thing, from the blind, white heat that stretches everywhere.

Beside him, the Indians sit straight-backed, framed by their heavy, colored clothes and long, obsidian braids, dark, seeking-eyed children swaddled in their laps and their hands nervously rising to finger the dense wads of rolled-up bills stuck inside their top hats to buy the week's or month's provisions; and the blacks, reminding him suddenly of home, loud and laughing in their sunglasses and old clothes, laughing when the driver tells them all how to act if the bus is robbed because they have less than nothing to steal and everyone knows it.

Somewhere in the country he has left behind, his father is dead, and somewhere in the country ahead is the lover who left him in the mountains, or whom he left there, he's not sure which, and now he is going to find her, and he might and he might not and he's not sure which he wants more. He is trying to take account and then he stops trying. Before leaving they told him to keep the window curtains closed so that the people who wait in the hills couldn't see how many were on the bus with enough time to come for it. When he heard that, he put all his money in the soles of his shoes, but he pushed the curtain back a little anyway and through it he sees an inch or two of the world that is slipping past.

The sun is yellow and flat on the grasses and the squat, far-off huts. Where there are cattle, they are drawn to ribs and sockets, huddled under the sprawled arms of stunted, starving trees. Three or four Easter-colored cinderblock shacks sit by the side of the road. Beside them, old, toothless men lay on hammocks strung between force-fed shade trees, while their grandchildren carry cups of rice and chicken legs, chewing gum and plastic bags filled with fruit and salt onto the bus to sell. He pretends to sleep because he suddenly can't imagine speaking, can't imagine leaving the tiny safety of his silence, a kind of vigil, really, that has lasted for days and become an almost physical thing, silence, a thing that he has found can fill the body, can delineate it and expose the innards, the specific gaps where this thing of flesh becomes his self, but he is hungry and he watches as the others suck the dripping fat and pineapple from their fingers.

In the afternoon, they stop in a ramshackle town where the buildings are bricked together by straw-colored mud. The streets are dry, white dust; dark slashes of spit or spilled water visible as scars across them. Shoe cobblers and decades-old refrigerator shops front the road, and two tiny children sit on a gutter in their mother's shadow gumming mango skins and then tossing the rinds to the filthy dogs that hover just out of reach. Young, whiskey-colored men in aviator sunglasses and truckstop baseball caps sit in front of the one café drinking liters of beer and passing around a jar of cane liquor, the walls above them plastered with the dark, naked women of advertisements for foreign beers. Several old couples and a few lone, bent-backed men climb onto the bus, dressed carefully in the collared rayon shirts and heavy cotton dresses held back for visiting grown children in other towns. They sit nervously in their seats, smiling to one another at the luxury of the bus and stacking and restacking the carefully newspapered packages on their laps. When they step down from the bus, it is only at the open mouth of another dirt road, and he watches them grow small, walking the rest of the way into the empty distance, into nothing.

By dusk they have moved into swamps. The road is raised and on either side of it, the land slips down into water. A collection of stilted, one-room houses stand high above the swamps ready for the floods that must come here. There are no bathrooms in the houses and he sees people squatting over the edges of the platforms they are built on and small boys standing in the doorways, the arced streams of their urine turned red and hot or a too-deep, golden amber depending on where they stand in front of the sun. On the surface of the water floats the refuse of the town, paper and cans and even broken pieces of furniture reaching their fractured arms and legs up through the surface, as if in some kind of stubborn, wordless rebellion, a refusal to disappear, and in between all of it, like discarded ribbons, are the shards of clear water, reflecting the color of the sky like scorching brand irons pushed under the surface.

The night comes so quickly it feels like a swallowing. The windows are black, with only the once-in-a-while shuddering light of an oil lamp or a television off in the hills. When he leans into the glass he can see the headlights of the bus lighting deep spoonfuls of the jungle that came with the dark, the wide, alien trees and plants that he has never seen before and doesn't know the names of. When they come to the small city, it seems to be birthed whole from the dark, immaculate. The wet neon lights and old cars and open barrooms, the frigate birds like massive, dark, hollowed-out chevrons cut into the lit ribs of clouds, and the black-haired men in shining trousers and tank-top undershirts, smoking rolled cigarettes and leaning against the lampposts, spotlit beneath them, the heat changing the air, turning it heavy and slow so that the women walking through the streets, slick-skinned beneath the small, loose clothes, seem to be swimming in it and the shouting and laughing seem to come from it, as if the right kind of air has a soul, a personality of its own, it all reminds him of what Havana or New Orleans must have been in the forties, the pulse and throb of a city in the heat, surrounded by jungles and the lapping of the ocean's water.

He finds a hotel room close to the bus stop, and his lover stayed there three nights before, and there is the room, with its close, white walls, so close that only the bed fits, and his three liters of sweating beer, bought downstairs, and his dollar packet of local cigarettes and the rank smell of traveling on his skin and everything else. A dance club thumps outside his window and already, somewhere in the blindness outside the city, the roosters are screaming, though the morning is still five hours away.

And he has never felt so alone in his life, never known what loneliness could be. He doesn't think about his family, his father, the slack-skinned eyelids or sutures in his almost opened mouth, not the rosary cross pushed like some tin boutonniere through the slit in his lapel, and he doesn't think about the girl, his lover, gone, held somewhere in this same steaming night. All he can think of, for some reason, lying naked on his bed, the thin, rancid taste of beer in his mouth, the thick strings of rough, blue smoke rising, rising above him, is that same dream, that same desiccate and imperfect thing,

America, that valley he lost, ran from, what kind of paradise are you that I am here.

And then there is only the sea, the rushing fact of it, and the black waterbirds floating through the clouds, and she is not here, his lover, and the long, black-gray sands reaching out below the cliffs, the cold wind coming fast off the water and spitting gray flecks of foam and sand onto his face, and maybe there is the one thing he is left with now, the one frightening and convoluted thought, that exile is not a place we come to at all but what we are left with, that we are all exiles, cast out and left to wander, that the country we've lost, the country we're searching for is gone, and that if we held it once it was already a memory, that the language we still hear whispering in our heads is a dream, the only one; and he is crying but for what, the pastel-colored skiffs turned belly-up down the beach like bright dream whales, and maybe the mestizo fisherman huddled between them, frayed and salt-scoured, empty nets humped at their feet, waiting, waiting for the surf to calm and let them out, and if life is to begin with this dissolution of what we were, and if all we have is this sea rushing over us, tearing us apart, then let me open my eyes and watch it rush, let me open my mouth and taste it. Let it clean me down to bones at least.

Eden

15. Hayden was still asleep as Robert sat in his car watching the day being born. First, the slow and pulsing lavender dilation, until finally the sun broke through the hills, a shimmering red crown bloodying the sky; thick, viscous colors spilling over the heavy night clouds in one gasping, spastic burst, leaving the sky clotted, and holding for one glowing, saturated, and shuddering second everything of the dawn collected above, all of what would then fall and become the day. Robert lifted the freezing bottle of bourbon from between his legs and his hands shook, rattling the glass against his teeth as he swallowed. Pressing the bottle back down, he could feel the stiffness in his crotch, his pubic hair and foreskin crowned together by the thick liquid that had sheathed them as it dried.

He had tried to make himself drunk out here, but remained strangely sober, only managing, with half a bottle of whiskey, to be sick out the window of the car. He couldn't stop shivering, the cold leather seats seeping through his pants to touch his thighs. Lying on the passenger seat was his grandfather's .45-caliber pistol, a slick, gristly shine clinging to the pearl handle in the dawn light.

He didn't know what he had come here for; certainly there was no absolution to be found here, no way, he already knew, of justifying anything, and he thought maybe in the end he just didn't know where else to go. He had taken the gun almost without thinking and a chill ran through him every time he looked at it sitting there. Perhaps his father or his grandfather would have known what to do with it, who to point to and say, yes, you, you will answer, even if it was only to themselves that they pointed. Perhaps that was courage. But if it was, then he was a coward, because he had nothing to point to, no one clean enough to answer, no one clean enough to do the pointing.

But, he thought now, maybe he had come here just to see the boy, maybe, in some specific perversity, they had only one another now, each left to the other to finally understand. Maybe the gun had nothing to do with courage, maybe the world had never been as simple as that, and really it was nothing but some kind of blunt, masculine talisman, what it had always been in the end, a flimsy metaphor for seeking solace in the only place left.

Robert wondered how long he had been here. Hours, he supposed; long enough to have watched the dew collect in the dark and then grow solid, bathing everything beneath it in the thin, silver sheen of frost that lay now like lace over the low plants, long enough to have watched the moon set and now the sun rise. Long enough that if he was leaving, he knew, he would have left.

The Mercedes was pulled deep into an overlook just past the

gravel and dirt road leading to the cabin, but still he sank down in his seat as the chrome bumper of a pick-up nosed out of the shade there. Inside it, Owen was lighting a cigarette off the car lighter, his first, long drag ripped from the open window before he turned down the road toward town, disappearing into the valley. In Robert's mind, the ghosts of too many images elbowed one another for room: Rachael in the doorway, a silhouette staring down at him, and her face as she shied away from his beating, Deb's quivering legs, stretched open on the bed, and his son's naked, pale hip and backside that first night, the antiseptic cleave of his skull where Peter Trapp had cleaned it. Hayden and the girl holding onto one another in the bar, the lights and the waitress, her face as he watched her, and his own hands, so weak and feeble in the dark, pressing against his wet penis. For some reason, seeing Owen seemed to topple it all over and Robert could feel himself almost beginning to cry again but he was empty, spent with crying, and he took another sip of the whiskey and thought he was going to be sick again. He waited for another minute and took a deep breath through his nose, starting the car and slowly backing out of the overlook.

The large trees that edged the eastern lip of the road laid the shadows of their bodies across the pavement. As he passed through them, the morning opened and closed on top of him. But on the small gravel road, it seemed as though dawn had not happened yet, the trees above leaning into one another and bathing the air in a dense, syrupy shade. The long, brown strings of summer vines still spiraled over the tree trunks, though fleshless, and the verdant ground ferns and lush weeds were huddled together at the sides of the road like the forgotten refugees of the season. Even in his arms and legs, the empty, unsteady nausea churned. On his right, deep into these woods, he knew, stood the clearing, to which he had not been back, and he tried not to look.

Robert sat in the driveway for a long time staring at the house, the still-dark windows and weathered poplar beams, the little white truck that must be Hayden's. He wondered what he was hoping this boy, just a boy, could offer. A long vegetable garden lay only half harvested to Robert's left, its bare stalks rising out of the dirt in long, skeletal lines. Between each one the earth beneath was crusted with the sheer, whitish gossamer of ice.

Hayden sat up quickly in his bed, though he only half heard the knocking. His breath was heaving, his body slicked with sweat. Beneath him, the sheets were soaked. The dog was barking. Though his eyes were open, he could still see the dream perfectly in front of him. His mother had been standing with her back to him, naked in the river, pouring handfuls of water over her head. Her whole body was wet and shining, her hair turned dark and straight by the water that dripped down her back and was caught in the backward, arcing spoon of her spine and returned again to the river along the cleaved curve below it.

As he watched her, she turned around and smiled. She was young, probably no more than a few years older than he was now. She ladled the water over herself, swallowing as it fell. Her breasts were small, the small nipples turned up above the half circles of flesh that came to rest against her ribs. He could follow her ribs descending her body, each one a gleaming scaffold, until they fell away into the flat, soft skin of her belly. Her hips protruded and cradled the dark mass of her pubic hair, which was halved by the water, doubled in its reflection.

He had wanted to touch her in the dream. Even now, in his bed, he was hard beneath the sheet. He had just begun to walk into the water when she stopped him, shaking her head. "No," she said. "Wait, baby. You can't drink this water." She smiled one more time. "Remember?" As she began to turn around again, Hayden woke up.

He looked out the window and could tell from the light through the curtain that it was just after dawn. The dog was baying.

Turning from under the blankets, he pulled the jeans on the floor up and over his legs. Even as the actual dream began to fall away, Hayden could feel its strangeness still, as you sometimes do after, the unease like a footprint against your belly. Only as he saw the dog did he come fully into waking, though. The baying had stopped and Sam stood with his muzzle to the door, his front legs straight and his hindlegs crouched behind him. His hackles stood raised in a line down his spine and what remained of his softened, brown teeth were bared in a gruesome, black-gummed smile. A low, terrifying growl escaped from his throat, his white eyes wandering over the door in front of him.

Hayden stopped. On the counter behind the dog sat the basket of tomatoes where he had left it last night. He could see them better now, the wide purple veins stretching through the red flesh, the green stalks holding their bodies like tiny, careful fingers. Leaning against the basket was a note his father had left, thanking him for bringing them in.

The door shook with another knock and Hayden jumped as the dog started barking again. The floor was cold against his bare feet. He felt like he couldn't breathe, his heart a scattershot rhythm inside him. Slowly, he walked toward the door, the same sweat from the dream reawakening over his skin, warm again. Sam turned as he came nearer, the cataracts staring up at him, his hackles resting. Hayden looked at the table in the back of the room, but the gun was gone and the table sat empty. He touched the dog's head and Sam turned away from the door and stood behind him.

The cold rushed in from outside and swirled over his naked chest in delicate slashings of winter. At first he was confused. He had expected maybe the sheriff. But it was Robert who stood leaning against the railing of the stairs. The skin on his face hung loose and misshapen, ashy and bloodless and swollen as though he had once been a boxer and was left now much older than his age, shapen only by the beatings he had taken. His dark eyes were wet and dull and the lids slipped down as though Hayden had surprised him by opening the door at all.

Robert wore a bird-hunting jacket and in the right front pocket something heavy pulled it askew on his body. Hayden looked down, and he saw the shape of the gun inside.

"Oh," he said. It felt stupid coming out of his mouth, but he had never thought of that.

Of course this is how it is, he thought, not grand, not vast, but all of it boiling down to the simple taste of tin in your mouth. He tried to think of his mother but he had lost the dream completely, as though there was room enough inside him for only one surreal moment at a time. He looked at the rosary hanging beside him on the wall, its beads like a picture frame without an image. What came to him was one of her letters, the one sentence scrawled onto the paper over and over again, *God is Here,* written furiously, the pen pushed down so hard that the paper looked carved, and it occurred to him that maybe she had been trying to convince herself, that maybe she hoped that if she pressed hard enough, He might appear from those welts.

Robert followed Hayden's eyes as they returned to the gun. "No, don't be scared," he said. He shook his head and looked down at his pocket. "Not of this. It was my grandfather's. That doesn't make any sense, but. No. I don't know why I've come here."

Hayden looked up at him. He had been crying, Hayden could tell, and a vein pulsed steadily in his temple.

"You know who I am?" Robert said.

Hayden nodded. He felt like he was trying to swallow the air. "Yes," he said. "I know."

Robert rubbed his face with his hands. Behind him, the morning was still dark, the sun not risen yet far enough to touch the valley still sprawling dark between its two spines.

"I don't even feel angry," Robert said. "Isn't that funny? Or, not funny, I guess, but strange. I'm not even angry with you."

"You know then?" Hayden said. "You know about Evelyn?"

"The girl? Is that her name?"

Hayden nodded.

"Yes. I know about her," Robert said. "I guess I know about everything. I was at that bar last night. That's how I saw you. I was right then, wasn't I?" Through the back windows of the house, Robert could see into the woods. He tried to imagine how close the clearing was.

He didn't wait for Hayden to say anything. He didn't have to, and Hayden knew it.

"Maybe," Robert said. "Maybe I came here thinking that you could explain this to me. Stupid, huh? That somebody could explain death. What it means. How you're supposed to find your way out of it. Are you cold? Your skin, it's all goose bumps."

"No," Hayden said. "I'm all right."

"I'm sorry," Robert said. "I know how strange this is. Do you understand, at all? Does this make any sense?"

He leaned against the railing again, weirdly casual. Hayden looked at him, how slack his face was, his eyes filling with tears. Hayden could smell the whiskey coming from him and it reminded him of his father and for a second he felt at ease, totally at home with this man standing in his doorway, gun in his pocket.

"Maybe," Hayden said. "Maybe it does."

Robert shook his head. "I'm just lost," he said. Tears began to fall from his eyes, his body shaking and his shoulders slumping beneath him. He wiped his face and Hayden just watched him. "I'm so lost," he sobbed. "I've been trying to figure this out on my own, but every step I take is wrong. You know? You live your whole life thinking you have enough for whatever comes, for anything, for all of them. But I didn't. I don't. I don't know where to look.

"And it's so fucking clear to me. How little love I have, or how little it means. And I can't love them well enough to stop any of it.

I haven't loved them well, not wisely, but so much worse. I'm so weak. And it's meaningless, isn't it? I mean, at every turn, I've failed. I was failed. I am failing, son. Right now, I'm failing to understand.

"This world, it's just too complicated, or something. You know? And we're too fucking human in it, aren't we? Isn't that what it comes down to? Free to fail in a world that doesn't care? Free to fail in a world that's desperate to give you the chance."

Robert covered his eyes, and leaned down into the railing.

"I don't know," Hayden said. He didn't want to look at Robert crying and stared past him into the garden. He shifted back and forth on his feet. The leaves had been gnawed off some of the plants, their tiny bald stems turned ragged in the hours since. Clouds coursed over the sky and the light was still muddy beneath them. Birds rose through the alleys between hills, shot into the open sky on the backs of warmer winds. "Maybe it's okay that the world doesn't care," Hayden said. "Maybe it just is, the world, you know? Maybe we make up the rest."

"Weather," Robert said.

"What?"

"Just weather," Robert said. He shook his head. "Never mind."

"My father told me this story once," Hayden said. Robert's breath was finally calming. "And I keep thinking about it, standing here. I don't know why. I guess that's fucked-up, huh? I mean, as far as this goes? To be thinking about a story right now?"

"Tell me," Robert said.

"What?"

"Tell me the story."

"I don't know it that well, though," Hayden said. "I think it's Greek, or something, but I'm not even sure. I don't know how to say it. I wish my father was here."

"Just tell me," Robert said, taking a deep breath. "Greeks." He sniffled and tried to smile. "Heroes, right?"

"I'm sorry," Hayden said. "I'm scared. I don't know what to say."

"Just tell me the fucking story," Robert screamed. His head shook as he yelled and Hayden took a step back. "I'm sorry," Robert said after a second. He wiped his lips of the spit that had come with the sound. "Please," he said.

Hayden nodded.

"I guess," Hayden said. "Its about a war. Or it takes place during one, anyway, the thing I'm thinking about. There's this famous soldier and everyone knows him. He kills the son of the other king, the one they're fighting, and he's famous, too, the son. They're the most famous soldiers in each of their armies. And the gods, they love them both, so no one knew how it would come out, their fight."

Robert was still catching his breath, and he adjusted his pant leg, leaning forward on the steps. He was looking up at Hayden, looking him in the eyes, and he nodded. "Okay," he said. "Go ahead."

"After he killed the king's son," Hayden said, "the soldier took his body back to their camp and wouldn't let them bury it. He did all kinds of things to it, defiling it or whatever. Even though the gods, they wouldn't let it rot because they loved him. But the prince had killed the soldier's lover or something. You know about the Greeks, right, how it was then? With men? And that's why he was doing what he was doing. Maybe he was trying to save him, still."

Hayden looked out at the hills as they took the light slowly, their solid mass thin as a ribbon torn in the wind.

"Anyway," he said. "The king, he snuck into where the Greeks were, into where the soldier had his son's body. Right into the tent, actually. And he came to the soldier and he told him that he had known his father. He asked him for his son's body back. Something happened between them. They were alone in the tent, and they talked. They talked about the dead, but also the ones who weren't dead yet, because his father, the soldier's, he wasn't dead yet. But obviously he would be, someday, and the soldier would be alone. They would all be dead and they would all be alone. I guess that's what the king was saying. He had been left alone, and what was even worse was to not be able to bury his son, to not be able to put him away right. Even being alone, it wasn't the worst thing.

"So, they cried together, the two of them, they cried for all these people. For everyone, I guess, just for people. And despite everything, despite that they were at war and all the death between them, they were both just trying to survive it. They understood, what each of them were, and why they did what they did. Because they had to. Because it was the only way, even if it wasn't right. They understood each other. No matter what had happened, no matter what either one had felt before. And the soldier, he gave the king his son's body back. And the king, he took it. He took it home."

Robert was staring at him. "But here's the only problem with that," he said. He had stopped crying and he shook his head. "I don't have anything to ask you for. And you, you don't have anything to give." He reached up and he put his hands on Hayden's arm. His fingers were wet from when he had wiped his tears away, and soft, almost warm against Hayden's skin. "You and me," he said. "We don't make much for heroes. Do we?" He squeezed Hayden's arm once. "Okay," he said, as he turned down the stairs.

"But I did save her," Hayden said. "Out in those woods," he said. "I saved her."

Robert turned back at the bottom of the stairs. "No," he said. He shook his head. "No, you didn't save her. You didn't save her from anything. There is no saving, son. Not in this, not for any of us. There's only what comes after."

Even as Hayden had said it, though, he had known he wasn't right. He saw too many memories now for that, had watched too many disparate moments coalesce to be reduced now to so simple and begging a thing as that. He sank down, steadying himself on the stair as he sat.

"I'm sorry, son," Robert said. "I am." He shuffled toward his car and didn't look back at the boy he could still hear crying behind him. Suddenly, a memory came to him. He was in the jungle, in Asia, and he was running. Even the metal of the rifle was hot. Beneath him was the dank, black earth. The sounds of animals screaming came from everywhere. As he opened the door to his car, he was suddenly certain that in that moment he had been remembering another time. Corn, heavy-topped and blinking in the sun, the soft earth of home beneath him.

The engine of the car was like thunder. Hayden watched as

Robert backed up and turned away from the driveway. They looked at each other one last time and then Hayden closed his eyes again. Behind him, Sam started howling, baying as the sun broke through the clouds. When he opened them again, Robert was gone.

And so this is how it ends, the knowledge beating blindly in your chest that your life is being set out in front of you, that you are not the whole thing you were but just this sad collection of what you can't explain, can't even justify, though you know it now, know that all of it is yours. The world rushing forward in front of you, the light fighting for supremacy above, the horizon in the distance like a jeweled gate set afire by the season, time's ringing in your ears like the sound of a gun.